Praise for *Sketcher*

"A funny, sad, atmospheric novel...
Captivating and characterful."
The Sunday Times

"Rollicking chronicles from the sticky side of Louisiana."
The Independent

"A richly textured evocation of life in the Bayou, lush with
fruitful descriptions and the tall tales of folklore."
The Literary Review

"A witty Mark Twain-like diversion that tells of superstition
and mojo-conjuring among the swamp folk of the
Bayou during the Reaganite 1980s."
The Spectator

"Funny, heartfelt and beguiling...
A tragicomic tour de force."
The Book

SKID

Roland Watson-Grant

ALMA BOOKS

ALMA BOOKS LTD
Hogarth House
32-34 Paradise Road
Richmond
Surrey TW9 1SE
United Kingdom
www.almabooks.com

Skid first published by Alma Books Limited in 2014
This mass-market edition first published by Alma Books Limited in 2015
Copyright © Roland Watson-Grant, 2014

Cover design: Jem Butcher

Roland Watson-Grant asserts his moral right to be identified as the author of
this work in accordance with the Copyright, Designs and Patents Act 1988

Printed and bound by CPI Group (UK) Ltd, Croydon, CR0 4YY

ISBN: 978-1-84688-363-7
eBook ISBN : 978-1-84688-326-2

SKID

PART ONE

One

Well, lemme tell you somethin' else. If they want pocket lint, I got lots of it. Yup. This must be a case of mistaken identity, cos, in these clothes, I only *look like* a guy with money. The only thing jinglin' in my pocket right now is a set of keys to our house on Hayne Boulevard. But here I am, Uptown New O'lins, miles from home, after dark, with four thugs tryin' to mug me and throw me into the Mississippi. Now, if you had told me that less than a year after we escaped from that swamp I'd be here runnin' for my life again – well, I woulda called you crazy. But that's the truth. I'm being chased by shadows. They're moving real fast, runnin' close to the ground, no sound coming from their tennis shoes. Meanwhile you should hear my clunky church loafers hittin' Washington Avenue like I'm a tap-dancer late for practice. It's real life that feels like one of those nightmares: you got nowhere to hide, but you can't keep runnin', and there's not a soul around except for the ones that are huntin' ya. You're on your own when you're in trouble, believe that.

Wait. A gate. Hell no – that's the cemetery. *Keep going Skid.* Glancing back I see the chained gates of Lafayette No. 1 disappearing in the dark – and believe me, that graveyard starts lookin' more welcoming than the dead stretch of road in front of me right now. I'm wishing that I had somehow busted those gates open, snuck in there and hidden real quick. Too late now. I dash left, onto a side street – don't know the name of it – you don't care when you're about to die. I have no experience of this part of the city anyway, even with my backing and forthing to Peter

3

Grant's house and all that. Good thing these dudes don't have a ride, cos they'd have caught me already. My heels are diggin' into the asphalt and sending shocks up my spine. Might as well be wearing a pair of pumps for God's sake. Now there's an old man watering plants behind a cast-iron fence. He doesn't even look up when I blow past his pretty little birthday-cake house in full Sunday best, gasping like a catfish and tearing up the pavement. Prob'ly seen weirder things in his life, living so close to a boneyard, the poor old guy. I'm clocking at least fifteen miles an hour I'm sure, but I slow down to dash left again. Now I know I'm on Sixth Street, cos, right quick, two high beams come on ahead of me, lighting up a street sign. Well, I'm thinkin': *Thank God, this might be my saving grace*. But the vehicle takes off, swings into the left lane and it's heading straight towards me. Dammit. There are more of them and they *do* have a car. Man, I'm done running and I've been out of luck for a long time. So I stand still, dip into my back pocket and hold my hands up as the headlights close in. Maybe I can throw my empty wallet to these hyenas and buy myself some time, even though this ol' thing is not so easy to part with. I'm sentimentally attached to it. Long story.

Thugs on foot to my left, car off to my right. I'm hollerin': "Awright! Awright!" so they don't ride the kerb and run me over.

Then I see another entrance to the cemetery. A back gate, similar to the one I bolted past earlier like a damn fool. So this time I decide to take my chances with the dead. I thought my hair would stand straight up as soon as I leapt into this burial ground, but it feels really peaceful. There are some old trees lined up along the concrete walkway, bowing down to graves on the other side. If the circumstances were different this would be a pleasant walk. Matter of fact the only strange thing I see is that the iron gates aren't just open: they're torn clean off the hinges and lying flat on the ground. As you can imagine, hours ago this place was crawling with tourists, posing beside burial vaults and smiling. Now there's nothing but Skid Beaumont dodging the blazin' beams of the car that just swung into the gateway behind me, making the graves grow long shadows and the trees look wicked.

I'm duckin' between mausoleums just far apart enough for me to squeeze in, with my chest heaving. *Hold your breath, Skid.* Impossible. Their own lights must have scared them too, cos those bastards they stop the car once they get inside the gate. An old Chevy – I hear the thing throttling. They're so close gas fumes are up my nose and hot headlights bounce off everything. Check the surroundings. I'm like a giant trying to fit into a small city. Four inches from my nose black mould is clinging to whitewash and rain stains are streaking off it all the way down the side of a burial vault. Pieces of marble tumble out the side of a tomb, and some ancient red bricks are peepin' through the cracks. Under every fresh coat there's something crumbling. The whitewash never wins.

Car doors open and close. Tennis shoes crunch dried leaves on the walkway. There's a low rumble. One of them has a pair of those new Rollerblades on. Prob'ly stole it off some dead guy.

"Yow, don't move, man."

The voice is above my head. One of the shadows climbed up on the vault behind me and tried to drop in, but the space wouldn't allow him. Right away a metal baseball bat comes down between the burial vaults and cracks open the plaster crust of a tomb right by my ear. Insects scramble out, surprised at the raid on their horrible little house. I take off again, and those punks, all half a dozen of them now, they scurry up behind me like cockroaches.

I'm tryin' to stay out of the headlights, so I crouch down and crawl into a space among a few smaller box tombs. They can't possibly find me here. And I hope they don't, cos this part of the cemetery is a dead end: up against a wall, one way in and no way out if they block me. Well, forget hoping – cos the bastards just found me. I'm in the corner with my knees right up under my chin and my head pushing so hard against a marble plaque I can make out the poor soul's name with the back of my scalp.

One of the thugs starts whistlin' and draggin' the metal baseball bat on the concrete like a real jerk who watches too many gangster movies. A leather belt is wrapped around a fist and the buckle is dangling. As they come in close, I grope around and grab a shoe-size piece of marble off the grass and chuck the thing in their direction. *Pow*. Baseball Bat Guy suddenly grabs his face and goes down. But he's not staying there. He sails it back in my direction. I duck, but not quick enough. Instant head throb and a warm trickle is crossing my eyebrow. My eyes slam shut. I'm so mad and scared I swear my bones are rattlin'. Burnt onto the back of my eyelids are the white graves: a photo negative of prob'ly the last thing I'll see.

Now look. I don't know – I must have thought about it, I guess. You know, one o' those crazy thoughts that crosses your mind when you're at the end of your rope? Or one o' those desperate things you do, like promise God a million things if he could help you make it from the bus stop to the bathroom? Yeah. But as those boys come charging in with the baseball bat in the air, I'm fixin' to fling the wallet to them again when the craziest thing pops into my head: *if only my guardian angel would stop makin' herself so scarce – that'd be great right now*.

Well, look. Right away I hear stone crumbling, and one of those tall marble monuments on top of a tomb, it just leans over and comes tumbling down right in the middle of the manhunt. *Brack. Boom*. The thing hits the rounded top of an oven tomb, sends plaster flyin', slides sideways and sets my teeth on edge. *Whoa*. What the hell. Stone splinters off in every direction. Those boys swear under their breath and pull back. Way back. Dust is in the air. I'm coughing. And that monument, it just settles in and sits there across the concrete path like the finger of God showing those punks the way out of the cemetery. So we're there, staring at each other over the massive piece of marble for a quiet minute before they curse some more and call me a ghost, and I holler back some horrible stuff about their parents. Tennis shoes shuffle out through dead leaves. High beams swing away, the Chevy engine roars off and fades to nothing, and I'm left sitting on a cold gravestone in my best clothes, with a terrible silence hanging between this twelve-foot monument and me. That's when I see that there's a statue attached to the very top of it: a mossy old marble angel. Down on her face, still holding a broken sword. Now I'm scared shitless.

I really should leave, but my knees are not in the mood. I reckon those boys must have got their balls back by now and are prob'ly waiting for me out on Sixth Street, mad as hell. Truth is, I don't blame 'em for hightailing it out of this boneyard. A ton of marble just took a nosedive inches in front of us for no practical reason.

Anyway, I'm finally up off the ground with my bones still shivering, but I'm heading south with my handkerchief over my eye. My head hurts like hell, but I reckon I can find that exit on Washington Avenue and avoid those punks. *Keep off the main walkway. Walk over some low graves if you have to, Skid.* Dead ahead is the iron sign that curves over the front gate with the words reversed in an arch like a bad spell. So I walk in a straight line with a slice of moon left over from last week following me through the trees. It's enough to help me see where I'm goin'.

The whole graveyard is a maze of cages and iron fences, rows and rows of spearheads gettin' red with rust. Someone left a string of party beads and cigarettes as an offering at a grave: prob'ly some poor fool prayin' to fix a mistake made on Mardi Gras night. I'm bobbin' and weavin' and brushin' away low branches while dead leaves shuffle in front of a breeze. You can smell the wax from the candles. I hold my nose. Then something makes me stop: a stone wall stacked to form an alcove. It's got this little garden, a well-kept lawn, and a tomb sits in the middle of it. No, not just a tomb, a small castle really: a beautiful thing, with shining marble columns and stained-glass windows behind a fancy fleur-de-lis fence. Fresh flowers are on the stone steps. Above it, a magnolia tree is sighin' and weepin' white flowers all over the green. Moonlight breaks through branches and tinsels down the front of the tomb. You can tell that this family didn't have to scrimp on the money to give their loved one a decent resting place. When the shadows move away, I see why:

BENET

I step up and, sure enough, carved into the marble are some names I recognize: "Orville Jacque Benet", "Herbert Francis Benet". Below that, their birthdays and a dash, followed by the date they got swallowed up by that sinkhole in the swamp.

So this is where Backhoe Benet laid his boys to rest. All the way out here, the legendary Broadway and Squash, the baddest bastards in the swamp. The tomb is brand-new too. For a second I miss them, no lie. But then... I get to thinkin' that that little dash between birth and death stands for all the years they did some real jacked-up things to people in the swamp, including us. One little dash full of so much damn trouble from these two hell-raisers. And here they are buried like royalty after all that. Matter of fact somebody even offered coins in front of the tomb, as if these two were dead saints or something. Well, look: I know a guy who could use the bus fare. So I'm just gonna go ahead and collect all the damn quarters I can find on the ground and even stick that one-dollar note in my wallet real quick. Don't feel bad. Trust me, these dudes don't deserve this money one bit.

Now, I'm trying not to get riled up, but right now I can't help picturing their big ol' fancy mausoleum all busted up. Yes, there I said it. I can't wait for it to crumble into one big mess. Let's see how many tourists ooh and ahh over a heap of marble. Well, right quick the wind comes up and washes through the trees and howls like hell and I start runnin' again, this time from about a dozen security guards. They're rushing through the cemetery with flashlights and nightsticks. Just before I slip under the arch and out onto Washington, I hear them hollerin' into walkie-talkies that *seven* grave-robbers just tore down both gates and busted open a brand-new tomb.

Two

There should be a law against reelin' in a man with a plate of scrambled eggs and then bushwhackin' him when he's eating. That's what people do to *rats*, right?

Well, the rat-catcher and part-time "Professor" Valerie Beaumont is lecturing again. This time the topic is "Survivin' in the City", otherwise called "Hell No, You Didn't Come in Here with Your Face Bleeding Last Night". I'm in her class of one, sittin' at the tiny round table in our "new" apartment kitchen. Well, ol' VB, she drops the plate in front of me, and goes to sit near the window. She's being real dramatic: opening the blinds, slumpin' down into that old tangerine fake-leather armchair as sunlight stripes the baby-blue walls behind her – the only wall we've painted so far. Coffee and a cigarette. Steam and smoke. She's pissed. Or scared. Prob'ly both. That smoke looks extra thick when the sunlight hits it.

"You think you're a man, huh?" That's how she begins, sounding real tired, even though she just woke up.

The fork hits my teeth, *clang*, like a boxing bell. Then it's the usual list of rules:

Get familiar with the RTA schedule. (Public Transportation.)

Don't hitch any rides. (There are weirdos out there.)

Avoid open lots, strangers and unfamiliar streets. (That sums up just about everywhere.)

Less TV and VCR. (You're a high-school senior soon.)

Try to get home before dark.

Lake Pontchartrain is right across the street, but it's not a playground, y'hear me?

Oh, and the city is not the swamp. Speak English. (Pay attention to words ending in "ing".)

The list does not include my latest violation. Over the last few months Frico and I, we've managed to break six of the first seven. So now there's definitely gonna be a new one:

"And don't go roamin' all around Uptown and Downtown like you're a tourist!"

"Great. Thanks, Skid." Frico's voice comes out of the bedroom and around the corner. That last stipulation should definitely mess with the guy's love life, even though Fricozoid hasn't really listened to his mother in years. Maybe she should make a rule about not playing hide-and-seek with muggers in the cemetery. I'm willing to keep that rule after last night.

Anyway, what's really funny is how these days when she starts givin' me the third degree, I actually welcome it. Cos it's like hearing my pops' superstitions coming out of my mother's mouth, I guess. I miss my old man. She has no idea that she's begun to sound like the man she's always criticizin'. The man she's fixin' to bury without finding his bones anywhere.

"You got into a fight last night, Skid?"

"No."

"Boy, you come in here with somethin' that might require stitches and you're tellin' me—"

"I got chased by some guys Uptown."

"What? What guys?"

"I don't know. It was dark."

"And they just chased you for no reason? And did this to you? Or you did somethin' to them first?"

"No, Moms, I swear. Those boys saw me waitin' for a bus and jumped me. They wanted money."

"You don't *have* any money for them to want."

"They didn't know that. And I wasn't gonna give those punks my wallet."

"Now you just sound ridiculous. You goin' to lose your life over an empty wallet, boy?"

"Pops gave me that wallet a long time ago."

"Yes, *I* remember givin' that wallet to your father for his birthday or something. He never used it, that man."

"Seriously? You gave your husband a wallet for his birthday?"

"Don't try changin' the subject, Skid. Wait – what's wrong with giving your father a wallet for his birthday?"

"Nothing, really. But would you like it if he gave you a bunch of pots and pans for your birthday?"

"Hell no, are you crazy? I'd think he was givin' me a hint or something."

"Exactly."

Pause. Smoke fillin' the silence.

"Anyway, enough about the damn wallet. That story about the cut on your face doesn't add up."

I smirk. She throws me a real nasty pair of eyes as usual.

"Skid, it's a sad day when your mother really wants to believe what you're sayin' and she just can't."

"You never believe anything I say anyhow, so…"

The ash is longer than the rest of the cigarette. It curls over and falls off. Her hand quivers a bit. The other one brushes at her lap. Deep breath. Fear smells stronger than tobacco right now.

"Terence, these are different days. Look outside. See those power lines? We're in the city now: it's all steel and stone and solid reality. Your father isn't around any more, and this place can be scarier than where we lived for twenny years. Don't forget how we ran from that murderer James Jackson to get here. Well, there's are dozens more like him out here."

Right. First of all, there's *nowhere* on this planet scarier than the south-east Louisiana swamp where my family lived for twenty years. That hole is the exact spot on this earth where the Devil fell foot first, I swear. You could have lost your life *and* your soul in there. Second, there's no gangster to be compared with Crazy James "Couyon" Jackson. And third, to hear her tell it, before she got to America that San Tainos Caribbean island was no damn picnic neither. Matter of fact, any minute now there'll be some serious quote coming out of her mouth courtesy of ol' San Tai.

"*Trouble never sets like rain*, Terence. You're never gonna see it comin'. And that ol' devil, he don't need no help raisin' chaos! So look here boy. I left the best parts of my days down in that swamp hole, dreamin' my life away with your father. All I want to do now is preserve a little piece of myself and make the most of movin' to where we could get an actual postal address."

I feel bad now, cos I really didn't mean to scare her. She has both hands massagin' her temples: migraine. And even though she's rantin' and that cigarette butt between her fingers makes it look like she's fuming real slow out of one ear, I know she's not really angry. When Valerie Beaumont is angry, it doesn't come out in an American accent. Anyway, I hear Frico getting off the bed in the room. He comes to the bedroom door and quietly pushes it shut. Just before it clicks, you can hear the headphones of a CD player cracklin' around his ears. Good. That's right. Turn up that music, Fricozoid. Cos as soon as Valerie Beaumont calms down and I pick my teeth, I got me a solo mission that works very nicely if you can't hear a damn thing.

Three

It's been a while, but we're still not back to normal after that night when we ran from "Couyon" Jackson's gang and got into this apartment. Some boxes are still stacked in the corner of the kitchen. The old KeroGas stove and my father's workbench are taking up space under the staircase out front. There's lots of swamp junk to throw out, but since my elder brothers Doug and Tony don't live with us any more, things like that take longer than usual. To be honest we haven't even given the prison-grey carpet a professional cleaning. So I guess we're still breathing carpet-freshener and the smell of who last lived here.

And whoever used to live here *really* liked sausages. The stench of it sticks to the rafters, just like the cheesy bunny-rabbit wallpaper behind the fridge and those greasy fingerprints on the kitchen cupboard. At least that's better than the smell of rat that was present when we first got here. The whole place squeaked even after we oiled the hinges on the cupboard, if you know what I mean. You'd walk into the kitchen and shadows would still be retreating into corners long after you turned the lights on. So Moms went out and spent a fortune on glue traps.

Then there's that ugly water stain in her bedroom ceiling. It's the last thing she sees every night before she goes to bed: deep brown like old blood. She says it looks like "a drop of swamp". Outside, along the corridor, you can see silverfish camping out in their dirty little sleeping bags. That's the official nuisance of the South, I swear. Soon they'll wriggle out and eat through books and boxes like we brought them lunch. Some nights you wake up, and when the streetlight hits the trees just so, you swear you're still in the swamp. You reach out and touch the wood and they turn into concrete walls again.

The good news is everything can be fixed – everything except maybe the tiles along the corridor outside. Those tiles are terrazzo, for godssake: little black-and-white specks of every stone known to man frozen in a square. It's the kind of thing that would drive a cat crazy. I mean, if you spill something, it's hard to tell if you really cleaned up.

Now, you know that my brother Frico can fix all the oldness with a pencil and paper. If y'all never heard, he's a hoodoo *sketcher*, a boy conjurer who can fix things with folk-magic drawings. But he's lazy. Apart from that, he's caught up with reading about this fancy art school in New York City. And that's one reason why Moms is crunching numbers like hell. Yeah, that bastard got a full scholarship, but she's still gonna have some expenses. It's a good thing she's finally opened her food business with Mrs Thorpe, a church sister of hers. A food cart really, but it's got ambition. Plus, like I said, she's planning Alrick Beaumont's memorial service, so all her time is taken up with a calculator and phone calls.

Yeah, we have a telephone now. Doug came and took the CB radio we used in the swamp. He said it's the Nineties now, and nobody uses Citizens' Band any more, but he wants it, cos a CB radio's a damn cool souvenir. I don't blame him: I loved that thing. And for the life of me I can't get used to a phone ringing off the hook every coupla minutes. It's frickin' *nuts*. I can deal with police sirens replacing swamp crickets at night and that neighbour we have who plays music all day and night – but, man, that – goddamn – phone! The only contraption I hate more than a ringin' telephone is a clock. All clocks do is hang around and point out the fact that you're late. Anyway, I tell

Valerie Beaumont I'm going to sort the boxes under the sink so we can throw out more stuff.

"It's about time, Skid," she says. And there's an Alrick Beaumont déjà-vu moment brought to you by Moms again. But I can't get distracted by thinkin' about Pops right now, cos like I said, I got things to do. Lemme break it down.

See, there's this old Frico Beaumont diary I found packed deep down in a box one morning after we moved into the city. He started it around 1981 and has been writing in it every now and then for years. I didn't get to read much when I found it. He was rambling on and on about being in love and all that. Anyway, as usual, his spelling and his grammar were all over the goddamn place. Maan, you should see it. It's hilarious. I reckon I'm gonna have some fun goin' through that whole diary with a nice red marker. It's my duty *to mankind*. Yep. I'm fixin' to do all the grammatical corrections cover to cover, then I'll pack it right back into the box. Imagine his face when he finds it a few years from now. *Ooowee*.

Well, I'm in luck. I was thinkin' I was gonna have to rummage around a bit. But in the second box of about seven, my hand hits the artsy-fartsy brass crest on the front of a hardcover book. See, my silly bro thinks the best place to hide anything from ol' Skid is in plain sight. Well, not today, man.

I'm sneaking out back when, without lookin' up, Valerie Beaumont asks me if I'm done with all the boxes already. I tell her I'm goin' to change the Band-Aid over my eye. She waves me away like she knows I'm up to no good, but she can't be bothered. I'm sixteen: gimme a break, Moms.

Now I got to find me a spot to look into Frico's diary. So I tuck it into my T-shirt before standing on the banister of the main stairs and hoisting myself onto the roof. This is actually the roof of someone *else's* apartment, so you have to take light steps to avoid somebody runnin' out onto a balcony to cuss at ya in a strange language. Up here reminds me of our tamarind-tree lookout spot in the swamp. Not as high, but at least you can see the shape of the complex.

It's a tight little space, these apartments – shaped like a short, fat crucifix. On the horizontal part of the cross you have all the units, one to fifteen, in a quadrangle, facing each other around a red-brick courtyard. A sugar-maple tree pushes up from a dirt square that's dead centre in the middle of the courtyard. It's a giant. Someone parked a beat-up ol' Toyota Tercel under it a long time ago. Now, after months of rain, dead leaves and bird droppings, you can hardly see anything inside that sorry car.

Then there's the vertical part of the cross: a red-brick walkway that runs from the abandoned backyard of the apartment complex, straight across the quadrangle and down into the road in front of the lake. There are no real security guards here, just a gate guy slash handyman. Most of the time this guy is sleeping. And he's not even here on weekends. He told us everybody calls him "Larry Lou". I'm sure every apartment complex in the world has some guy named Larry. But *our* Larry is the one known for havin' morning breath all day long. He's an OK guy, but job-wise Larry is as "faux" as the French fixtures around this place, like those hollow aluminium fleur-de-lis fences pretending to be cast iron.

Anyway, I'm sitting in the shade of the maple tree that comes all the way up and hangs over part of the roof, with my red marker, ready to read, but the sun is splintering off the lake across the street and hittin' me in the eyes. I turn south, but the tiny cars silently crawlin' over the I-10 Highway are just as distracting. Far west, Downtown New O'lins keeps rising full steam under clouds piled high and cranes paused halfway to heaven. Hayne Boulevard is one long road into the city. Follow the poles and power lines trailin' off into the haze and you'll hit the highway. Over the Connection Bridge my elder brothers have a place like real city boys. That's where I'd like to be eventually: way out west, nearabouts where they live. But here we are, still far east. Not enough city. Not "city" enough. It's as if we ran as fast as we could from a great big blob, but the mud on our shoes became hard and weighed us down, so this is as far as we got. This far is close to the tail end of the great snake, Hayne Boulevard, a place full of construction crews, mom-and-pop shops and dust. So much dryness you'll prob'ly get thirsty just by looking out the damn window. To be honest, in some ways, this part of the city still feels like the swamp. The main reason is that same lonesome lake across the street, right alongside the train tracks. One of the largest in America, they say. I swear there are secret places along the shores of Lake Pontchartrain that haven't felt the pressure of a human foot or soaked up someone's shadow in years. But these are the places Valerie Beaumont banned, for godssake, and since I had enough adventures last night, I refocus on the journal.

I'm just a few pages in, putting "*sp*" or "*(sic)*" every second line or so, when I pause to look at a sketch Frico's done of Teesha Grey, his girlfriend. It's not realistic. Her chest is more impressive in real life. He's obsessed with this girl. Anyways, I'm flippin' through the book when somethin' pops out from between the pages and drops onto the roof tiles. It's a small plastic-covered card with a circle sketched on it. Words in a foreign language curl around the rim of the circle, and in the centre there's a hexagon. Other diagrams and random numbers fill up the inside. The whole thing looks like the electrical circuits my father used to draw when he was building some electronic contraption, or the type of thing you'd see in a do-it-yourself manual just before you go berserk.

Now, once I laid eyes on those strange symbols and letters, I knew what it was: a hoodoo-magic seal, one of those objects my father used to bury in the ground at night when he was busy tryin' to conjure up oil or gas in the swamp. Now, this one looks different. More complex. Like it was from outside the galaxy or something, no lie. The whole card smells like the swamp though: raw, mildewy. And yeah, you're right. It's one of those dark things my mother warned us *never, never, never* to bring into the house. But there it was, stuck in between the pages of Fricozoid's personal lovey-dovey diary, right up there in the woman's kitchen. The boy doesn't listen. Even ol' man Pa Campbell told us not to play around with folk-magic spells and this kind of hoodoo stuff.

So right then I reckoned I'd have to do the right thing and confiscate it. Keep the magic seal out of Frico's reach for his own good.

Well, it's getting hot up here on the roof now, 'specially since everybody in the apartment complex is awake and cookin' breakfast. Trust me, at breakfast and dinner it's an international cookoff in these parts. When we just got here, Moms could stick her nose up in the air and say what was being cooked and where, and whose cooking needed more parsley or less MSG. Yup. My mother's nose knew we had Greek, Indian and Mexican neighbours long before we met 'em. And she could tell who the superstitious ones are. They're the ones who burn frankincense or basil oil every weekend to chase ghosts. And once they start that shit up, you'd better burn some frankincense too. Cos those ghosts, they're like cockroaches. Somebody sprays Raid somewhere and they just come bargin' into where you live, is what I heard.

Before I can climb down, Frico suddenly comes around the corner of the apartment building carrying two blue coats. He walks down to the end of the walkway and looks up to the roof like he knew exactly where I was the whole time, and hollers out:

"Which one do you want to wear... to the service?"

Slowly, I put the book beside me. He didn't see it. I hesitate too long. Damn.

"I'm comin' up."

I swear the boy can fly. He's at the edge the roof in two seconds wearing both coats. I tell him I want the blue one, so he shouldn't have put his sweaty self in it.

"They're both blue, man, be more specific."

"Darker blue. And preferably without your body odour, if you don't mind."

He's stepping towards me. Maybe I should tell him not to come too close. Too late. He has his hands out like wings to help him balance across the peak of the roof. Most days he's a jerk, and when I really want him to go away, that's when he gets friendly.

"'Sup, Skid?"

"Wondering."

"'Bout?"

"Should we really call 'em train tracks since they were there *before* the train came?"

"Wow. Deep. But really – whatcha doin' up here?"

I know he just wants to find out more about what happened last night. Boy's a bastard. So I throw him another curve ball.

"Countin' cars."

"OK, I'll help you out when you get to ten."

"Hilarious."

His usual joke about me and mathematics isn't even funny. The boy is boring. So what if I hate math. People only need mathematics to count money. Anyways, I condescend the guy, cos I need the fake laugh and the sound of a passing car to cover my next move. When Frico steps up, I drop the diary and the red marker over the side of the building like a pro, but the damn book lands in the swimming pool. Yes, we have a swimming pool, but please don't get excited. Remember this place was hotshot waay back in the *Seventies*. It was for people on the up and up – almost bourgeoisie, Pops would say. Nowadays the whole place, including that pool, is as rundown as a racehorse. Matter of fact, the pool is empty except for a nasty green puddle down at the deep end, where it says "9 ft", which I find really funny, since there's no water in the damn thing. Once upon a time the whole thing was covered in "Greek blue" tiles, but now it just looks like a mechanic's dirty overalls. Maple leaves litter the inside, but not enough to cover up the noise of Frico's diary when it fell. Now he's walking straight to look over the edge. Dammit. *Think fast, Skid.*

"So… guess what happened last night, Fricozoid?"

It worked. He ignored the nickname, but he stopped his tight-rope-walkin' towards the edge. Now he's half-smiling, genuinely interested in my damn business again.

"Well, from the looks of that gash over your eye – you got beat up. Or you've been up here playing punch-buggy with yourself again. And losing."

"Now *that's* funny. By the way, I could use your help gettin' rid of this cut with a hoodoo sketch or two."

He's patting all his pockets like a smoker who can't find matches. He shrugs. "Oh sorry, Skid. Looks like I don't have a pencil up here."

"Yeah? Well I no longer have a story for ya."

"Suit yourself. Just remember when you're running around with Peter Grant and them – your mother doesn't want to do a double funeral this year."

"She doesn't have to do even one. We don't know that Pops is dead."

"We don't know that he's not. I hope he isn't. But he was 'exposed to imminent danger', so he *can* be declared dead. You should read more."

(So says the guy who can't even spell to save his goddamn life.)

"Well, did she do it? Declare him dead?"

"Well, that night in the swamp… Pops got caught among the gators and the gunshots and the most notorious gang there is.

We know he got shot *and* lost his leg in deep waters full of killing machines. Nobody's seen or heard from him since. So, wouldn't you think 'bout declaring him dead, Skid?"

I keep quiet, cos I got nothing to compete with that kinda logic. He sits down and pats my knee.

"Momma wants to move on. She stopped wearing her wedding ring. She wants to close that book, man."

Move On. Close That Book. This guy is the cliché champion of the world, for godssakes. I want to tell him he missed a big opportunity to say "Start afresh", but he prob'ly wouldn't get it. I waste my time on this damn boy. Glancing over the edge I see the diary down in the pool. The stupid book is wide open. The wind is fanning out the pages, showing it off like a little paper peacock.

Frico turns to get off the roof. *Good. Go away.* Then, when he's holding on by his elbows and his feet are dangling off the roof trying to find the banister, that's when he chooses to give me advice. "Seriously though, Skid, be careful in those parts. I said nothin' to Momma, but it was on the news that some grave-robbers tore down the gates of Lafayette No. 1 last night. They ransacked a brand-new tomb and tore down a hundred-year-old monument."

"For real?"

My head is on fire, but I keep my cool. That angel toppling over. Those two gates flung down and lyin' flat on the ground. Broadway and Squash's tomb – was it even possible?

Four

This church is as old as the Book of Genesis, I swear. "First Tabernacle" on Hayne. The newest thing in here is the calendar on the back wall. It still says July 15th, 1990. That was a week ago almost. Down front they have a painting of the Lord looking down at us. He has a lamb across his shoulders, and his face is stern or happy, depending on which eye you close. A scroll across the top of the portrait says "Be Silent before Him" in gold and royal blue. Then they got some noisy ceiling fans installed on poles that drop down just below the old chandeliers. So you have a nice little flicker every time you're trying to read something. That's not as annoyin' as the termite sawdust or the pieces of baked bugs that fall onto your funeral programme from the chandelier. My father's face is in a large frame right below Jesus. The man is handsome. I'd forgotten what he looks like. He didn't take that photo too long ago neither. Maybe at a photo studio downtown when he took a break from cheating on my mother. Anyway, we're all here, sitting in the front pew in birth order: Tony, Doug, Frico, then me. Four pieces of our father.

Families always get the front row at funerals. There's more privacy for crying when your back is turned, I guess. Moms is at the end of the bench with all her facial expressions switched off. It's her funeral face. Looking around you can see that the church isn't packed. Even if she thought nobody would come, it's obvious Moms made the effort. She splurged on a memorial-service package that comes with lilies and lavender-coloured flowers and some white paper fans that aren't too corny at all. There's flowers all over the place. The funeral home chose the church too, since Pops never really had membership anywhere.

Now, this service started minutes ago, but people are still filing in. Maybe because it's a weekday, so they'll pop in from work and then go away and get on with their lives. Or maybe it's that many people are reluctantly comin' cos they don't think Alrick Beaumont's really dead. And maybe all those pretty ladies who came in late and stayed in the back – maybe they all just want to avoid Moms.

The officiating minister is up on the podium trying to para-phrase somebody: "Flowers are to comfort the living. Funerals are for those who remain." Deep. I look around, and those who remain are about to die in the heat. All the way to the back, people are flippin' futile paper fans back and forth. Men take their coats off and we follow suit. It's a miserable summer. The minister welcomes my pops' former customers, former employ-ers, co-workers, CB radio buddies – most of these people I've never seen. But even as the place fills up, I can't shake the feelin' that the most important people didn't make it. I try not to be sentimental, but it's like the world emptied out after we left the swamp. People just fell off the edges of the city or got devoured by airport terminals and evaporated into the clouds over New O'lins. Sometimes the loneliest place in the world is the whole goddamn world, trust me.

Ma and Pa Campbell stayed for a few days to file police reports and just calm down. Then family members came for them and they headed off to Arizona. Haven't heard from them since Ma called from a rest stop on the way to say they were almost there. After a few months Doug went off farther into the city to live with Tony. I guess I could say I see Peter Grant and his girl Suzy Wilson often enough, and Mai – well, you know that story. My ex-girlfriend is away somewhere in New O'lins, one year closer to becomin' the nun she wants to be. But I haven't called her at that number she gave me. I left it right there etched into the porch of our old swamp house. She found out where we now live from Tony, who saw her carolling at Lakeside Mall last Christmas, and she's written to me twice, always ending with "The Lord Bless You and Keep You". And as you can imagine, ending her letters like that just discourages all the sinful, lovey-dovey lyrics I was planning on writin' back to her.

I think she knows it, that girl.

Meanwhile Harry T, my other friend, he came around a few times since we moved into the apartment. He'd just turn up on his bicycle like usual. But there were no swamp crawfish for him to get (Moms said she didn't want to see another goddamn craw-fish in her life – she'd rather die of starvation), and it generally wasn't much fun for the guy any more, cos he loved the swamp. So you'd see him appear to tell you about the latest New O'lins dance moves and then he'd leave. The last move he made was to Fort Polk for basic training. Yeah, he joined the military like he'd been sayin' for a while. That means, apart from Peter and Suzy, Frico's the only one left from our circle of friends. But you know how weird he is. I swear, if I could talk to the guy, I wouldn't be snooping around in his diary all the time. OK, maybe I would, but whatever.

Speaking of which, you shoulda seen me hustlin' off the roof to go get the diary out of the pool that day. Eventually, though, I decided to leave it inside one of those little inlets where water used to go in or out when it was a respectable pool. I reckon it would be safer there, sheltered from rain and everything, as long as the weather was normal. People in these apartments only visit the back of the complex to use the laundromat. And that's not very often, cos most of the nine washing machines are as useless as the swimming facilities, and that fake handyman Larry Lou-*ser* can't even fix his giant wedgie, for godssake.

But maan, you wouldn't believe how much I'm learning from this boy's book – even though originally I only wanted to correct his bad sentences. I never get to read the thing for more than three or five minutes at a sitting though. But last time I sat down real low in that pool, I read something *interesting*. He was writin' about Teesha and some argument they had, when all of a sudden on the next page, he just dropped a line straight outta nowhere:

"Trust me, my brother Terence is not what anybody thinks he is."

Well, first off, I was thinkin' it's based on some crap I said to Teesha – but I wasn't sure. (I say lots of flirtatious things to Teesha – can't keep track). So my mind was tickin' again like crazy. But right then I overheard our noisy neighbours fighting again and I got distracted and almost didn't see when Fricozoid jumped down into the damn pool and nearly caught me red-handed, so to speak. So that's all I got to read: him griping about me again. But that quotation had me goin' nuts. For the rest of that day I sat on the driveway looking out at the Ponchartrain levee, thinkin': "Terence is not what anybody thinks he is." Man! Why use the word "*what*", like I'm an animal or something? Well, that night I listened to lazy buses dragging themselves up and down Hayne Boulevard, still thinking about the phrase. Got up next morning and damn near pulled up all the nutgrass forcing their way up through the cracks in the apartment-complex concrete just to stop myself goin' crazy.

Now here I am, in church, at my father's memorial service, for Heaven's sake, still obsessing over it, since I haven't gotten a chance to read anything in the diary since. Well, the minister just ended his welcome. I guess I daydreamed through two readings, including one I should have done. Damn. My brothers are

lookin' at me with their faces all ruffled up. The minister invites
Moms to read the eulogy. She stands behind a tall mahogany
podium decorated with deep carvings and adjusts the microphone. There's feedback. You're not really in church if there's
no microphone feedback.

Moms takes a deep breath and starts reading: "Alrick Julian
Beaumont was born on June 11th, 1943." Well, that's about all
she manages to say. Now, if you look real close, you can see the
soul fall out of a person. Just watch the eyes, man. You'll see
something disappear, like curtains falling away from window
frames. If you ever witnessed a phone call where somebody went
from a happy hello to horrible news, then you've prob'ly seen it.
Well, that's my moms right now. Her shoulders drop. She's gone
quiet, but her love for my pops is turned up so loud it's drowning the squeaking church fans. She can't let go so easily. So she
just stands at that podium and stares ahead, her eyes glistening.
And all the women who tiptoed into the rear benches late, they
all start squirming in their seats. Cos now they prob'ly think
she's gonna give it to them in the house of the Lord. I guess it
makes sense to expect anything from a mourning woman with
a microphone. But no, my mother isn't even looking at all my
father's ex-lovers. She was beyond them. She was staring off over
the long, murky miles of time and space. And I'm sure somewhere
in those reruns in her head she saw herself and Alrick playing
on the beach in San Tainos. In the sun. A time long ago, when it
was just the two of them and their love – before real life rushed
in and laid down the law. She said as much before, and the older
I get, I have more reason not to gag when she talks about being
in love and losing someone.

Anyway, the minister, he gets up and holds her shoulders
from behind. She nods and steps down, leavin' her paper on the
podium. I hold my head down, cos I feel bad for her and worse

for myself. If *I* miss my old man, I can't imagine what she's feeling. I look up again and Frico Beaumont, of all people, is now at the podium, in my mother's place, coat back on, ready to read. I dry my eyes with the back of my hands and look again, just to make sure. *Seriously?* This boy can barely put a sentence together even if you gave him all the words on goddamn flash cards. And now he has ambitions to read in front of a whole church? At an important event like this? And of course, without his glasses. But I'm the only one making a fuss, so he begins: "Alrick Julian Beaumont was born..." Before long, he's so boring I wander off in my mind again, thinking how it seems that soon enough every damn thing in the world belongs to the word "was". Even a man who has not been confirmed dead. "Alrick Julian Beaumont *was*."

Well, after a while ol' Zoid's reading picks up and it's going fairly well, to tell the truth. People are starting to sob all over the place because of some of the details. I wish they'd stop, even though some of it is pretty sad. I learnt that my father never knew his old man. Grandpa Beaumont died when Alrick was just a few months old – and that could prob'ly explain why he's so wonderfully screwed up family-wise. But then, just when I'm beginning to feel proud of the reading, Frico decides there's too much snifflin' and sadness in the place. He doesn't stick to the script, but instead goes off in the middle of the eulogy and tries to be a stand-up comedian. In church. He leans forward and grips the podium with both hands, tryin' to look all cool and relaxed.

"Of course, if you're like my brother Terence, you'd probably say there's no reason to cry."

Maan, I may be shocked, but my mother is *mortified* right now. Her hand is crushin' her handkerchief. She glares at the guy from the front pew and shakes her head slowly from side to side. It doesn't stop him. Frico's on a roll.

"Cos Terence, he doesn't think our father is gone."

There's a buzz in the church. I don't know where he's going with this, but for a second I wonder if he knows about me correcting his journal, and maybe this is public revenge for all that red ink.

"But you have to forgive Terence. He's the little one."

Uncomfortable giggles here and there.

"A *little* stubborn, a *little* too opinionated, a *little* loopy from time to time."

Now the whole church is laughin' a little, like they think this is a planned part of the show or somethin'. Or maybe people laugh when they feel awkward. Well, my mother, she pulls herself to the edge of her seat and stares at him. Then, still without saying a word, she looks over her shoulder. Her eyes scope the church and the laughing dies down. Cos the woman has San Tainos amulets around her neck and bracelets on her arm, and her head is wrapped in white like a voodoo high priestess. So she looks like she's fixin' to hex anybody who dared turn her husband's memorial service into a circus.

It's prob'ly the first time she's kind of stood up for me, but it's too late. Cos now it's really awkward for everybody. And me? I'm mad as hell. So I start thinkin' he's damn lucky that old podium he's leaning on can still hold him up, even though he's so fulla shit. Trus' me, soon as I run that through my mind, the top part of the podium, the flat part, it just slides out from under his elbows – with perfect timing – just as if I'd gone up there and dragged it out from under the bastard myself. The thing slips off and lands on the church floor, makin' one hell of a racket. It bounces towards us in the front row. My mother claps her hand one time, and the thing wobbles off into the corner like a lost hubcap. The congregation gasps in unison, then starts buzzin' again. But Frico? That guy just steps away from the other piece of podium and doesn't even miss a beat.

31

While the officiating minister and his deacons try to gather up the busted part, Frico comes right out front like a pop star talkin' to his fans. He looks me dead in the eye and continues his routine: "Termites! Ladies and gentlemen. They're evil. Overcome them with good! Give generously."

The congregation bursts out laughing and clapping like they forgot where the hell they are. Then, when the deacons put the top part of the podium back on, Frico, he gets back to the eulogy with a straight face, as if nothing just happened.

"Alrick Beaumont was a brilliant man who gave generously of himself. And many admired and loved him – y'all included."

Applause. His timing is perfect. Then everybody quiets down and the congregation loves him, that jerk.

Five

At five o' clock in the morning it's a little chilly out, even during this Louisiana summer. My denim jacket works, though, so only my cheeks tighten against the wind coming up off Ponchartrain. I didn't wash my face. No time. And I'm sure my hair is a seriously bushy "bed head". But no one in the apartment complex comes outside this time of morning, and that's the point. So I pull the apartment door shut and head across the quadrangle in the dark. I've been questioning myself these past few days on account of those weird occurrences and that line from Frico's diary. And that's exactly what I'm heading for.

I left the red marker in the room this morning. What I really need to look for are some answers in this boy's writing. Well, it's all quiet in the corridors 'cept for 5A, where our noisy neighbours are moanin' and breathin' all heavy, even this early in the mornin'. That's what woke me up in the first place. Don't know how the hell Frico and Moms can sleep with all that bouncin' around behind the wall. Moms says it's just disgraceful how they carry on over there. Sometimes Frico calls Teesha so she can listen over the phone, I swear. Me, I just feel bad for that neighbour guy. His love life sounds like a terrible fight.

The maple tree shivers against a gust when I pass it. There's a "FOR SALE" sign on the ol' beat-up Tercel. Yah, believe it. Still scanning the area, I jog down some steps to the old pool at the rear of the complex. There's been a few showers of rain, and the diary is safe there, tucked into the inlet. Frico hasn't missed it either. Seems like he stopped writing in it just after we left the swamp. Suddenly a blast of cold goes from my head to my heels. It's not the wind. It's because right on the edge of the empty pool, under the dull poolside lamp, I can see a girl. She's sitting with her head bowed down. She's in pyjama bottoms, bedside slippers and one of those Madonna T-shirts with a windbreaker over it.

Now, lemme tell ya, this is the strangest sight to see at five in the morning. And I freeze, cos I feel like heading back to the apartment in a hurry, no lie. But she looks like she's sleeping, and I'm curious to find out who the hell she is. Well, soon as my foot falls on the next step, she holds her head up and I can't see any eyes behind that curtain of curly hair. I stop. She pauses. Crickets. Heavy breathing. I'm not moving and neither is she. It's as if we can both just reverse and slink back into the holes we came out of and pretend we never even saw each other. I'm beginning to think she's not human, but she brushes her curls away from her face and hollers out to me as if it's broad daylight and we're long-time friends:

"Wow. This guy Skid is a real freak, huh?"

I'm wondering how the hell this girl knows my name, and now my feet are completely convinced it's time to get goin'. Then I see she's found the damn diary. Would you believe it? She has it wide open in her lap, reading out Frico's private business.

"Where'd you get that? And who are ya anyway?"

"Some idiot left it in the pool. I'm Claire."

"Hm. So why're you out here, Claire?"

"I love reading by lamplight, I guess. That and my uncle and his wife are having a little fun and I don't wanna hear how much."

I stop a few feet from her and I hold my hand out for the diary.

"Those noisy folks are your family? Really sorry to hear. Anyway, gimme that now."

"Oh it's *yoours*?" She stretches to shake my hand instead. "Well, congrats. Nice hiding place you got here."

She has an accent – I can't make out what it is. But she beat me to saying it.

"You have an accent."

"Yeah, my pops is… was Cajun." I'm wondering why I'm even talking to this girl who I've never seen in my life.

"Awesome. But naw, it's not the Cajun accent. It's something else."

"OK. Big deal. Lemme get that book, please."

"Who's asking?"

She's really annoying. Worse than when I met Mai years ago.

"My name's Terence—"

"Wait, wait. You mean, Terence 'Skid' Beaumont? The freak from this book? Wow. Whoever's writing in this journal does not like you *at all*."

"It's a *diary*, and I don't care what people think about me."

Dammit. I forgot that just a few pages in, Fricozoid wrote my whole goddamn name in the book, or I would have told her my name was Frederick or Wilfred or Clark or something. (No offence if that's your name or anything.) Anyway, I try to grab the journal, but this girl flips out a cigarette lighter with the longest frickin' flame I've ever seen in my life. She holds the book out over the pool with the fire waving under it. The edge of a page turns brown and smoke curls away. This chick is actually tryin' to bully me. I swear she's slightly neurotic, but no one's told her yet. And now is not the time.

"Sit down Terence. You can either let me read to you like it's a bedtime story or you can put the ashes back together when I'm gone."

Goddamn girl is *irritating*. But to be honest, she's bangin' too. Yup. Really, really cute, and she knows it. That's why she's been laughing and throwin' back her head like she's at a goddamn model photo shoot. Women… man! She got deep, honey-coloured eyes. And I hope it's not just because of the gold of the poolside light. She's a smoker, though. Smells like it. Smoke and perfume. I like that for some reason. (I'm messed up, I know. We've been through that already.) The fire leaping from the lighter shows more of her dark-brown curls.

Thick, rich. Long enough to hide her eyes when she leans forward. But it stops at her nose and leaves her mouth peeking out like the last strawberry on the bush. *Ooowee.* Girl waits till I take a seat on the edge of the pool a few feet away before she puts the book down and lights one up.

"Are you old enough to be smokin'?" (I'm just checking her out, age and all.)

"Aren't you too young to be my dad?" You can hear her voice coming through the smoke, muffled.

"Me? I'm not too young for anything, period."

"Pshhh!"

Pshhh? I hate when girls do that. It's the worse thing. You try to be all mature and suave and they go: "*Pshhh!*" and roll their eyes. You can feel your balls shrinking, I swear.

Now I'm really thinkin' of grabbin' for the diary again and making a break for it, but she starts reading, and that catches me off guard.

"Anyway, listen to this," she says. "*Believe me, my brother Terence 'Skid' Beaumont* – that's you – *is not what anybody thinks he is…*"

She's picking up right where I left off last time. I'd really rather read it by myself, and I'm pretty riled up, but I reckon it's better to hear something than nothing at all, cos this weird girl looks like she's nuts enough to burn the damn book for real. To my ears, her voice is peanut-butter smooth. Like somethin' you'd lick from a spoon. And she puts on a British kind of English when she's reading. You know, the kind that forgets that the letter R was ever invented? But just when I start listenin', she flips the pages back and forth and suddenly stops reading. Somethin' caught her eye. She's scanning the whole page like crazy and her big honey eyes are sparklin'.

"Wow. Wow. Oh wow," she's says to herself, really getting on my nerves now.

"What? Read it for *godssake*!"

Can't believe I'm allowing this shit. The term "jerk" is usually reserved for Frico, but this girl is *pushing* it.

She leans forward over the pool. Drags on her Newport. A cloud is swirlin' around in her mouth. Words force it over the edge of her lips when she begins to read again:

"We didn't have a TV for years, growing up... and that's because of Terence. My father would fix it and Terence would break it, even though he was barely a year old. I wasn't quite sure how, but he did. And he got away with it. The last kid always does. We always had to pitch in and hurry and fix stuff before our parents found out, or just keep the baby away from things so that life would be less miserable for all of us. Tony made toys for Terence and Doug gave him a savings box and tried to teach him about money. Kids love money once they learn you can exchange it for candy. But all that didn't help. He still broke stuff. Over the years my mother and father argued about it all the time, because my father's repair jobs were taking too long or some customers were getting their appliances back more torn up than they brought them in. So soon there wasn't a hell of a lot of money. The biggest thing Skid broke in my family was the bank."

She's resting back on her elbows, and I'm fidgeting cos of what I just heard. Maan, I don't remember it being *that* bad when I was little. I mean, I *do* remember my family always hollerin' out my damn name for every little thing. To this day I still think my name should always be written in big block letters with a permanent exclamation sign on the end of it. Well, now I do a double take, cos this Claire girl is staring at me. I look down into the pool and up at the winking stars, trying to avoid her eyes. Damn weird. She leans her head and smiles, then brushes her hair back and starts giggling.

"*What?*"

She laughs out so loud I swear she woke up all of Hayne Boulevard. Her eyes are wet when she points the cigarette at me and shakes it to emphasize what she's sayin'. A few tobacco sparks fall off.

"So… wait… ha ha… you single-handedly bankrupted your family as a baby? Daamn. Who wrote this? Your brother… your sister? They're hilarious!"

The tips of my ears are getting hot, and I think meeting this girl is turning into a disaster. A man appears on the poolside stairs.

"Claire! Get back in 'ere! You only here for one li'le summer, and you out here all by you'self so early?"

It's her unbearable uncle – thank God. He hobbles down the pool steps. Dark-skinned dude. Bedside slippers, boxer shorts and socks. That T-shirt and leopard-print robe are barely covering his gut: really charming guy.

Claire hands me the diary and gets up.

"Uncle Mattis, you two really need to make up during the day, OK? Do your boinkin' in the *day*."

He puts a fat finger to his lips, glances at me and looks back to her. "Shhh! Why you lettin' everybody know your family's private business, eh?"

He talks funny. But when he sticks out his hand and introduces himself to me officially, the guy switches into real standard English: "Mattis, George Mattis" – as if he thinks his leopard print became a business suit.

I wave hello from a distance: "Terence."

They walk off arguing. Mattis takes a break from laughing at Claire. He points at the Tercel under the tree and hollers:

"Hey Terry, tell your ol' lady I'll give her a good deal on the ol' limousine. I'm selling it!"

This guy doesn't think it's too early for anything. And people shouldn't call me Terry.

I dust off the diary and head home. Now the sounds of the city are rising with the sun. It's 5.45 a.m. when I get back in. I know cos there's a blackbird that raises hell on the window ledge of Moms' room every morning at this time. He's loud and as hoarse as a hawker, but she encourages him with sunflower seeds, so he keeps comin' back. The woman loves anything with feathers. She'd prob'ly throw seeds to the goddamn vultures if they'd eat it. I sneak into her room. She fell asleep with the calculator in her hand again and her feet danglin' off the edge of the bed. The memorial-service pamphlet is beside the pillow. You can see she's been sleeping on a layer of hard work and worries. Her body does not relax into the bed. But her face is peaceful. Pointy nose and high cheekbones with skin polished like a carving.

The soft morning light is getting a cutting edge now, and those white lace curtains, they're breathin' the breeze from the lake, in and out like lungs, in time with her groanin'. Valerie Beaumont says groanin' is the most natural chant in the world, a sleep spell for the sick and the weary. She should know. Many nights that's what puts her to sleep. Between my father and raising four boys I wonder sometimes how her heart managed to get this far. The early bird is gettin' into his second verse behind the glass, marchin' back and forth and singing for seeds, but she's not even stirring. When I was seven or eight and she fell asleep dog-tired, I used to put a little mirror under her nose to see if she was still alive. She doesn't know that. Just like she doesn't know what I just found out by the pool.

* * *

I'm making my own breakfast. It's only cereal, so I fix a bowl for Frico and wake him up. He's surprised. He takes it and digs in, even though one time I gave him a big, fat garden slug concealed in a glass of milk. Don't remember why, but he deserved it, I can tell you that.

"OK" (*yawn*) "whaddya want, Skid? I don't have a dime."

"I wouldn't ask you for money, you're always broke... a starvin' artist, like they say. Teesha pays for every damn thing."

"Yeah, you're right. That's why I'm going to college come fall. Make somethin' of myself. You should start plannin' for that."

"College. Yeah, I guess I should."

And he knows I'm brushing him off, so he rambles on a bit about scholarships and SAT classes and how I'm no fool and I'm a Beaumont and we're survivors and we always work things out and Moms is doing her best.

"I want to make money like Doug."

"Well, Doug got a business head," he says, slurping the milk. "That's his talent. You have to be more realistic than that."

Be realistic. Says the hoodoo sketcher who makes impossible things happen with a goddamn pencil. I so wish I had another slug.

"By the way, speaking of money... did you miss this?"

He reaches into a drawer and tosses me my old wallet.

"How'd you get this, man?"

"Seems the coats we wore to the funeral got mixed up at the church. I had yours on at the podium."

I checked to make sure everything was still in my wallet (you don't know that guy Frico), including the buck I took off Broadway and Squash's grave. It wasn't.

"So where the hell's my money?"

"Oh, sorry, I gave that to the deacons when they passed the offering plate around."

40

"You gave *my* money to the deacons?"

"Yeah, big deal. It's only a buck, man. I couldn't in good conscience stand up there and say 'give generously' and then give nothing. Plus it's only a buck, and I gave it to God, man – chill out."

At this point I can't possibly tell him that I took the money off two devils. I change the subject.

"So how's Teesha?"

"Funny you should ask. Wanna roll with us to the Wildlife Refuge today? We're planting swamp grass."

"Wow, exciting! I'm really lookin' forward to mud on my tennis shoes and bird shit on my shoulders. Look, it's a Sunday, man. People *sleep* on a Sunday."

But in my head I'm thinking how the last time I saw Frico's girl she was *so* fine. *Hubba hubba*, as Pa Campbell would say about beautiful women in his nasty old-man way. Wouldn't hurt to see her skin glistening under some swamp sun. God knows I need the adrenalin. So even though I want to see more of that girl Claire who seems to be staying with her uncle for the summer, I say "OK". Frico hijacked me with all that scholarship talk anyhow. Imagine, I make the guy breakfast just to see if I could learn anything more about the diary from the horse's mouth, and the damn horse chomps down the whole conversation.

Anyway, I sleep for about an hour, and when I open my eyes Moms is up. I look out into the kitchen and… the Incredibly Wonderful Teesha Grey is sitting there with a cup of tea, talking with Valerie Beaumont. How can a girl look so good in dumpy jeans and a big ol' T-shirt? She's blessed, I tell ya, *blessed*. And she's got this cool complexion, like she pops into the shower every hour or so. Mysterious, hot as hell and smart. That's too much power for one person.

"You could have told me she was here, man."

He ignores me at first and pulls on the new hoodie that he got in the mail from the art college. "Lannaman's Institute of Art, NYC" it says across the front.

"She's driving her old lady's car, Skid. How else did you think we'd make it to the refuge? That's halfway to where we used to live."

It's a good thing he misunderstood me, cos what I meant was that I wanted to freshen up before she arrived. Well, when we're heading out, Frico takes off the Lannaman's hoodie, cos his girl says it makes him look like a rap reject. I think it makes him look all preppy and artsy-fartsy, and that's my problem with it. I might be artsy. But I'm not fartsy. Fartsy is the pretentious part of being artsy. Like people who walk around braggin' that they're poets or whatever else. They wear frilly shirts and carry around books and everythin'. It's annoying.

Anyway, Teesha gives Frico the keys and we're backing out in her mother's old Land Rover. It's one of those original Rovers that look like a tank: grey, with rivets all along the side. You can't break that vehicle, you have to wear it down until it dies, man. Well, halfway down the red-brick slope, Frico suddenly decides to mash the brakes and we all get jostled a bit. That's because turning off Hayne Boulevard and into the apartment complex is a long, black Lincoln Town Car. The thing waddles up the driveway with the engine almost quiet. It squeezes past us on the left, in slow motion, and we all look across. Behind the wheel is a big bearded guy, and the veins at the side of my head begin to throb a little bit.

Six

Seabreeze is a soft sandpaper. You should see how it slowly scours the fishing huts along the Gulf Coast till they're as brown as the herring hangin' inside of 'em. The Gulf goes on for ever. Blue water breathin' out raw fish guts and salt. Far out the horizon line is raggedy. A fat cloud with rain bristling out of it is scrubbing the colour out of the sea. When you're caught between the rain to the right and sun sizzlin' over the swamp on your left, they say the Devil and his wife are havin' a bitch of a fight. But all the way to the Wildlife Refuge, Teesha and her boyfriend soak up the scenery and smile at each other like lovers on vacation.

Meanwhile, over in the back seat, Skid Beaumont is not havin' half as much fun. It's all coming back to me now – the reasons I hate the damn swamp. Dry heat. Black and grey mud. Giant clumps of fermenting swamp grass. Bugs beatin' the windshield and buzzin' round your ears.

Well, at least this wild atmosphere is helping me keep my mind off the fact that Tracey "Backhoe" Benet just drove up in our driveway, one day after my father's "funeral". Lord knows I felt like staying home when I saw his mug in the rear-view mirror. And when he crawled past us along the driveway, you could see his wrist on the steering wheel, and it had a big ol' ganglion. That's like a swelling right at the wrist joint. But his was huge, like a hunchback for your arm. So yeah, I'd rather be at home right now. Cos apart from Teesha's curves, the only reason I'm here today is cos Frico needs a replacement to plant grasses when he goes to school in the fall. And that means money in my pocket.

Now look, this Wildlife Refuge has grown. It's the first time I'm seeing it properly, cos the last time we passed through here you could say we were in kind of a hurry. Under the reality of the muck and the muddy waters you can make out Frico's magic sketching of nearly a year ago. Every now and then, a clump of mangroves or a clearing in the trees looks exactly like a corner of the L-shaped island we used to live on in the swamp. It makes me dizzy, like what they say happens when you see a ghost. Surreal, man. My brother prob'ly resketched everything from swamp photos that he took. Inside the Refuge the birds are in frightening numbers, and I hear in the wintertime it's worse. There's always some bird showing off with a song about nothin' or some silly water fowl racin' across the surface, leaving a trail of circles. These critters have nothing to do, I tell ya. Above our heads they bend branches, then leap off to dive-bomb some fish. Then there's the bayou itself: savage water standing still for miles, green crust on top. Sharp things break through every now and then. A sudden splash, jaws up, slammin' shut, swallowin' things whole.

I watch Teesha Grey bending over in the boat and jumpin' into chest-deep water for about an hour or so, and that also helps me not to go nuts. She makes plantin' water grass a beautiful, beautiful thing. But now it's almost midday, and I swear I'm so bored I'm beginnin' to listen to evaporation taking place. The world around you gets all wobbly, and your shirt sticks to your back. There's a ring around the sun now: a white-hot bulb in a steel ceiling. I'm happy when it's time for lunch and some shade. But I'm not happy with the *kind* of lunch these Conservation Lands people serve. So I'm picking through it slowly until Frico goes to the portable craphouse on the grounds. That's when I get myself into trouble. I finally brave up and I ask Teesha if Frico's pencil has anything to do with her looking so wonderfully curvy up on top.

44

Well, look man, she didn't take it as a compliment. The last thing I saw was those lines in the palm of her hand comin' up so close I could read her future, for godssakes. Then *pow*. Stars. She slapped me so hard the whole world went dark before I came to my senses and took off.

Now there are strict Wildlife Refuge rules about how we use the motorboats, but I'm really mad at myself for being so stupid. I have no idea where I'm going. But wide-open water allows you a lot of options. When my face cools down, I recognize an old friend lying on top of a levee. It's those train tracks that slice through the swamp. I used to run alongside them all day when I was little: a horizontal piece of the city cutting through the wilderness – beautiful nuts and bolts taking you to civilization. Today, though, it's quiet and rusty, cos they stopped using it. And I hear they're about to come and rip the whole thing up pretty soon as they develop the Refuge further. But I'm just as excited as if the Gulf Coast train itself was rumbling past me in all its mechanical glory. Cos now maybe I can follow these tracks off to my left, back to where we used to live. It takes me a half-hour of backing up the boat and goin' around swamp debris and tangled roots. I have to keep the tracks in sight or I swear I'll get lost. Well, after a spell, the boat slides through a stretch of mangroves and I'm there: L-Island, as I used to call it. Well, if this is the part where a heavenly choir is supposed to sing out, it'll be a sad second-line chorus, I'll tell you that.

L-island is more of a mess than it ever was. The Gulf rolled in and pushed the lake onto the land, so it looks like there's a permanent high tide. The extra water rolled over those sandbag-and-mud levees we'd build right before a storm. The whole place is a brackish brown pond. Beneath this boat are places where we used to walk and play and run from trouble. It's funny how you can come back to a place you lived in all your life and not feel welcome. Through the trees I try to make out where the creek was. I can't. It's completely swallowed up by the flood. And vines hang from the trees right above where the sinkhole opened up and took in Broadway and Squash that night. White flowers flare all the way down one vine. The lowest blooms drop just above the water, almost kissing the reflections on the surface – bells swinging without makin' a sound.

I cut the motor and steer the boat through traces of oil on the water: colours running together as if a rainbow melted in the heat. Between the trees, spiders built sky cities and highways of silk. The place looks weird, man, no lie. It's like those train tracks might as well have been a goddamn brick road that takes you into a forbidden forest or a jacked-up ghost town. Suddenly all the critters keep quiet. Dead silence makes my ears ring. The swamp is tryin' to keep a secret. Flowers force open and rivers keep comin' through, like they want to forget all that happened here.

I ditch the boat on a mudbank and slop through shallow water on foot for a minute. The shack we used to live in should be just south of the train tracks. Sunbeams come slidin' down all around through the trees. On a nearby bush, buds bloom into butterflies. The shack should be just ahead. I find it sittin' low, half-submerged in the bayou. The windows are sad eyes peering over the surface. Under the porch, the front door is open, in a gasp. Our house has drowned.

I wade towards it. Tadpoles wriggle away. The ripples around my shins become brown waves bouncin' off the shack as I climb onto the porch and peer in through the door. It looks like someone had been using our house as a fishing hut before it sank. Maan, I don't know – but right now this shack seems so small. Like how did we fit six people and all their ambitions and arguments into that little space? Even the swamp itself seems all cluttered up: full of déjà vus, I guess. It's like at every turn I keep grabbin' hold of the tail end of a memory – somethin' really important that I should be remembering – but it's too slippery, and so it slides away before I can get a good grip. Anyway, I have my eyes peeled, tryin' hard to see inside the shack. I can hear chains draggin' right about the same time my eyes finally adjust – and shit, all I can make out in the far corner of the room is a white face, two long horns, a long beard and some beady eyes shining back at me. Well, on my way back down from leapin' about five feet into the air, I figure out what the damn thing is: a stupid billy goat that got away from Ma Campbell during the last few days we lived out here. That bastard is still alive even in all this mess. Of course, me realizing that it's not ol' Beelzebub himself livin' in our abandoned house doesn't help me one bit, cos fear is crawlin' up my back right now, and it's time to go. Clouds are cuttin' off the sun, and all around there's a gurgling. Brown bubbles comin' up from the bayou like burps. I panic. Two steps back and the half-sunken porch gives way. I grab the rail and it comes off in my hand along with a thousand termites that look like rice racing up my arm. There's Mai's faded address and phone number still carved by ballpoint pen into the wood. It's funny how things burn into your mind at the worst times. I can see the information in my head while I'm slapping at bugs and runnin' like hell through the damn trees with that goat bleating after me the whole way. There's blood in the mud now. You can smell it. My chest is a drum and my head is a wreckin' ball tearing down Spider City. I pretty much dive into the damn boat with a faceful of web and blaze out of L-Island. I'm heading in no particular direction, just *out*. Motor's sputtering – must have picked up some roots – but I keep going.

Well, as soon as I get out into open water, the motor goes dead. I'm pulling hard on the starter rope as clouds come over in a hurry. Rip it once, twice, three times: nothing. *Grab the paddles, quick. Turn, turn.* All around, critters keep chanting like it's feeding time. Trees are shuffling. A powerful current sloshes waves against the boat and pulls on the paddles. Strange circles appear on the water, like ripples from invisible rain, and the boat is turnin' around by itself. Then over the bow all I can see comin' to the surface are plastic-covered cards. Hundreds of 'em, floating to the surface while the boat turns like a clock gone crazy. The swamp goes silent and, in a second, I'm dizzy and fixin' to fall overboard into the sea of hoodoo-magic seals surrounding me: decades of my father's dead dreams suddenly belched up by this bayou.

I have to paddle the whole way to the Refuge. I get back with the borrowed boat when the sun is ripe and ready to drop. Teesha and Frico are sitting on the landing with their feet hangin' over the water. Suzy, Peter Grant, Doug and Tony are behind them. Looks like they called out the whole goddamn cavalry on account of me being gone so long. They don't even look relieved when I paddle up. Matter of fact nobody says a word. A wildlife ranger storms out of an office behind them and throws his thumb over his shoulder, motioning for me to get the hell out of the boat and give back the hip boots. He jumps straight off the landing into the boat and roars away. Teesha tells me I'm "officially banned from the Refuge". *Banned?* I used to *live* around here, lady. Big deal anyway. It's just a weird ol' swamp.

Seven

There's a Meat Mart just two blocks away from our house that kinda reminds me of Lam Lee Hahn, minus the pretty Vietnamese girl who I'm still crazy about. It's where Moms gets all her smokes and stuff. They sell lottery tickets and liquor behind the cash register too. Ask Frico, he knows all about that stuff. On his eighteenth birthday, the boy went out and bought lottery numbers, cigarettes and a bottle of beer just because he could. But you can't even mention these things to Valerie. Especially about the lottery.

"You might as well chuck all your dolla' bills into a blender and press purée" is what she says about gambling. And let's not even start on the drinking, man. Drinking is drugs, as far as she's concerned.

Anyway, I'm only at the Meat Mart today because of Suzy Wilson and Peter. You should see 'em. Peter's profilin' in a pair of Ray-Bans that he won't even take off indoors, and he's talking real slow, like a douchebag musician doing a TV interview. Suzy's still sweet. She's a blonde now (bleach), and so self-conscious of her hair you can tell she's fishin' for a compliment. It's nice – shows up her green eyes. I'd tell her I like it, but then I'd have to go ahead and compliment her whole outfit and, to be honest, that neon-pink off-the-shoulder top with her white leggings and green leg-warmers make her look like a slice of watermelon. Maybe it's just sour grapes, since Pete ended up with her and not me, but I'm not gettin' into all that stuff today.

Anyway, these two are plannin' to defy their parents and move in together once they reach eighteen, which is soon. They got no other plans in life but to be wild and free and run around town annoyin' people by speakin' about culture and sports and music and food, all in full French. That's lame. I mean, Claire learnt French and a bunch of other stuff along with her ABCs, and you don't see her goin' on and on about it. Anyway, those two drove up to the apartment today and met Claire for the first time, and the two ladies get to talkin' girlie stuff.

Then all of a sudden Suzy wants honey biscuits. You know how girls can get: they always want "something sweet", especially after lunch. Man, I'd buy somethin' for myself and Claire, but Frico, he gave away my last dollar in that church-offering stunt. Plus that stupid "rewind or get fined" policy at the video-rental store really cleaned me out this month. Well, good ol' Peter says he'll get us some snacks while we shoot the breeze. The Meat Mart guy doesn't like teenagers hangin' out in front of his place, cos it encourages drive-bys – so he says. Peter tells him his statement is racist and the guy cusses us out properly in Spanish and goes back inside. So, we're hangin' out, I'm chewin' on a piece of beef jerky that could double as a leather belt, while bourgeoisie Pete is listenin' to all the troubles of my life.

"Man, I'm happy y'all came by so I could bail, cos I got banned from the Refuge, so I got nowhere to go. And that guy Tracey Backhoe Benet is back at my house today again. Just need to avoid him and my mother for a while. I mean, two days in a damn row! And he's gotten into my *kitchen* this time – him and his ganglion that's the size of the Superdome. I mean, las' time it was just the parking lot. That's one of the bad things about living in the city. It's easier for people to just show up on your frickin' doorstep without notice. Y'all shoulda told me, Pete. Well, I swear if he comes around tomorrow I'm gonna mount a verse from the Good Book on that refrigerator, right where he can see it: 'Withdraw thy foot from thy neighbour's house, before he gets tired of you and hates your guts.'"

Well, while I'm looking over at the lake and yappin', I'm expecting Pete to say: "That's in there?" – but he doesn't. And I notice Claire's gone quiet too. So I turn around and Peter and Suzy are French-talking and French-kissing each other with food in their mouths. See? This typa thing is the real reason the Meat Mart guy doesn't want people in front of his goddamn store. It also means that it's time to take off.

"C'mon Claire, let's bounce."

"Where you going, Skiddo?" Peter wants to know, mid-kiss.

"Just think I'll take my English-speaking ass back to *el maison*, if y'all don't mind."

"It's *la maison*, Skid. It's French, feminine gender."

"It's *annoyin'*, is what it is, man."

"What's wrong witchoo man?"

"No, what's wrong with you two? We can't hang around here in the middle of your goddamn tongue-switchin', man. We're bailin'."

"Easy, man, I was hearing you. I don't listen with my lips, dude."

"Look, I couldn't be Frenchin' with my girl if you were babblin' on about the New O'lins Saints' upcoming season or jazz or some shit."

He looks hurt that I said "jazz" and "shit" in the same sentence. Obviously missed my point. So the boy gets spiteful.

"Awright man, bail. But don't forget you owe me some dough, from before... and for the beef jerky. Gas money, you know."

I can't really tell why, but I get a little annoyed at this boy asking me about his money so soon after he said it was cool and I could give him back whenever, and especially since the jerky tasted like it came from the cow's hoof. So I just whip out the wallet to show him I had no cheese whatsoever. I find a grubby old penny in one of the pockets, so I flip it at the guy and walk off in a huff. Well, all I know is I'm halfway home and Claire is tellin' me not to walk so fast, when all of a sudden we had to duck and Claire lost her honey biscuits, cos one of those manhole covers in the middle of Hayne Boulevard just popped out like a Coke cap, flipped high into the air, came down, landed sideways and rolled into the goddamn Meat Mart window. Now there's glass and sausages and cuss words everywhere.

We run back to see Peter and Suzy kissing dirt. At first the Meat Mart guy thinks we had something to do with it, so he comes out cussing *en español* again. Pete is up off the ground, but you can see his ego is still flat on the concrete. So he goes off on the guy in French, and all of a sudden we're locked inside a language sandwich. Good thing the foreman from a road construction crew saw the whole thing and hopped across the street to squash all the drama.

"Easy, man, it ain't these kids's fault. It's those manhole covers again. Happens all the time when there's rain closer to the river. Water pressure builds up underground and – *bang* – soon you got yourself a sewage cannon."

Sure enough, there's murky water spewing out of the manhole right now. So we're all joggin' back up the street to avoid gettin' soaked, Claire and Suzy still moaning about their honey biscuits like they didn't see we just escaped being clobbered by a cast-iron Oreo.

Back inside, I pass Tracey Benet and Moms. I try to be pleasant and pretend I don't see the dozen red roses on the kitchen table. Benet is drinking lemon-rind tea, which I know he didn't take to our house in his own thermos.

I stop at the sink and mess around a bit, just to listen in on what they're talkin' about. But those two are keepin' quiet now that I'm here. It's funny, no matter how long we were neighbours in the swamp, I can count the number of times I came so close to this guy. It's a strange sightin', sort of. You kinda expect a man like Backhoe Benet, with such a huge reputation, to fill the room with a presence as suffocatin' as a sulphur mine. But now the biggest thing in the room is his ganglion, I swear. And seeing him sittin' there at our kitchen table with his hair thinning on top and my father's simple old teacup in his hand, you can't tell he's one of the richest guys in south Louisiana.

Now, I'm trying hard, but I can't remember what his voice sounds like. It's like when you're goin' about your business and you suddenly run across a rockstar and you try to remember even one of their songs but you just can't, cos your brain is so damn distracted by their star-ness.

"H'llo Ter'nce, haw tha hell are ya?"

That's it. Deep Southern drawl comin' through a mouthful of mashed potatoes and bullshit. And he's loud.

Yeah, now I remember: his voice is what takes up space. He's one of those blowhards who speak full volume with the hope that his voice can echo in your kitchen long after he's gone.

"Doin' alright, sir, thank you very much. You?"

Dammit, I hate when my mother hijacks me with people I have to force myself to talk to.

"Oh, I'm here. Tryin' ta make the best of it."

Yah. I heard your company, Earnest-Benet, just hit another natural-gas jackpot. White suit, silk shirt, hundred-dollar haircut. Making the best of it my ass.

"Yew grown so big though, Ter'nce. Yew a man now!"

Oh jeez. You saw me a year ago. And you're still swallowin' one of the Es in "Terence".

"So sorry about yer father, Ter'nce. We go so far back, me and him."

OK, this guy is blowin' much more smoke than Moms' ciga-rette. I'm out.

I mumble a response, then barge into the bedroom and slam the door. Frico is hugging the phone and whispering to Teesha on the other end.

"Dude, off the phone. We need to talk."

Even with the whole Refuge episode, he looks relieved to see me for the first time in for ever. He puts the receiver against his chest. I hit the high-speed button on that little metal-blade fan in the room – that thing chops up your words like an Osterizer, so it sounds like rain on the roof.

I point towards the kitchen with my thumb. "What the hell?"

"The woman's lost it," he says. Sometimes Frico is capable of great clarity.

"We need to—"

"—do something, I know." He mumbles into the phone, hangs up and puts both hands on his head. Well, before we can come up with any idea of what action to take, we hear the chairs in the kitchen being pushed away from the table and Backhoe Benet's fancy shoes making tracks back to his car.

"Maybe he got the hint."

"Prob'ly got scared."

We're high-fivin' when Moms opens the door to our bedroom. She's in proper-English mode. Mad as hell.

"Frico, Terence. None of that is necessary or appropriate behaviour."

"Well... we were saying the same thing, Momma. Not appropriate behaviour at all, especially after a funeral."

"Mr Benet came by to apologize for not being there and to offer condolences."

"Guess those red roses are for Pops too, huh, Mrs Beaumont?"

Soon as the words come out of my mouth, I feel like a total jerk. She just looks at me and walks away. Aww, man. Fricozoid, he shakes his head and goes tut-tut-tut, all self-righteousey, like

54

he wasn't *thinkin'* the same damn thing I was honest enough to say out loud. So he goes out there to apologize, but not before we smell cigarette smoke. In about twelve minutes, him and Moms, they're out there laughin'. Well, Frico's coughin' more than laughin'. He can't stand Moms' smokin', and he'll be glad to be rid of it when he goes off to college. But today, he's playin' the hypocrite.

Now I'm in the room by myself watchin' the day turn rusty-red and I'm thinkin': "That charmer really knows how to fix *everything there is in this life*. What am I gonna do when he's gone?" Well, I reckon it's a good thing the bastard is *still* here, cos our noisy neighbours' bed just started creaking again. And now their headboard is bangin' down our bedroom wall.

PART TWO

Eight

I was wondering when Valerie Beaumont was finally gonna snap on account of all that hammering. Well, she's over there right now, beating on the neighbours' door. It's Claire who answers. She shrugs and apologizes to Moms, puts her head back inside the apartment and hollers out her uncle's name. The racket stops. I swear, suddenly you can hear traffic on the streets, birds in the sky, the refrigerator hummin', the toilet tank fillin' up and everything. I can just imagine Mattis getting up and saying "This better be damn good", like they do in the movies. He comes to his door, and Claire steps outside in front of him and walks along the corridor. She's passing our apartment when I pull her inside and half-close the door. She's grinning.

"Shit! Your mother just walked up and banged on the door—"

"I know!"

Frico nods to Claire, but he's more interested in hearing the confrontation than in meeting somebody new. Moms is in her calm, killer voice. And she left somethin' on the stove, so you know she's gonna make a quick job of this. She starts off talkin' about how embarrassing it is to have visitors over with all that hammerin' on the wall, and how she has "two impressionable young boys" and was wondering if he and his wife wouldn't mind "keeping it down in the honeymoon suite".

Well, look man. All of a sudden I hear Mattis go from zero to frickin' ten. He's on top of his voice, as loud as the trumpet of the Lord, cussin' at my mother. But not for the life of me can

I understand a word he's sayin'. He might as well be speakin' French.

Frico knows a bit of French. And he's lookin' at me blank. And that ain't Spanish neither.

To make matters worse, Valerie Beaumont cranks her voice up to the same level and starts hollering right back at Mattis – *in the man's own doorway* – but worse, in the same strange language. What the frickin' hell.

We look around and Claire is on the floor laughing her ass off.

"This is too funny!"

Well, I'm happy somebody understands this mumbo-jumbo, cos all I'm hearing from Moms and Mattis is:

"*Somethin'-somethin'* – eh? Eh?"

"*Somethin'-somethin'-somethin'* – eeeh? Eeeh?"

Claire is up off the floor, eyes wet, trying to catch her breath. Then she starts translating.

"They're cussin' in Caribbean patois. San Tainos dialect, to be specific."

I should've known, but last time I heard that stuff we were in the swamp. And it was nothin' as thick as this, trus' me. This one must be from the country parts of San Tainos, no doubt.

"Your mother is saying my uncle is a worthless goat with no manners."

"Woah."

"He thinks she's out of order and he can damn well do what he damn well wants behind his bedroom door – it's a free country et cetera."

"Oh man, keep going."

"OK, she just said being his neighbour feels like living between the songs on a goddamn rock-'n'-roll album – you know the silence ain't gonna last."

"Nice."

"Oh oh… she just called his apartment a cockroach farm."
The dialect goes into overdrive.

"What are they yellin' about now?" Frico wants to know.

"Oh, nothing specific. They're just exchanging the worst words you can tell somebody in San Tainos. Trust me, you don't wanna know."

Now, when we're all in the middle of enjoyin' this argument, those two cussers, they fall silent all of a sudden. Then Mattis starts laughing first. One of those belly laughs you thought only belonged to rich old people. Then Moms gets into it. Laughter. Tears. Happy ones, though. Turns out they lived side by side for a year and didn't know that they're both originally from San Tainos until they started hollerin' at each other in freakin' Caribbeanese. Then they just get boring and nostalgic. Mattis goes to wash up. He puts on some clothes and he and his wife come over to our apartment and it's all warm and fuzzy now. Damn, I hate that. Mattis and his wife are wearing corny San Tainos T-shirts, the type tourists wear, with a beach and the flag across the damn front. It's like they never heard that the guy who wears a San Tai T-shirt all day long, seven days a week, is prob'ly not from San Tainos at all. They brought over pepper and curry and tamarind balls (that's tamarind preserves in an overdose of brown sugar) like it's a Caribbean Christmas or something. Funny how the Mattises have a whole cupboard full of spices but you never smell them cookin' a damn thing over there. I also can't believe how these people find so much to say about a little crumb of land in the sea that's barely a hundred miles long. But they do.

Mrs Mattis: San Tainos is an open-air museum full of good old things.

Moms: San Tai is next door to Mexico, right at the corner of the Caribbean and down the road from New O'lins, that's why it sops up the sauce from all three.

Mattis: San Tainos made a deal with the Devil, and the Devil didn't like his cut (ha ha ha, et cetera).

Those were the less corny ones. Now they're out in the living room takin' up space and tunin' in to local Caribbean radio. You can hear them overdoin' the dialect and talkin' with Frico and Moms about the good ol' days while I'm kissin' Claire in the kitchen. (Yeah. Didn't see that comin', did ya? Look, it just happened, man. I guess we got caught up in the whole Carnival celebration thing too, what the hell.)

Well, that was the end of the fun and games. Now lately my mother's going over to Mattis's apartment too regularly, and I'm sure people are starting to talk, especially with her also accommodating Benet these days. Claire says it's nothing. They're just catchin' up on island culture, and her aunt doesn't even mind. At the same time, my mother's been buttering me up. Don't know why, but she wants me to go with her next time she goes over to Mattis's. Maybe it's about the Tercel. I hope she's not plannin' on buyin' that thing. In any case, Doug or Tony can give her advice about a car better than I can. As a rule I don't like giving people advice, man. You give people advice and ten years from now you might see 'em again and they'll tell you how they've been in jail or bankrupt on account of what you told 'em. Screw all that, man. Don't give anybody advice. And don't take advice from nobody, trus' me. Not even family. Especially not family. Matter of fact, I think I just gave you some, so feel free to go ahead and scratch all that crap I just said, for godssake.

Moms figured out I like Claire. I've told her the details a hundred times, I swear: Claire is from San Tainos originally. Her father still lives there. She's an only child. Military brat. Her mother is a PhD from Baton Rouge and works with the Army Corp of Engineers around the city. "Wherever there's a crane or a drain, her mother's prob'ly worked on a project there." Claire's going to be a senior in the fall like me.

Well, Valerie Beaumont is using that information to her advantage. And I'm not complaining. I make at least two trips a week over to Mattis to collect things wrapped in brown paper or to hand him tiny packages of stuff. Come to think of it, I'm not quite sure what's in them. I feel through the packages, but still no clue. Well, Claire remedies that right quick. She lets me know one day in a whisper that her uncle was a folk-magic worker back in San Tainos. Powerful guy. An *obeah man*. That's what they call hoodoo conjurers on the island. It turns out my mother, that hypocrite, is workin' on "one final spell", even though she's all born again and whatever. Claire defends her, though.

"Give her a break. I don't know the whole story, but it's very important from what I overheard. And while I don't personally believe in that stuff, Uncle Mattis is known for it. People come and consult with him all the time. If he stayed in San Tainos, he'd be rich by now."

Yah, right. Anyway, I asked her to try and overhear some more stuff and let me know. Cos I'm hoping to Heaven that this top-secret final spell by Valerie Beaumont is the one that will keep Tracey Backhoe Benet from coming around this damn place.

Nine

You're not supposed to be able to smell stuff in a dream. And dreams are usually blurry or take place in some black-and-white world. But still, I know I'm asleep. We're in the swamp, and someone's hiding behind a tree. I tell them I know they're out there, cos they smell. Yeah, some serious sweat and whiskey come through on the wind, and Pa Campbell appears from behind a tree, laughin'. He's going on about how if we had a water tank he could take a bath. I tell him we don't live in the swamps any more. We live in the city.

"Ah, well, theah's some swamp under all that cement."

Man, you get to say all kinds of nonsense when you're old and in a dream. Anyway, he's not in his wheelchair any more. He's walking upright and strong for a sick old man. That's weird, so I ask him about it. He says: "If you think dat's nuts, you should see the daylight where we live. Sunset all day long."

Yeah, I've heard that about Arizona before. It's good to see the old man, though. My memory couldn't do a better job if I was wide awake. He says he's not having any pain right now, but he feels like "a mannequin in a Mardi Gras mask" – ready to party, but stiff as a board. Ma Campbell's keeping him locked up. That's rough. He was never the stay-inside type.

"So how's the city, kid?"

"Not what I expected. I feel like the stone that somebody tried to skip across a pond and it plopped down right in the middle instead."

He laughs out real loud, and I wonder if what I said was even that level of funny.

"Plopped down in the middle. Don't we all feel like that, sometaams."

He's sorry that he and Ma Campbell couldn't make it to Pops' memorial service.

"That's OK, it wasn't all that anyway."

"Your father was a good guy. His game plan was like his hoodoo. Could never quite get it right. Had his priorities all mixed up, so he made mistakes. But his heart was in da right place."

Oh man. I see he's fixin' to jaw on and on about my old man, and I'm not feeling up to that right now.

"Now, that's deeper than a shark tooth in a slow swimmer, Pa. So I would ask you to explain, but I know as usual you ain't got the time."

"Oh yes, I got the taam, kid. Heh, I got all the taam theah is. Ain't doing nothin' but sittin' around like furniture over theah."

Dammit. He sits down on a tree stump, gets real comfortable and licks his lips.

"Remember, back in the swamp, how I used ta take you crawfishin' and tell you 'bout the good ol' days?"

"Yeah, I guess those were *my* good ol' days."

"Shuddup and listen. I didn't come all this way to get all nostalchical witchoo. What I didn't tell you… is that the good ol' days is where we all make some really bad moves. You're livin' your life, and before you know it taam is swingin' her three swords at you and your good intentions are all in pieces before you on the floor."

"Wow, Pa. Maybe you should write an agony 'Uncle Pa Campbell' column in the papers."

"Put it in the suggestion box, kid. I'll read it when I give a shit. Don't get smart with me. Now I was talking about makin' mistakes. For example, in the good ol' days I made mistakes with

James and Ma, kid. And your old man, he regretted some of the things that he caused with Valerie and with Benet. Your mother loves y'all, but some days she prob'ly wishes she never left San Tainos. And Benet… well, he got punished in the worst way for his transgressions. But once you're breathing theah's no escapin' mistakes, Terence. That just how life is. But it works out, kid. Cos those mistakes make us do better… if we're smart."

Now I know he's making sense. But I'm focusing on the fact that he said "*Terence*". He used my real name. That's proof that I'm off in La La Land. He never, ever remembered it in real life. What's more interesting is to see the old man's face really close up in this dream light. Lemme tell you somethin', man. The force of gravity is a shabby ol' bastard. I mean, you can see how gravity hangs on to Pa's upper lip and drags it down over his top teeth. Meanwhile it's pulling his bottom lip down over his chin. And as you can imagine, all that pulling and draggin' makes it difficult to see the top row of teeth. But it's left the bottom row stickin' up over his lower lip like a rickety picket fence that needs painting.

"Pay attention son."

Oh, I'm tryin' hard. But Pa Campbell, he's one of those people with a face that fascinates the hell out of you, until you can't really concentrate on what's comin' out of their mouth. He's so beautifully broken and old, with laugh-lines deeper than the wrinkles on a Danish roll. I can't picture him young and without those wrinkles. Perfect skin would spoil the guy. And when he's tellin' you a story, even a sad one, it's like you're having an orange – one of those pulpy ones that soaked up the whole damn summer – and you can't keep all that juice from running down to your wrists.

"Like they say: 'time turns us into caricatures of what we really wanted to be and shadows of what we could've become'. Your father got into a heap o' trouble cos he had big dreams for himself and bigger ones for y'all. Most of the taam he was half-aways down the road with some fancy, expensive idea, before he realized that dream wouldn't work! Dreams... dreams are watery things, kid. So Alrick damn near drowned your mother with all that confoundid dreamin'!"

The guy's a wreck, but he's funny as hell too, looks and all.

I wake up laughing. Or rather Frico wakes me up *because* I'm laughin'. Can you believe that?

I rub my eyes and try to look at Fricozoid in the dark, standin' over my bed.

"What?"

"You were laughing in your sleep."

"I was laughin' in my sleep... so?"

"So I woke you up."

"Wait. You woke me up because I was *laughin'* in my sleep? Listen, this is how it works, 'Zoid: if a person's screaming, hollerin' or rolling about in their sleep – *then* you wake them up. But if they're laughin'... leave 'em alone. They're havin' fun. It's so goddamn simple."

I can't see his face, but I can tell his silhouette is looking at me like *I'm* the jerk.

"OK, Skid. Just pray that nobody ever tries ticklin' you to death in your dreams, man, cos I won't hear a damn thing."

"Pshhh. *Nobody* ever tickled anybody to death, man."

"Wish they would though."

That bastard couldn't just go back to bed and lose an argument. He had to take a cheap shot.

"Ha, I bet you were probably dreaming about Mai tickling you all over."

I wanted to tell him I was dreaming about his girl Teesha bending over in that boat back at the swamp. But that's a definite midnight fight, so instead I said:

"Ain't nothin' wrong with dreamin' about your girl, dude."

"Everything's wrong with it. Night 'n' day you're dreaming about Mai, and she's your *ex*, for godssake. Seems like everything reminds you of Mai. If I put on a damn wig, *I'd* remind you of Mai."

"Depends on the wig, man."

I get up, grab my denim jacket and soon I'm outside walking towards the ol' pool again. It's one of those nights: a deep-purple syrup poured over everything. I reckon it's close to morning rather than midnight, so I hope Claire will be out here. She isn't. Maybe I can wait with the crickets. So I hop down into the pool and walk over to the shallow end looking up at the stars. I really should thank the guy for wakin' me out of my sleep. Lord knows after that dream I'd pro'bly just stay awake goin' around in circles in my head, cos I'm tied to my thoughts like that damn billy goat in the swamp. I'm enjoying the thought of draggin' some red ink through Frico's diary as payback for what he just said about Mai. But I can't find it in the inlet. Maybe I put it somewhere else. I stick my hand way in and feel around and check a couple other nooks and crannies. Nothing. That girl Claire took my book, no doubt. Damn. It's not for casual reading. And I'm sure this pool doesn't look like a library or nothin', so you can't just come up in here and borrow shit. I'm so annoyed right now, I almost don't see that there's a brand-new blue sky erasing the electric lights along Hayne Boulevard. Claire really shouldn't touch my stuff. She's not family. She's not even really my girlfriend yet, man.

Ten

We're into August now, so it's almost back to school. I can't stand this time of year, cos here's how I feel about school: "Let's be done with it already." To me, high school is startin' to look like one long detention for something I didn't do, no lie. And it's not the teachers, man, it's the kids. Kids are mean, all the way from kindergarten to high school. And look, I'm not a wimp who's scared to get beat up or nothin'. But I'm no jock either. Of course, if I had to choose a label, I'd be a damn nerd and a wimp instead of a big, brawny dude walkin' round with my head hollow because my brain fell down into a bag between my legs. I like reading – so what. You got some people who break out into hives if you as much as crack open a goddamn book. I'm not one of those morons. I've been weird my whole life. I know, cos I actually make my bed in the morning. I mean, who does that? Sorry, I'm ranting.

Anyway, back to kids and their meanness. Just before summer break, for example, some punks did the worst thing. Now, this is a stupid wannabe gang who can't even piss straight. And they're pathetic. They name themselves after Couyon's old gang, like folks who watch TV and slip away from reality. Now these dudes, they used to hang around leaky bathrooms and do crap like push you into the urinal mid-piss and take your wallet while your hands are occupied. So I walked in there on a Tuesday and I see 'em gathering around. I go into a stall instead and close the door.

"Shouldn't have gone into our stall, Beau-moront." (These guys are *so* clever it gives me goosebumps.)

71

"Oh it's your stall? Didn't see your name on it," I answer back.

Well, that was a bad choice of words, cos their names were *definitely* scrawled on the inside of the stall, and so they start spray-paintin' "Couyon Crew" all over the door while I'm still in there. So the place starts smellin' like an auto-paint shop in an alley. I can't breathe.

Soon as I popped out of the stall, they're waitin' for me. So I told 'em I'll slap 'em with the hands I haven't washed yet, and they back off. Now that should tell ya, these guys are not badass. They only feel like they've got some kinda power cos their parents prob'ly own something disgraceful, like a sewage-disposal plant or whatever. Funny how parents do the dirty work so kids can show off for generations. In any case, people don't know that nobody's as badass as Valerie – and I'm her son. So I told 'em to dare touch me and they can watch their whole family fall apart. Well, they laughed, cos their families are perhaps already in shambles. But when I dip into my pocket and they see the hoodoo seal come up in my hand and I'm chantin' like Valerie Beaumont, they take off, slippin' all over the place like a bunch of three-legged puppies on a polished floor. Well, by Thursday morning that same week, there was an announcement about an emergency assembly for last period. Now that's the last thing you wanna hear, 'specially with the new assembly hall smellin' like wet cement and fresh paint to set off your sinusitis.

Seems like the school authorities wanted to know who committed the latest crime in the boy's bathroom.

No, they weren't talkin' about the graffiti those boys did on the bathroom stall. They were talkin' about the mean, five-foot diamondback water snake that Skid Beaumont caught and stuffed into the toilet bowl in the same stall. They were talkin' about how I got margarine from the cafeteria and buttered the damn toilet seat so the snake couldn't climb out and, worse, when one of those bastards came in and sat on the throne too fast, well, he just slid down into the bowl right on top o' that reptile. And if *you* were the snake, you can imagine how you'd feel to see a full moon comin' down on top o' your head.

Now relax, cos I gotta tell ya, diamondback water snakes aren't poisonous, but they *do* look like rattlers and they hiss and spit and behave real rowdy when you corner 'em. And who the hell's got time to identify what kind of snake it is when they're busy tryin' to get their behind back into a pair o' trousers? Nobody. That's why those wannabe gangsters and various other kids just kept emerging from the bathroom in half their birthday suit.

Of course, before long, some idiot in the assembly hall suggested to the Dean of Discipline that those diamondback serpents come from east New O'lins, closer to the lake.

"And there are only a few people here who live on Hayne. Terence Beaumont is one of 'em."

They couldn't prove it of course, but that doesn't stop the whole assembly hall from lookin' at me real suspiciously.

So now I took the opportunity to save my own skin publicly by reporting the serious concerns for my personal safety and the fact that those boys continually harass other students and deface the bathroom. The long and short of it is: I got off scot-free and those boys took the rap for the snake incident as well. In retaliation, they got hold of my home phone number from the principal's office and scrawled it on the bathroom wall with instructions to "Call after six p.m. for special favours". Damn.

Well, I went home and, as you'd expect, my old lady was answering the phone all evening and askin' me who I gave her phone number to and why the hell everybody thinks this is a goddamn massage parlour. All night I listened to the phone ringin' off the hook and Valerie Beaumont cussin' and carryin' on. And I just wished I'd get to school and all that damn graffiti would be gone.

Now, there was no need for me to borrow a paintbrush and some lacquer from Larry Lou to take to school after all that powerful wishing. Cos look. By that Friday, there was a whole wreckin' crew gathered with sledgehammers and a crane. They were getting ready to tear down that old bathroom that same weekend. Come to think of it, that was a while before Lafayette Cemetery and prob'ly the first time I got a hint that some strange things were going on around me.

Anyway, I just got back from looking for Claire (still can't find her or the diary) and there's an old lady sleeping across Frico's bed with his pillow over her head. I can't see her face, but her dentures are on Frico's nightstand. (You should see the guy's face.) He got home half an hour before me. Now he's just sitting there staring at this stranger on his bed and her teeth over in the corner. I go over and try to peek under the pillow. Her hair looks full white. Skin-and-bone fingers. Huge blue veins fan out across the back of the hands that clutch the pillow. I'm just about to ask him if his mother knows he has a girl in his bed when he blocks the joke.

"Airhead, it's Ma Campbell. She's not well, so shut the hell up." Damn. One year with Pa being sick really made Ma Campbell wither away.

"Momma said not to wake her. She's gone around to where she opened that deli stand or whatever. Said she'll be back in a sec."

"Back in a sec? Did Benet take her?"

"Nah, haven't seen him today."

"Good."

"Nope. Not good."

"Whatchoo mean?"

"She drove her own car."

"Moms bought a car?"

"Well, just about. She's getting that Tercel from out in the yard."

"What the—"

"Yeah. Mattis cleaned it up and told her she can take it for a test drive."

"Man, that car is in no condition to be on the road."

"It's seen better days. But I guess it's holding up. Now it's like a shopping cart with a key."

"What's she thinkin'?"

"Dunno. Maybe that she needs to do something drastic to escape the twenty years she spent sloshin' behind her husband – in a swamp."

"Yeah, I guess. But what's up with Benet comin' here? That's not cool, man."

"Look, I'm not judgin' the guy, but I don't like him snuggling up to Momma either."

Ma Campbell turns in her sleep.

"Shh."

I look around. "By the way, where's Pa Campbell?"

"Oh, Pa? You didn't pass him just now? He's with the luggage in the kitchen."

I step back out into the kitchen half-smilin', cos the old man is playin' hide-and-seek with me like in the dream. That's when I see the luggage on the kitchen table.

One bag. And from the lilac looks of it, it belongs to Ma Campbell. I stick my head back into the room.

"Look behind the bag," Frico says, before I can say anything.

Pa Campbell is too old to be bending down behind luggage. But there's a *cloisonné* urn on the table where Benet's roses used to be. Chinese design with red-and-gold dragon scales. And there's a cover on it.

"See him now?"

That boy Frico is *cold*. He comes out of the room and stands in the doorway with his hands folded. "That's what you call an urn, Skid. It's for ashes."

The kitchen is spinning now.

"I know what an urn is for."

"Yep. Sorry Skid, and from the looks of it, Ma is not altogether here neither."

Ma Campbell is up. She drags herself out of the room. She looks worse standing up.

"Oh, theah you are, Lobo." She picks up the urn and takes it back into the bedroom without looking at us even once. I call after her softly.

"Hey, Ma."

"Shhhh."

I guess that dream was worth paying attention to. But I dare not tell ol' Valerie Beaumont. You know she'd be up in arms about me dreamin' about talking to the dead – like I was supposed to know Pa had gone and died.

We're eating dinner with plastic forks tonight. Yep. The first order of business for Ma Campbell was to comb through the kitchen and hide all our silverware. Where? We don't know. Why? She's going senile. That's not the worst thing. It was the police who took her here yesterday. Old white woman wearing African print with silver hair to her shoulders wandering barefoot up Hayne Boulevard huggin' a Chinese urn: that's gonna get some attention. They assume she took a train or a bus from another state and, once she was in New O'lins, she rambled about looking for "Valerie Byfield". It's a good thing she had the address right.

Something tells me she'll be here a while. And that's gonna be interesting. For example, right now Pa's ashes are on the table, where it can tip over into the tossed salad. And we can't move it. She's a bulldog about protecting that thing. Moms leaves it alone. She's doing her best to make Ma comfortable under the circumstances.

"More rice, Ma?"

"No, no. You cook a little too salty for me, Valerie. B'sides, I can't even get a good grip on these cheap plastic forks you use. You gotta do betta, chile. Maybe if you stopped draggin' on them cigarettes you'd be able to afford some decent cutlery for once in your life. It's just a suggestion, though. Me? I can up an' quit smoking—"

"Yes Ma, you can up and quit smoking whenever you feel like it, I heard you a hundred times."

"That's right, me and my smokin' is all right, but you about to *kill* me with this salty rice."

Truth is, the rice isn't salty. It's worse. It tastes like Tide. But that's because Ma Campbell took it with her from Arizona and prob'ly packed it too close to some laundry detergent in her luggage. Moms sucks in her lower lip to hide a smile.

"Anyway, I was sayin'. I always used to tell Pa that we live in a swamp but we ain't hooligans. We eat *at the table*. And we use *good silverware*. I used to have the finest things. God knows these days I cain't find them 'em anywheah."

Ma Campbell's really far gone. All the precious stuff she was referring to was burnt up that night when her son's gang torched their house in the swamp.

I look across, and Moms' lower lip is not coming back out. But the smile is showing now. Ma Campbell was never her favourite person, but she can deal with this. Plus, it's the charitable thing to do.

"Goddammit, Valerie!" Ma throws down the plastic fork. "I'm going ta get a decent fork over at our house. Be back soon."

"Damn!" Frico's eyes are wide. "She's in the swamp right now!"

He's laughing until Ma comes back in with a gleaming knife and fork in a white napkin. Ma stuffs the napkin in the neck of her house dress and chows down. Moms knows her cutlery when she sees it, but she's gonna let it slide.

"Awright now, heah we go. Y'all can be hooligans if y'all want. Eat with your hands, for all I care."

"So... can I borrow some of your silver, Ma?" Moms is making a joke of it.

"Oh no, not a chance. Your husband never ever gave my husband back his electrical tools, so I'm thinkin' that's like, you know, a family thing."

Moms is taking a sip of juice when Ma says this. We all nearly get showered with punch. You shouldn't laugh when someone is losing it, but I swear Ma Campbell is a comedienne. Well, that's when she's not telling us how Pa died. She strokes the top of her neck while talking and stares off at nothing, like Pa used to do.

"The day he died, we were goin' through the desert in Arizona, if I remember c'rreckly. First he's goin' on about how he cain't wait to get to Arizona so he can grow some huge blue agave plants to make his own tequila. I'm tellin' him blue agave takes years, he's tellin' me he's got the taam. When it's about a hun'red degrees out theah, he tells me he's cold and freezin', and he's lettin' me know who I should call in case of anything. He says I should tell James he's sorry for all he did to him that made him grow up and go against the law. Then he's insisting that Valerie should get the 1960s San Tainos picture album, and his tackle box and fishin' equipment must go to Skid. I'm laughin' at him, tellin' him he's gonna live until he's two hun'red, so he should stop depressin' me with all the details of how to divide his estate. My grand-nephew and grand-niece are up front drivin', and they're laughin' too, cos they know Lobo and his usual melodrama. Well, I'm in the back with him. He has his head restin' on the seat and he's lookin' back at me and laughin' real soft about my joke – ha ha ha – until I realize that one of those 'has' – one of them – is goin' on for just too long."

At this point she tears up, the poor old lady.

"He died happy."

Maan, when she said that, I'm thinking: poor Pa, he got the swamp swishing around in his veins. But he goes and dies in a dry ol' desert. I can imagine him laughin' at the irony while the sunset turned a few clouds into live coals over his head: final fire-works for a great ol' guy. And of course all I can hear in my head is his old rancid harmonica wailin' out a tune, until my eyes get hot and I don't know if I'm mad at the guy or sorry for myself.

Ma puts down the fork. She touches the urn and looks at us real serious.

"Now I think we gotta pray for him. Cos somethin' tells me my Lobo didn't quite make it all the way to the other side." She says Pa Campbell is plopped down somewhere in Purgatory right now, raising hell. She's sure it's easier for James Jackson to get out of prison than for Pa to reach the Pearly Gates. Well, if all that is true, I can't help thinkin' that maybe he ended up stranded in the middle because he never said he was sorry about shooting my pops in the leg back in the swamp. Never said it even once. Not even in the dream.

Eleven

"Get up Terence." That's Valerie Beaumont. It's clear from her tone that you don't want to mess with her even if your seventeenth birthday is next month.

"Wash yourself and get ready. We're going to the deli."

That means I'm going to get a passenger-seat lecture today. And it could be about anything. People will see the Toyota in traffic, a handsome guy sulkin' in the shotgun seat and a finger-waggin' woman naggin' him all the way to work.

Meanwhile Frico gets to stay home with Ma Campbell and his girl's coming over. I'm still half asleep, so I blurt out that it'll take a little while to get ready, cos I'm waiting for Claire, cos she should've met me outside by the abandoned pool last night with a book that she borrowed but she didn't show up. Well, that just set off a round of interrogation from Ma Campbell.

"Girl? What girl? She was out there witchoo, at night? You know her well? What's she look like?"

Meanwhile Moms wants me to ignore Ma and do what *she* told me to do. Frico gets involved. When two women gang up on you, you're dead.

Frico: Book? What book did she borrow, man?

Ma Campbell: Laawd! Valerie, your boy done gone and had relations with a ghost!

Frico: What book, Skid?

Moms: Ma, Frico, quiet please. Terence and I have had words about his night-time activities a'ready. Plus, Tracey was tellin' me the same thing recently. All kinds of strange people runnin' around this place. Terence, I'm leaving in, like, one minute. Let's go!

Of course, to me, all that "ghost and strange people" talk is less scary than the fact that my mother is now on a first-name basis with Tracey Backhoe Benet. So I go for that part of the sentence.

"'*Tracey*', Moms? You mean '*Backhoe*'. You mean '*Mr Benet*'. You mean '*Captain Benet*'. Right, Moms?"

"Get your clothes on, boy. Now."

Inside, the old Tercel smells like a taxi. A taxi with four wrestlers comin' home from the gym. The car creaks when goin' up and down a slope, and you have to lift the door to close it. It's missing a hubcab. Make that two or three. And the paint job is so jacked up from the birds, anybody can tell it's been sittin' under a tree. Belongs in a junkyard, no lie. But it's got a wicked sound system, man, cos apparently Mattis takes his music seriously. Frico says Moms prob'ly just wanted a decent car radio and the guy just threw in the rest of the car to sweeten the deal. The radio's playing some good music, but Moms turns it down once we hit Hayne Boulevard. I reckon that for her the sound of clanging pots and squeaking styrofoam cups in the back is much better than Simply Red.

"So, Terence..."

Oh oh. Valerie Beaumont has that "I'm your buddy so I can confide in you" voice. I know it anywhere. Ol' VB wants to talk about the car or Benet or that spell I hear she's working on with Mattis.

But nah, she surprises me.

"I'm thinking of giving the food cart a name, you know. Small enough operation, but it's got ambition... so I need a name. Furthermore, we're competing with a Hispanic food truck in the same spot. They just have a sign that says 'Tapas', so we gotta be more official than that. Whaddya think, huh?"

Truth be told, I like making up names for stuff. So I won't show it, but my mind is working from the word go. I take a shot.

"How about 'Crossroads', cos it's close to the intersection of Bullard and Lake Forest—"

"No, that's too hoodoo. People might think I'm working magic over there."

"But that's the point! Here's the slogan: 'Where the Taste Is Magical'."

"Nah. Cute but corny."

Says the queen of corny San Tai folk tales. Imagine I hand the woman a gold nugget and she says "corny". I dare her to come up with one.

"I was thinkin' something more Caribbean…"

Oh boy, here we go.

"Something like 'Hummingbirds… Food on the Fly'."

"No, Mrs Beaumont. That sounds like *flies are on the food.* C'mon, Moms, leave the slogans to me."

"OK, your turn, Mr Beaumont."

I suggest the name "Alrick's" and she just glares at me and looks out the window for a long time. Damn. Nice going, Terence. Very sensitive.

We stop by Mrs Thorpe, who's retired and a widow. Prob'ly she was a teacher or something. She has that whole "neglected pedagogue" look going on: glasses with a safety cord, close-cropped hair, white at the temples. And she's so tarnished you know it's because she's spent her whole damn life making other people shine. Nice lady though.

Anyway, she used her retirement money to build a large fancy kitchen and invested in Moms' idea. So this is where the food gets made. Mrs Thorpe doesn't care what we call the food cart. We settle on the name "Bo's", a shortened form of "Beaumont", otherwise called "Bo's Caribbean Kitchen" or BCK. I think it's wicked, man. No slogan, though. That name says everything. It makes you think that the place is owned by a regular guy with a deep laugh, who just wants to serve you good food. Everybody will like "Bo's". Especially since we're serving lunch near to a big ol' construction site where they eat like horses.

Well, we get down to business, and I was thinking that my display of creativity in the car was going to make me some kind of Innovation Director or something. Pshhh. That's a long way from me hollering out ticket numbers through the window so customers can come collect their goddamn San Tainos fish soup, sandwiches and Jamaican-style patties.

Me: Number 28 and 29! 28? 29?

Some other guy: How 'bout 30, man? Call 30. I got 30!

Meanwhile Number 28 is adjusting his hearing aid and Number 29 is at the gas station across the street taking a long leak. This is hard work. Doug would be proud to see me making money with Moms – but look, I'm not feeling like a businessman yet. Far as I'm concerned, this is not a job. Working for the family business is just household chores with longer hours and a logo, trust me. And to prove it, I get to go nowhere *near* that cash box. Anyway, now Number 28 is complaining about not hearing his ticket called, and 29 is rushing back across the street still pulling up his zipper. The whole time Valerie's watching, so I gotta be polite. Especially when Number 30 starts hollering that he was here *before* 28 and 29, but he just saw them getting served first. Man. Now 28 is whining that his soup is cold and 29 says the stew is not what he ordered. You should see the look Valerie Beaumont's giving me, cos she thinks I'm fixin' to cuss at her customers. So I start being real polite and using the brand name: "Sorry about that. Thanks for making it Bo's, come again." But customers, most of those bastards are mean. They just grunt and walk away sipping soup. One guy even said: "*Bo's* – yeah, right, kid… more like: *blows*."

Anyway, with all that, the thing I hate the most about this job is dipping into the deep freeze. You have to bear the frost and then the heat and then the frost again when you go back down in there and rummage around for the right cold drink that the customer ordered. So, in the lunch-hour rush, I have my head in the freezer and there's this customer that keeps changing her mind about what flavour she wants.

"Grape. No, I mean grape*fruit*, you got grapefruit, boy?"

"Yeah, I got grapefruit." My head is down in the deep freeze. I wonder if she can hear my teeth chattering. I can't feel my fingertips when I grab the grapefruit can. She hollers again: "Hey... you know what? Make that an orange – or an orange-*pineapple*... no, hey, gimme a Coke."

So I look up to see who the hell is the flavour chameleon at the window – and lo and behold, it's Claire, messing with me the whole time. She smiles and I play mad, but something inside of me is happy to see her.

"Where's my book?"

"We got to talk."

Moms is not amused that I need a lunch break. But she's letting me off just this once. So I grab my food handler's cap off (damn thing makes you look like you're taking a shower and serving at the same time) and I go to a payphone to call Mrs Thorpe so she can come take my place for half an hour. She'd do anything for Moms. I've hardly hung up the extra-rancid receiver when I see her steering the big brown Ford Terravan into the intersection. Claire and I, we cross the street and push the door to the diner, and music hits us hard.

Inside is like day through a dark filter. Red and white neon lights glow through smoke from a grill in the back. Something smells delicious. Claire knows the dude that runs the place. He slides her a few menus and some tokens for a *Charlie's Angels* pinball machine in the corner. While I'm tryin' to choose from the menu, I'm watching people play. They hit the buttons at the side of the pinball machine and the girls bounce it with their hips, and I'm thinking how the Eighties passed us by in the swamp and now it's almost too late to be living in the city. Breakdancing is near-corny now, graffiti is noise on a wall. Rubik's cubes just piss people off, and nobody balances beat-boxes on their shoulders any more. Now the beatboxes have wheels on 'em: cars that roll around the Ninth Ward blasting beats day and night.

I order the same thing as Claire. It tastes like my mother's cooking, no lie. But I don't get to finish. Claire goes over to a corner and puts money into a jukebox. Sounds like blues with more box guitar and a bass line in it. Slower too, like somebody was playin' the blues on a car stereo and they passed you on the street and you got that Doppler-effect feelin' from it. I'm no dancer, as you may remember, and people are look-ing – but this is easy. All I have to do is put my back against the jukebox and let her lean on me. She's singin' the lyrics in some kind of creole, so all I catch is the word "drop". Or maybe I can't keep my head straight cos she's playin' with my hair and dancin'. She's twisting herself around me and she's sweet and smoky and soft like a pretzel. Then just when it's goin' good and she's singing in my ear, I go and say something stupid.

"Now you sound like my mother."

Soon as I said it, I repeated it in my head: *Now you sound like my mother?* What? Well, she just rolls her eyes and wheels away and goes to sit at a table. I swear, sometimes my mouth and my brain break up, and by the time they get back together it's just too damn late. Claire pats the seat beside her.

Cigarette.

I try to explain that I meant her *accent* or her *patois*, or whatever the hell they call it.

"You've never had a girlfriend, have you, Terence Beaumont?"

"Um, yeah. But – well, she became a nun."

She let out a laugh louder than the jukebox.

"Ah, it figures."

Now those words are worse than "pshhh", cos it means she's been psychoanalysing me.

"Ah, it figures? Wha' does that mean?"

"You'd drive anybody to become a nun."

"You know nothing about me, man."

"That's why we're here, handsome."

Wow. She knows how to pull my strings and make me unravel, especially after taking my book and criticizin' me and all.

"Now, about the diary. Why don't you come over tonight? I wanna ask you something."

So Valerie Beaumont and I are heading back home with that stale-food smell in the car. Up ahead sad clouds are coming down low and jagged, like somebody ripped away the bottom part of a paper sky. And you know that when rain starts hitting a windscreen it's time to miss people or fall in love, right? Well, not tonight. Cos even though I'm thinking about later on with Claire, my mother, she's driving and distracting me by talking about the day. Boring things like how sweet and genuine Mrs Thorpe is, and what supplies we need to get for the week. No joke.

"We need to step our game up, cos that damn Tapas truck is stealing our ideas. I'm thinking we should make tomorrow Customer Appreciation Day. I already put up a sign on the cart."

That's Moms. Always taking everything too seriously, even though she says Ma Campbell is the worrywart. Well, "Customer Appreciation Day" is the last thing I heard, cos as the Tercel turns onto the red-brick driveway and the headlights wash the shadows off our house, we see too many cars crammed into the parking area out front. All the lights are on in our apartment. So I know something weird is up.

Twelve

Imagine coming home to see your kitchen full of people. No, not just people – "Prayer Warriors". That's what they call the women visiting from my mom's church. Mrs Thorpe is one of them. It's what you could call a prayer ambush, a real Holy Roller intervention.

But look, these Warriors, they don't play around. They cover all the bases. Soon as we come in the door, they gather round and block the exit. They raise their hands up to the ceiling and then down to the floor. Some of them swoop down and anoint Moms and Ma Campbell with oil. Moms doesn't look surprised. The Warriors, they all got basil leaves waving and frankincense smoke comin' out of a honey jar while they're walking in a circle around the kitchen and singin'. Oh man. I was hoping to watch some TV, but I reckon it's gonna take all night to banish the ghosts of Alrick Beaumont and Lobo Campbell.

They say both of 'em have been wandering around our house of late. I notice they spend a longer time prayin' away my pops' spirit, informing him that he's a ghost, so he should stay out. Ha. If I remember correctly, my pops was doing a damn good job of that while he was alive. Anyway, there's this one guy in the Prayer Warriors group. He's walkin' around with one hell of a hardcover King James that could clobber the Devil out of you if you got too unruly.

Now, Ma Campbell's praying for a miracle for James "Couyon" Jackson, her son: "Throw open the gates o' that prison, bend those iron bars!" I scan the room. Moms is sitting there with a spot of olive oil on her forehead. She's a little uncomfortable. I know it's because of the mention of James's name as well as all this ghost talk. Somethin' inside my mother wants my father to be *alive*. But maan, can you imagine the mess he'd be in if he actually turned up here tonight, alive and in the flesh? For the first time in his life he would *not* enjoy being chased by a bunch of passionate women.

Anyways, I look across at Ma Campbell, who's hobbling around with the group hummin' a psalm with a small palm branch in her hand. She says it's a "wand for banishing spirits". I grin and tell her it looks like a dead palm branch to me. She taps me on the head with it.

"Get behind me, Devil!"

She's so cute. And as fascinating as Pa. It's as if the years fell softly on top of her like flowers, one by one. But now the weight of it all is crushing her body into a ball. The lines around her neck are so deep and dark they look like rings choking her. But forget all that; I'm wondering what exactly it was that set her off in the first place and made her and Moms call in the troops.

She doesn't take long to let me know. Ma Campbell tells the Warriors what I said this morning, only she lets on that I had met a ghost out by the pool and that I'm prob'ly the one attracting all these spirits into the place with my "riotous living". Well, before I can escape to my room, those church ladies stop the conga line and they strike. Valerie Beaumont is on her feet trying to stop the prayer gang, but it's too late. They plunk my ass down onto the living-room couch. Sixty fingers land on my head and oil is running down my forehead already. King James Boy comes close, fixin' to clobber me. I glare at the guy, and he backs off real quick. Out of the corner of my eye I see Teesha and Frico, on their way out the door, stopping to enjoy the scene of me gettin' hijacked.

Well, look. Those Prayer Warriors are more like *assassins* when they start straight-shooting at my sins:

"Deliver him, Lawd! These teenagers and their *lust*!"

(Direct hit.)

"The *dirty curse words*, Father! Listenin' to *nasty* song lyrics!"

(Between the eyes.)

"These young *boys* and the *indiscipline*!"

(Bull's-eye again.)

"The *disobedience*! *Back-talking* to parents!"

(Bull's-eye. Bull's-eye.)

Man, they couldn't leave soon enough. They hurried off to a prayer meeting at the church, and Moms and Ma Campbell went with them. Ma wanted to drag me along, but Valerie Beaumont thought I'd had enough. Frico laughed at me a little bit – OK, a lot – then left with his fine girl. So I'm sitting here with my sins all shot full of holes, head throbbing and guilt crawling all over me. I'm really considering taking church more seriously and changin' my life, when there's a knock at the door. It's Claire. With all the drama, I didn't remember that she wanted me to come over. Damn.

And just when I was planning to behave myself.

I get into Mattis's living room still wiping my forehead. The place is full of candles and sweet incense, with flower petals all over the coffee table. The sofa is really a love seat: cosy and close. Perfect for people like Suzy and Peter, who want to smush up against each other all day long and combine facial features. So when I'm thinkin' Mattis and his wife are away and Claire is up to something romantic, I notice the shelves all around the room. Honey jars are all over the place with labels on 'em. I can barely make them out by the flashin' light of the TV.

"Rosemary", "Rose Petals", "Angelica", "Marassa Oil".

On the shelves above those honey jars, statues of St Michael the Archangel, St Raphael, a Chinese Good-Luck Buddha and Santa Muerte, the Mexican skeleton saint, are all hangin' out together, covered in beads and silk flowers and rosaries. Crystals catch the colour from the TV, and two metal incense burners gleam in the half-light. So I reckon I prob'ly walked into a special hoodoo scene, and therefore this visit is not the make-out session I though it was going to be.

Claire is at the far end of the couch looking at the ceiling, while Mattis's fridge and his air-conditioning unit bicker back and forth. When one trips out the other trips in, like two short-fused people having an argument about nothin'.

"Electrical trouble," says Claire, real awkwardly, like she's feelin' around for conversation. "Larry Lou should be coming to look at it."

"Yeah, that's all Larry will do. Throw on his blue overalls that's still as crisp as a biscuit, come *look* at the wiring and go: *ahh, hmm*. And then go back to sleepin' in the guardhouse."

She smiles and goes silent again. I feel like I'm waiting to get mugged. I'm gettin' up to go when Mattis walks into the room in his boxers and socks as usual. He's got his head wrapped in red, and somethin' is under his arm. It's Frico's diary.

"Where's your modda, eh? Thought she was comin'."

"Dragged off to church by Warriors."

"Oh yes, I heard them prayin' for ya. Couldn't hear my TV for a while."

Got some real nerve, this guy.

He goes on: "Roughed you up a bit, eh? Your modda means well. She just wants to leave nothin' untried."

I'm wondering what this guy's talkin' about when he plops the diary onto the table and suddenly Claire starts babbling that she's sorry for all the trouble, but this might be for my own good.

Mattis sits down and looks me in the eye, like a doctor who's got a bit of bad news.

"Terence, your modda came to see me about helping her. She is very afraid for you."

Claire can see that the look on my face means I don't like this pokin' into my business one bit, and I'm fixin' to bail. So she jumps into the middle of it again.

"Terence, it's my fault. I was telling my uncle about what I read in your brother's diary, just because it was funny. Then while I was talking, it hit me that children would call each other 'skid' in kindergarten back in SanTai."

"For real?"

"Yes, it was like the biggest insult, because it meant you were… stupid or clumsy or a kind of jinx."

She laughs, kind of uncomfortably, and her uncle, he gets impatient and starts waving her off.

"Claire, Claire, please. Terence, I told her already: that whole skid thing in San Tainos is an old folk tale, eh? Way back on plantations, people used to believe you could cast a bad spell on a traitor or a slave master and turn them stupid. Accordin' to them, you could make a 'deliberate mistake' in the recipe of a spell and put a hex on somethin' that they handle, like a handkerchief, eh? Or give them a dark-magic seal, concealed as a gift, and that would make dark angels haunt them for life. So the belief is, you put powers on a person that make their lives get out of control – like a carriage or a car, eh? Hence the term: *skid*. But nobody believes that any more. So, like I told Claire, that name is of no significance."

"Well it was just a guess, Uncle. I was thinking that maybe something could have happened in the past that Terence doesn't know about and somebody called him that nickname as a warning or—"

"Somebody, something, somewhere. Oh, Claire. Heh, heh. Now you just sound like you're wasting your mother's money at school, eh? My sister would hate to hear you now, cos all of that is pure rubbish, eh? A magic mistake? No. Powers don't work like that. Centuries ago, when people couldn't explain how things work, they came up with that. They claim hurricanes and tremors in the Caribbean were caused by skids who called up demons from the sea and the earth and all that. They blamed skid spells for everything. If they called you a skid, you better leave the village, eh? Quite a few people were killed on that island because they were labelled like that. But modern-day people in San Tainos don't even know about those stories, let alone Americans like your old man…"

"Whoa. What do you know about my old man? My father is white. And he's American. But he might know more about San Tai magic than you do."

"Well, accordin' to your modda, he wasn't that good with the ol' magic wand."

I'm looking straight at Mattis right now, cos I'm mad at Claire, but more pissed at my old lady.

"My mother discussed my father with *you*? And what exactly did she tell you about me?"

"She didn't go into details. The problems you're having, Terence, are far beyond superstition. That's why she came over here to talk to me about you. She believes that there may be danger lurking around you."

"Ha. Oh, that again. Yes, she thinks the whole city is about to get me. Did she run her mouth and tell y'all that some punks attacked me?"

"No, but is this true, eh, Terence?"

Well, you know, at this point I'm thinkin' this guy Mattis is not my favourite person in the world. And he should have put on a shirt. He's just big and hairy – a spiky kind of hairy. I mean, if you wanted someone to imitate a hairbrush, this would be your guy.

"Look, some dumb dudes wanted money, they came at me and—"

"Well, I think people get robbed all the time, eh? It can't be that. This is deeper, eh? She wants me to do a protection spell for you, to guard you against a spiritual kind of evil."

Mattis's face is over a tall red candle now, his scruffy beard almost catching fire. If this guy is tryin' to scare me – he's doing well.

"Tss. I'm in my teens, for godssakes. All you old folk think somethin' evil's goin' on with us teens, right Claire?"

Claire looks down at the coffee table. The girl leaves me hangin'. Then she flat out starts helpin' the guy.

"Well, maybe Terence. But seriously, forget the San Tai stories. Have you seen anything strange of late, like what happened at the Meat Mart for example?"

Maan, I hate that she switched on me. And that she mentioned the Meat Mart. Worst of all, I hate that these two are starting to make sense.

"OK look, man, I haven't told anybody this, but I guess I *have* seen a few things – but it's nothing *that* crucial for my mother to come consult somebody. I mean, I haven't even told her."

Mattis leans forward. "Told her what? You can tell me, eh?"

Claire holds my hand. I thought she didn't believe in all this stuff. I'm thinkin' at this point I should backpedal and joke about how strange and hairy Mattis is. But the time for jokes is gone. So I tell them both about the cemetery and the podium at the church. He looks bored. But when I mention the swamp and me nearly fallin' overboard into all those hoodoo-magic seals, Mattis jumps up from his chair.

"Yes! I knew it. You're the one who collected them, eh?"

I shake my head up and down. He hollers louder.

"That's it. You are flooded with power!"

I'm startin' to think he's the one who's full of it.

Then he leaps across the room and brings back a bunch of magic seals bound with a broad elastic band: my father's seals. All the ones I could collect from the bayou that afternoon. Yeah, I didn't tell you, but I brought a couple of 'em back and left them out in the pool inlet with the diary. Didn't want to take them inside and scare ol' Valerie Beaumont. Well, just my luck, Claire found 'em in the pool and brought them in to her *obeah-man* uncle. Genius, that girl.

I reach out for the seals from Mattis. "OK. Those are mine. Thanks." He pulls back.

"Oh, you can have the diary back, but these... these are dangerous. These must be destroyed, eh? These are sig seals. Used to summon powerful angels. Matter of fact, they're supposed to be the signatures of the angels. Angels wrote these down themselves long ago... with fiery fingers."

(*Oh jeez. My father scratched those down with a Paper Mate pen.*)

"And these angels are not those little Valentine's Day cupids, eh? No, no. These are the reapers – Special Forces, the ones responsible for screechin' down, shaking the ground and takin' out the first-born of Egypt. Horrible creatures with four heads, like ol' Ezekiel saw. You can't handle all that power, eh? And dat must be the danger your modda's talkin' about."

Now I'm curious, so I ask Claire. "So, why didn't you mention that you found them when you invited me over here?"

"I saw them and I knew what they were. I don't usually believe, but I got scared. I was afraid you wouldn't come talk to my uncle. And I was thinking you should, just in case."

Mattis jumps in.

"Furthermore, for me to break the spell that's on you, you have to declare all secrets truthfully. So I suggest that you tell your modda all you told me and then find all the seals in the swamp and take them to me for destruction. Then we can start workin' immediately. Awright?"

Now my mind is workin' overtime. See, I'm thinking on the one hand that maybe I could declare all the happenings to Valerie Beaumont. I should tell her I found her husband's hoodoo seals floating in the bayou. Tell her I went lookin' for him, cos I know he's alive. Get it all out in the open once and for all like I did in the swamps back in the day. Tell her the truth about the cemetery and all of it. Just get it off my chest. Maybe she'll finally believe me this time.

But on the other hand, maybe I shouldn't say a damn thing. Not with a big business opportunity fallin' into my lap right about now.

See, I think Terence Skid Beaumont is about to sell second-hand hoodoo seals to this sucker Mattis for about three fifty each. Yeah, he can keep the free samples. But I'm fixin' to fish those things out of the bayou by the hundreds, and then I'm gonna go retail on this guy. Cos something tells me he's not gonna destroy a single one of 'em. No sir. He wants to use 'em in *his* hoodoo. And that's the other thing about Mattis. I don't care what my mother thinks – it's clear as day he's not up to snuff. Just about anybody who's anybody in conjurin' could take one look and know that my father's magic seals aren't good for anything. So Mattis? He's a funny guy and I like him in spite of everything. But the fact that he can't see that those seals are useless? That tells me he's fake and his hoodoo is just as half-assed as Alrick Julian Beaumont's.

Thirteen

So. I have this business plan drawn up and everything. There's a lifetime supply of hoodoo seals in the swamp and my client wants these things like yesterday. Now look, if I thought these seals were any good, I wouldn't be selling them to ol' George Mattis. He wouldn't deserve 'em. Now, just to be safe, I'll use one of the old busted washin' machines in the laundromat as a storage bin and hope that handyman Larry Lou doesn't suddenly learn how to fix somethin' besides his breakfast. The only challenge I have now is how to get the product out of the bayou. I mean, transportation and time-wise, that is – you know ol' Pa Campbell taught me how to handle myself in a boat – God rest that man's soul. Loved him to death.

So anyway, like they say in business: "worst things first". I'm writing the sweetest letter of apology to the Wildlife Refuge people about how sorry I am for my "misuse of their property" and how I'm "experiencing deep remorse for borrowing their boat over an extended period, which was tantamount to belligerence on my part". (If you ever have to write an apology, don't forget the one-two combination of the words "belligerence and remorse". They go a far way in saving your ass, trus' me.) I ended by assuring them that "I recognize the need to be cognizant of safety procedures while on Conservation Lands for the sake of wildlife and human beings". Hell, I even threw in a compliment about the "delectable lunch" they serve over there. Damn. I meant some of that stuff, though, and you shoulda seen the smile across Teesha Grey's face when I read it to her and asked her to drop it off for me. Meanwhile Frico's just lookin' at me like I'm a show-off. Hoodoo-sketcher-boy has issues with my language skills.

Well, Teesha came through for me. It's been less than a week and I'm back in a boat draggin' magic seals out of swamp water. (*Ka-ching.*) It's hard work though, no lie. This is August, so you know the sun is pipin' hot in the early afternoon – that part of the day when everything just hangs around doin' nothin' like a lazy teenager, as they say. They should see this teenager sweatin' for his bread. Now I reckon those Conservation people, they're tryin' to get the last laugh. Cos they gave me a real rickety pirogue. You should see the thing. If I lost this ol' saucepan of a boat, they'd just say: "Ah well, let's hope a rescue team finds that Terence guy before nightfall." I'm sure that right now, back in their air-conditioned offices, they're all laughin' at me.

But seriously, I've never been in a boat and seen it crab-walkin' before. I gotta hold the thing together and keep an eye on two gators resting at the bottom of the bayou, all grey-green and muscly. Anyway, I thought some of Pa's fishing equipment that Ma brought back from Arizona would come in real handy, but I hardly need it. As soon as I get back close to that spot where the magic seals came up last time, I can feel the current in the water. I lash the boat around a mangrove and decide to swim out deeper with a net. But as soon as I touch the water with one foot – up come those seals from the bottom of the bayou, floating towards me almost as if I called them up to the surface.

Now, Alrick Beaumont has me wondering if I underestimated his magic, cos those plastic-covered cards seem to be playin' with me a bit. They bob up to the boat, I reach out, pick a few of them up, but the rest sink away, then come up farther downstream, like they're playing hide-and-seek. Well, I quit early, cos I get a bit spooked and I'm not takin' any chances with my life.

Anyway, I figure that while I'm here behind God's back I might as well make one more visit to the swamp shack and look in on that ol' billy goat I ran into. I reckon that runaway quadruped could be my contingency plan to mitigate the shortfall in my finances when I fail to deliver any magic seals today. Yeah, you got it: I plan to catch and sell that bastard. Now, I don't have it all figured out yet, 'specially the part about how to take this critter across the water. Lord knows he's not gonna be excited about sharing a boat with the likes o' me, but I'll work somethin' out.

I'm almost at the shack again, and the more I think about selling that goat, the more I'm convinced it's a brilliant idea. Here's why. Once I take him home, I know I'll have at least two people lickin' their chops, ready to buy him. Those two buyers would be that same Mattis and his wife. See, they're Caribbean people. And Caribbean people, they *love* that stuff. My ol' lady? *Oowee* – nothing to her like some good ol' goat meat. So as soon as I can bring this critter into the city, they're gonna put on their San Tainos T-shirts, break out the rum and have a "curry goat feed". That's like a party for no real reason, where they invite friends over and cook the meat with curry powder and spices and all that stuff and they eat the whole goat, 'cept for maybe the horns. Goats are not safe in San Tainos, trus' me. Pa Campbell used to tell me: "Skid, they use the whole head to make soup. And they roast the nuts too." Some people believe that roasted goat nuts would be good for a guy like Mattis, who wants to break down your bedroom wall every two days or so. Something tells me it puts lots of hair on your chest as well.

Well, anyway, soon as I crab-walk up to the shack in the ol' washtub, I know something's off. I hear water sloshin' and hoofs in the house clump-clumping around. But it sounds like two, not four. So 'cept my billy goat's gone and learnt to walk on two legs, I think there's somebody trespassin' on my goddamn property. Now this is not goin' down like last time. I'm facin' this like a man – a man who has seen some strange things so far this year. So here I go: leaping out of the boat, splashin' through the water, jumping onto the porch and kickin' in the goddamn door with a paddle in my hand.

There's a tall dude in the middle of the room. Can't see his face, but I know that kinky hair anywhere.

"Goddamit, Skid! What're you doin' out here by yourself? Who took you? Did you come from the train tracks? Momma here?"

"Easy, Doug. Leave spaces between your questions and maybe I can stick a few answers in 'em, huh?"

"Look man, I'm serious. Why're you all the way out here?"

"I used to live here, remember?"

"Shuddup. It's not safe out here. And I thought I heard you got banned from the Refuge."

"Nasty rumours. Matter of fact, I came to check on the wildlife. You seen a billy goat round here?"

"No… just a jackass with a paddle and no goddamn boat."

I lower the paddle.

"Har-har. That was not even original, man. Moms know *you* out here?"

"No, so don't say a word. I don't want her to worry."

"Well, tell me what you're up to, then!"

He looks at me sideways. Boy knows when I'm twistin' his arm.

"Let's just say I'm looking for money that Benet left around here."

"Benet left money?"

"It's actually none o' your business, boy. Calm down."

"Sad. I was just about to tell you the real reason I'm in the swamps. It's about money too. Maybe we can join forces and make a fortune."

"Um, no. Let's go."

The boy's looking around tryin' to find the muddy strip he used to get to the shack. He's so lost right now it's hilarious.

"Looks like you need a ride outta here. Me and my boat'll give you a lift if you tell me more about that Benet buried treasure."

"Never said anything about buried treasure. Where's the boat?"

"Right over here. And just so you know, there's only room for two. So if we find my billy goat, you're walkin'."

"You're outta *your mind*."

We're pickin' our way through the sogginess. He's walkin' in my footsteps by the time we get to the boat.

"Ever had curry goat, Doug?"

"A few times."

"Whadya think?"

"A bit gamey. But it's OK."

"Well, soon I'm gonna invite you to a goat feed at the apartment. You can bring your girl."

"My girl doesn't like goat."

"It's free."

"She still doesn't like goat."

I get him to do the rowing and I drop him off along the train tracks. He hops out of the pirogue and climbs up the levee. I'm shielding my eyes and lookin' up at my big brother. He's tall as hell for his age.

"So this is where I'm leavin' you?"

"Yeah, I'm cool. I got my motorcycle on the dirt road just beyond here."

Yah. The boy's such a cheapskate it's prob'ly a one-wheeler. "*Money's the only magic there is*" – that's his slogan. And that means that presently he's powerless.

"Tell Tony I'm gonna call him later," I holler after him. But I don't think he heard me.

I didn't find my goat today, but that's OK. And that buried treasure Doug talked about is intriguing, man. Anyway, in the meantime I can't wait to ring up ol' nerd Tony Beaumont when I get back home, so he can give me a scientific reason why those hoodoo cards seemed to have a mind of their own. I won't tell him specifically about them, though. All he needs to know is that I was cleaning up garbage from the bayou and saw debris popping up and down from the water. Well, on the phone the boy's a genius. At first.

"Hmm. Some people say the underground water in the swamp is connected to the tidal currents out in the Gulf, Skid. I'm not so sure. But if we assume that's true, you might definitely see the ebb and flow of ocean currents even on the surface of the bayou."

I'm ready to jump for joy and click my heels when the guy says:

"Of course, some oceanographers have debunked that theory. They say it's rubbish actually. What you're seein' is displacement caused by more sinkholes openin' up in the swamp. More space underwater, plus more things like trees falling in, means more movement of everything. As a matter of fact…"

Well, the guy lost my interest almost immediately. I dropped him off somewhere around the word "debunked".

"What do *you* believe Tony?"

"It's not a matter of what I believe per se, Skid. I just try to listen to all the scientific theories and see what evidence there is to support each. I try to *understand* rather than just *believe* somethin'."

Well, you know I hung up soon after that, right? I mean, really. Thanks a lot for nothin', man. I need some scientific assurance that I can get back to work and this guy just wanted to display how much he knows? But see, Tony Beaumont's a bit like toilet paper. Sometimes he's on a roll and other times he's just full o' crap, no lie. I mean, you either believe in a thing or you don't, right? Pick a side, man. Jeez. That's one reason I'm gonna miss Pa Campbell. That geezer was a practical guy. He knew how to build a strong porch on stilts, and he could prob'ly fix a couple outboard motors with a hairpin if he had to. But he believed what he believed. I might not have taken on half of his mumbo-jumbo, but at least he wasn't lookin' for permission from nobody anyway. Gotta respect a guy like that. Meanwhile my eldest brother has all the theories in the world and sits in the valley makin' no decision whatsoever. Funny how all he wants to do is road-trip all across America instead of becomin' a big hotshot scientist or whatever. I think that's just his way of still searchin' for my pops, though.

Well, look. Come hell, hoodoo or high water, I got a business to run. So I go to the laundromat to take inventory. I count off how many seals I got and it turns out I didn't do too badly. So I make sure Claire is nowhere around when I call Mattis and tell him to meet me by the pool, stat. Now I've got to formulate a strategy for effective negotiation.

Soon Mattis walks outside. For the first time he's wearing a T-shirt, thank God, but he looks lumpy, like what would happen if you poured cold oatmeal porridge into a sweatsock. From down inside the pool I can see him looking around, cos he doesn't see me yet. I call out to him and he comes and looks over the edge. His mouth is greasy as hell, like he's been eatin' half a pig all by himself.

"Heeey Terence, what's goin' on?"

"Got some seals for ya."

"Good, we need to get rid of them as soon as possible. So we can start workin', eh? You mother paid me an advance, you know."

"Oh, she did? That's good, that's good. Well, I agree, we need to get rid of these then."

I point to the seals, all eleven of them, laid out at my feet. He sucks some grease off his fat fingers and is fixin' to practically leap into the damn pool to get his hands on the goods.

That's when he sees that I also got this brand-new jerrycan that I borrowed from Teesha Grey's Land Rover at my feet.

He pulls back a little.

"What is that?"

"Oh that? It's a jerrycan. People carry gasoline around in it."

"I know what it *is* Terence. I am asking what it's *for*."

"Well, I reckon if we gonna destroy these things, then the best way is by burning and the best place might be right here in this empty pool."

He stops and grimaces, like when you bite down your own tongue and not even God can help you for the next few minutes or so.

"What's the problem? Ain't that what you said we're supposed to do, destroy the seals?"

So now I'm pouring out that jerrycan all over the cards.

"NO!" Mattis has his hand in mid-air out towards me and looks like he's about to pass out. Veins pop out the side of his head. I literally see his blood pressure shootin' up.

"Tell you what, Uncle," I say, still pouring. "These things are still awright, more or less, cos they're covered in plastic."

Then I take out Moms' stainless-steel Zippo lighter real dramatically and back off a bit.

"But if I was to drop this lighter here, they wouldn't be of much use. So whatchoo say? How about, hmm, three fifty... each?"

Easiest deal I ever did. The guy didn't even negotiate. So I tell him I'll clean them up with dishwashing liquid and drop them off later. Soon as he swears and disappears up the steps, here comes Fricozoid. He just shakes his head when he sees me drinkin' from Teesha Grey's jerrycan.

"*Apper joosh*," I say, with my cheeks full and my lips prob'ly lookin' like a goldfish.

"Skid, I really don't care if you're guzzlin' gas or apple juice. Momma's been hollerin' for you for ten minutes."

Well, just when my business is up and runnin', my other lame job gets in the way. Yeah, Moms suddenly needs me full-time at Bo's until the end of summer. Damn. This is bad timing. You can see how that's gonna be a conflict of interest. I swear, my mother has a monkey wrench in her back pocket, ready to throw into my business when I least expect it. Now I'm walking around behind her, telling her how much they need me at the Refuge and how it's for a good cause and I thought she cared about animals. She's popping in and out of the bathroom, gettin' ready and telling me to do the same.

"Those alligators already have their meals planned out, Skid, we gotta look out for ours."

She comes back with a cup of tea from the kitchen asking me how come I'm interested in the Wildlife Refuge all of a sudden. And she could have sworn Frico said I got banned. I'm so happy that you can depend on good ol' Ma Campbell to cut in and start knackerin' about something completely irrelevant.

"Valerie, did you burn some incense in that car before you got behind that steerin' wheel? Cain't be too careful with San Tainos people. You said so yousself. Maybe you should hang a sack of St John's wort from the rear-view mirror to protect you from that Mattis fella. You San Tai people, don't do so well livin' close together. Not even on the island isself these days. That's exac'ly why the whole country is upside down and close to civil war right now, I heard. Imagine, there's an active volcano, but it's the people who're blowin' up—"

"The volcano is active?"

"Yes, Terence. And Ma, you let me worry about our San Tai neighbour and where I come from, OK?"

"I'm just puttin' a stake in the ground, Valerie. That neighbour of yours ain't all that neighbourly. Don't you watch his white smile. Look at the eyes. Them eyes got red – whatchoo call it – um, red laser beams comin' out of 'em, cos he sees you prosperin'. Evil eyes, Valerie."

"Ma, you know I got nothin' for that man to envy me for. So stop it, please."

"OK, honey. I'm just sayin' I don't trust him any further than I can shoot him. And that's me cuttin' him a lotta slack."

Well, we have a sack of St John's wort swingin' from the rear-view mirror by the time we get to Mrs Thorpe's. That's supposed to chase all the bad luck out from the Tercel. Well, it's Ma Campbell that Moms can't wait to get out of the car. We drop her off, and when we finally get to our lunch cart, maan, the whole sidewalk is a circus. That Tapas food truck is having a goddamn Customer Appreciation Day. I like the word "livid". Moms is livid. We're walking across to the food cart. A guy tries to offer Moms a mini-taco and she just glares at him. When we get into our cart, as soon as we open the window and look out on the intersection, we really see what we're up against. The Tapas people have been working hard. They hand-painted their food truck overnight, in the rain. A sunray-and-rainbow design. God knows how they dried it. They have girls in tennis skirts and summer shorts handing out samples and flyers. This one guy standing on a couple of crates is dressed like Elvis with a guitar and a microphone. He's tearing it up – singin' out what they're doing for their customers and what they got for discounted prices:

"One day only,
One day only,
Quesadillas, tacos, guac–a–mole!"

I'm grinning until I see Moms ripping down the Customer Appreciation Day sign she put up just yesterday. There's a long line stretching from the Tapas truck past the Walgreens on Lake Forest Boulevard, and people are excited. Some of our customers are in the line. They look like they want to tell you: "Hey, don't worry, I'm still having lunch with you guys, I just want to check this out." Well, not Number 30 from yesterday. He just wants to flip me his two middle fingers from behind his half-price taco and free guacamole. Maan, when these Tapas guys rip off an idea, they go all out. Overnight.

Valerie Beaumont starts criticizing everything on the Tapas truck: the paint job, where it's parked, how it's parked and all the people who are serving.

"Listen to them rattlin' them pots and pans like amateurs. And you'd think somebody over there would smell that those mushrooms are burning. Might as well serve the people charcoal, for godssakes."

Then she grunts, puts on her business voice and tells me to get busy. So I'm outside wiping off the windows and packin' out hot cups, but you know I'm really watching the Appreciation Day proceedings, right? Moms keeps motioning to me to hurry up. She's getting antsy, and people start noticing. Then, just when you think it can't get worse, the Tapas truck turns it up a notch. Here comes a pickup with street tap-dancers. Bourbon Street performers. Now, these guys are serious. Look. They got flattened Coke cans nailed to the bottom of their tennis shoes, and when they perform, they *kill it*.

Now I know "tappers" has nothing to do with "tapas", but nobody cares when those boys start tapping on the kerb and rapping about tapas, pickin' up where Elvis left off. One guy, he's tap-dancing while beating a tiny tin drum. The top of it is beaten so bare you can see the steel under the white paint. So they're tearing up the sidewalk and clapping out a beat, and I swear nobody in the line would notice right now if the truck suddenly doubled the price on every damn thing. The truck is in good shape too. Corrugated-steel steps. Stainless-steel everything. Hotplates and a sink with a dish drain. A flat-top cookin' griddle with a vent on top of the truck to let out the heat. Wow. Even the bees are crowding over there. They huddle around the syrup bottles even as a Tapas girl is serving sweet colours over crushed ice. Sno-balls. I want one. They're half-price today, and the place is boilin' already. But I couldn't do that to Moms.

"Go get a sno-ball, Terence, it's OK."

"Nope, it's not OK," I say, wiping the counter and swallowing hard.

"Terence, it's OK."

Well, while I'm walking over there fishin' for my wallet, I feel even worse. I got some money from Mattis, but today Bo's suffered a serious loss. Not even the "FREE Mexi-Caribbean Spring Rolls" sign brought any customers over. Moms spent the day on her calculator. The Tapas truck people, they beat us. Not fair and square, though: they bootlegged my mother's idea. So when I stop at the Tapas window and look at what they were doing, I see Moms' business dream. That's where she's heading, and then even higher. I know one day she'll get there and I can't wait to see it.

But the competition ain't playin' fair. So I reckon I'll just stand here and wonder what it would take to start a kitchen fire in their truck, to make smoke pour out from the vent, until their line of customers breaks up like ants who lost the scent of the sugar bowl.

Well, the sno-ball bees just started goin' berserk, cos a water bottle burst on the flat-top griddle and oil flames are leapin' up to the roof of the truck. Somebody's slappin' at the fire with a wet dishcloth and hollerin' for *un extintor*. Maybe I should have pointed out the extinguisher beside the stainless-steel cupboard that's going soot-black right about now. But I reckon they're gonna need the smoke to calm the bees. Someone kicks open an extra window and the Tapas people, they bail out of their fancy truck in all directions like the smoke. I'm happy to make the mayhem happen.

We're going home with too many cups and leftovers, and the smell of smoke and cooking oil up our noses. Ma Campbell's in the back now saying what a wretched woman Mrs Thorpe is.

"And she's stingy on top of it!"

Moms takes the bait.

"What happened over there, Ma?"

"Caint find a goddamn fork in her house! And I had to eat soup with a plastic spoon taday, you believe that?"

You really shouldn't laugh at old folks, cos the joke's on you in a coupla years, but Moms tipped off Mrs Thorpe about the trouble she was taking into her house. Ma figured that out, and she doesn't take too kindly to that, so before long she's looking for a way to get back at us. When Moms mentions the Tapas truck burnin' and us making a loss, Ma Campbell comes in for the kill.

"A-ha! Yes! I told you, Valerie, but nobody listens to a half-deaf woman! They put a hex on you and it turned back on them!"

Moms rolls her eyes.

"Fix it. That's what you need to do, Valerie. Let's stop at Lam Lee Hahn and get some cinnamon, some lemon juice and some laundry bluing. Sprinkle the pavement round your food cart with this liquid for nine days and round 'bout this taam next week, they're goin' down. Now, all that is free advice. This ol' lady ain't even gonna charge you, since you say you didn't make even a daam taday."

Ma Campbell is right, though, in a sense. Moms hasn't done one ritual since we got into the city, 'cept burn frankincense in the house. Not to mention using any folk medicine. In the swamp, if you as much as cleared your throat, you'd get a cocktail of bush medicine that'd cure all the ailments you were about to catch. Nowadays? Pssh. Everything my mother uses has a plastic cap, a "Keep out of reach of children" sticker and a name you can't pronounce. Well, Ma's done it. Now, Moms' face is as dark as the soap-scum clouds settlin' in over the Lake. God's trying to clean the earth of some nasty con-jurin'. Or maybe it's residue from all the dirty laundry these two've been washing.

"Ma?"

"Yes, Val'rie."

"You might not remember this, but we left the swamp a long time ago."

"We did *what*?"

"Yes we did. And some days like today, when I listen to you talk, I feel like that swamp is chasin' me. Like the marsh is catchin' up to me. It's comin' up around my ankles and draggin' me down again. Like I'm a giant but somebody's hacking at my legs bit by bit, you know?"

Ma keeps quiet for a long time. Then, like a radio that just found the signal:

"Well, Valerie Beaumont. You say you left the swamp – but you ain't out o' the woods yet. Least you can do right now is continue ta pray hard and do hoodoo too for your bidniss' sake. You made a mess o' your marriage. Don't make a mess of your bidniss too. I mean, if you didn't like ta do all that deep con-jurin' any more by the taam your husband was runnin' around New O'lins cheatin' on ya, then you could've at least tied nine knots in a string the length of his thing. And that woulda kept his zipper up until he got home at night. Hell, you'd prob'ly have ta shove him out tha goddamn house in tha mornin'! But your husband is none of my bidniss. Mine is dead and gone. All I do now is pray for a decent crossin'-over, so I can join him in the right place at the right taam. Best you do is keep on livin' and marry that Backhoe Benet and all his millions like I see you been fixin' ta do."

Fourteen

Never hug somebody too soon after they been hurt. Your pity might become part of the pain. My mother's eyes are shimmerin' by the time the bumper scrapes the bottom of the driveway, and I know better than to say anything. Give it a day or so. I trail behind with a pack of hot cups. She turns around, takes them and tells me to get the rest of the stuff.

Inside, you can hear her room door close. Now there's some muffled exchange between herself and Ma. Frico is asking me what happened, while I'm trying to listen to those two. He drags my attention away by mentioning that Mattis's hot niece came looking for me today.

"Yo Skid… she's almost as sweet as Teesha. When she knocked I was checkin' her out through the peephole before he opened the door."

"OK, easy, man." Guy has no respect. "Don't *tell* a guy you were checking out his girl, man."

"She's not my type, though. You notice she has a chipped tooth, right?"

Funny, I never really thought about Claire's chipped tooth until this guy mentioned it just now. It's so slight and kinda cute, really. Especially since when she laughs she slightly covers her mouth, cos she's prob'ly conscious of it. But she shouldn't be. Cos she's beautiful. And these days I admire girls with little quirks. I still love older women too, cos older women, they have all these beautiful dents and scrapes and they're so set in their ways with all their love-life superstitions and rules and broken hearts and life lessons. So only a real jerk would look past a woman's wonderfulness and focus on her chipped tooth. That guy can appreciate broken things from behind a camera, but he can't accept faults in people up close. Damn.

Well, Mattis really needs to talk to me, Frico said. And by the way he's smilin', I know he's gettin' interested in my damn business again. I lose interest in Moms' argument and head for the door.

Open it up and there's Mattis, in the damn doorway with his back to the sunset. He couldn't wait until I got over there? Worse, he turns up at the door, holding Frico's diary, like he missed the point that that was supposed to be a secret. I'm trying to push him out into the corridor, but it's too late. Frico sees it. He forces himself past me and snatches the book out of Mattis's hand before the *obeah man* even knows what's going on.

"Skid, we need to talk, man," is all Frico says before glaring at the guy and stomping back inside the apartment.

I'm looking at Mattis in the doorway like "what the hell, man?" And this big man in his forties looks at me and shrugs. *Shrugs.* Like it's something simple. Like we're in Phys Ed class together and he just fumbled a ball or something. No big deal. Cos it's not like it's a real game or anything.

Anyway, he motions for me to come out into the corridor for a business meeting. The meeting takes like thirty seconds. Turns out his client needs a *dozen* magic seals, and he just realized I only gave him *eleven*.

"Eleven, twelve, big deal," I say. "The difference is only one. I'll get you a hundred more later this week."

"No. Look. They need all these seals *tonight*, eh? It's full-moon time, and twelve is significant."

"Awright, I'll work something out."

Back inside, Frico is asking his mother for the car keys.

"As long as y'all clear the stuff out and wash up, you can take it," is what she hollers out through her room door before starting up again with Ma. She closes the door again, and they sound like they're shouting from inside a can. Moms prob'ly wants us both to get out of the house so she can really give the ol' lady a piece of her mind. Well, it's the fastest Frico ever washed pots and pans, man, cos he's got Valerie Beaumont's car keys. I know he's pissed about the whole journal thing, and I want to smooth things over. So when he says to roll with him around Paris Avenue, further west, I'm ready. In less than half an hour we're heading out just as it gets dark. Frico is trying to find the headlamps. Windshield wiper comes on. Twice. Now I'm wonderin' if it's a good idea to let this guy drive. At least he knows how to turn on the car stereo. It's Toto.

"I love this song, man."

"Skid. We ain't here for the Top Twenty countdown."

I try to change the subject from his journal before he even starts talkin' about it. "She's plannin' to marry Benet, man."

"What?..."

Caught him off guard. Good. But then I realize he knows more than I do.

"Oh, that. Well, not really but—"

"What? Not really?"

"I mean she's not *planning* anything. Who'd you hear that from?"

"Ma."

"Ma Campbell's flipped, man. Momma asked Ma Campbell for her opinion 'bout whether or not she should go into *business* with Benet. Backhoe has four businesses across the city. He knows his stuff. Momma used the words 'business proposal' and poor Ma probably took it the wrong way. Thinks Benet is trying to marry her."

"Well, doesn't that make you uncomft'able? That she's at least thinking about being in some kind of relationship with him?"

He grunted and shrugged.

"I hate it when you do that."

"What?"

"The gruntin' and the shrugging. What does gruntin' and shrugging mean?"

"Relax man, Moms and Benet used to be involved a long time ago, you know this."

"Like I was sayin', though, for some reason your shrugging really annoys me. Annoyin' like people who tell you a movie from start to finish before you watch it. Or they do all the voices – like they never heard 'bout reported speech, y'know?"

"Um, what?

"More annoying than whoever writes 'Wash Me Please' across the Tercel windshield every time we're at Bo's."

"OK, wait... stop."

"Just venting, man."

"Relax, Terence. Get a hold of yourself."

"And that's another thing. Why do I always hear that *I* have to control myself?"

"Maybe it's cos you're outta control, Skid."

I feel the tips of my ears getting hot again. I take a deep breath and get back to the original topic.

"Anyway, what are we going to do about Benet, man?"

"We? *You.* I'm leaving in less than a month, dude."

Shit. With all the drama I forgot all about him leaving. That knocked the wind out of me for sure. So we're closer downtown now, and I'm looking out at all the twinklin', silent cars lined up across the toll bridge like robot fireflies. A car slides by us going in the opposite direction almost without a sound. We stop somewhere on the east bank of the Mississippi and get out. In the late sun, the business district is blazin' bright across the river. A bunch of crystal buildings growing straight up out of the earth. I hear Frico sigh.

"Terence Skid Beaumont?"

Under my breath, still looking straight ahead: "'Sup, man?"

"Forget Benet for now. I'm leaving in a coupla weeks. You're gonna have to take charge."

And as the night lights come on in the skyscrapers across the river, my brother, the hoodoo-magic sketcher that makes everything OK, is actually telling me I have to become the man of the house.

"You really got to stick closer to Momma. Keep her safe and don't go running around doing those crazy late-night stunts of yours. I don't mean to scare you, Skid, but sooner or later that guy 'Couyon' Jackson is gonna be back in New Orleans. And he's gonna come looking for his ol' lady. And his mother lives with ours. You got to step up and do what you can to let this guy know that a man is around. I hate leavin'. But you got what it takes, man. You're no slouch. And you should call on Doug and Tony for back-up more often."

Now I got lights goin' off in my head just like those buildings across the river, but I'm not sayin' a word.

"Go on, man, I'm listening."

"All I'm sayin' is that I believe in you, Skid."

Whoa. Are you hearing this guy? He might as well have said: "*I believe you're a skid.*" There's something in Claire's story, man.

"Ever wonder where my nickname comes from, Frico?"

"Huh? Have you been listenin'?"

"Of course man. Just asking a question."

"Well, to answer your question, Terence: not partic'larly, no. I don't care. Even though I heard that in some parts o' Canada that's what they call kids who act like bums. Pops' ancestors are from Canada, and you're on your way to being worthless – so, the whole thing follows."

"You're a trip. No, it all has to do with folk magic. In San Tainos, a 'skid' is somebody affected by a deliberate folk-magic *mistake*."

"A 'deliberate mistake'. Are you even listening to yourself?"

"Now you're just pickin' at the words as if your English is perfect. In other words, a *skid* is caused by a spell gone wrong... powers out of control. People struck by San Tai magic."

Frico's lookin' at me like I'm all kinds o' crazy right now.

"You are struck stupid indeed. But it ain't magical! Ha, that's so funny."

"No, it's not."

This bastard is takin' a long time to recover from his own joke.

"Anyway, you *are* a bit outta control. Moms says that all the time. But 'Skid' is just a nickname, man. Get over it."

"So you think I'm just turnin' windmills into monsters, huh?"

"Turning windmills, whassat?"

"You think I'm making up stuff in my head?"

"Ha. You're much worse than that, man."

Silence. I swear I can hear the world rumblin' around. Stale sunlight has half his face burnished like old gold. He sees I'm as serious as a sudden thundercloud. So he looks at the ground for a long time and sighs a little bit.

"Terence? Do you remember what Momma did when you told her I could sketch on paper and somehow fix things?"

"Hell, she didn't say nothin'. She just patted my head and went lookin' for that shrink's card."

"Exactly. Please don't put her through that again, man. Momma is different these days. She's happier. And you know what she always says."

"Yeah, 'Life is like a broken tooth. The worst only shows up when you're happy' – I know."

"Good. So if you're havin' strange ideas about your nickname, please keep 'em to yourself. Maybe you're just super-weird and super-clumsy or probably you got Post-Dramatic Syndrome from livin' in the swamp."

Trust me, Frico's a malaprop machine going off to *college* in the fall. It's so sad.

He's checkin' his watch.

"We should get going. It's prob'ly really dangerous out here now."

We're heading back home, and he's switching on the wipers again when there's no rain yet. He's nervous as hell. Like he figures I know he was trying to tell me about the skid without really tellin' me about the skid. Cos that must have been a deep family secret, a cover-up. Somebody in my family made a folk-magic mistake back in the day. No, not Valerie. Maybe Alrick Beaumont. And it's been hush-hush all these years. But Frico's diary is the biggest hint. Now he wants to come clean, but he doesn't want to be known as the Beaumont who spilt the beans, so to speak.

It's one of those nights when the sky is dark but you can still see white clouds right over your head. The Toyota Tercel is slurpin' up those spaghetti lines in the middle of the highway. I'm staring out into darkness. Every few seconds sheet lightning flares in the clouds across the lake, blue and silver at the same time, like the flash of a welding rod from afar. Maybe God is fixin' somethin' that broke off this ol' spacecraft we whirl around on. In my head other things are breakin'. I'm remembering Broadway and Squash drowning in the swamp. I'm seein' that sinkhole tearin' open and those boys scramblin' up the sides and never making it back to the river banks. I'm seeing that marble monument with the angel coming down in the cemetery again. *Brack. Boom.* Barely missin' those muggers. I'm picturing Peter Grant ducking down at the Meat Mart cos that incoming manhole cover is cuttin' through the air like a coin.

Dammit.

I am a skid.

I look over at Frico, and everything becomes clear. Mattis was on to something. The magic seal I found in Frico's diary is prob'ly the cause of the hoodoo mistake itself. My old man buried everything else. Maybe I played with it as a baby and got zapped or somethin'. Why else would 'Zoid be hiding it all these years, 'cept to keep my wings clipped? Now he knows the genie is out of the damn bottle. Matter of fact he's seen the power himself. He was wearing my coat at the church when the podium popped off and fell to the floor. The wallet was in the coat. The seal is always in the wallet. Yeah. That's where I stashed it real quick after I found it in his diary.

Maybe I can still get this guy to tell the whole truth.

"I found one of Pops' old hoodoo magic seals in your diary. I've been walkin' around with it in my wallet for months."

"OK. And?"

"Remember that hundred-year-old monument breakin' in Lafayette? Maybe I did it."

He looks over at me this time. His eyes are shifting all over the place.

"Jeez. Just let it go, Terence."

"And that podium at the church. And the sinkhole in the swamp. I remember that night clearly now. Broadway and Squash – fingers on the trigger, ready to shoot Moms and Doug and Tony. I yelled out over the rain and the gunshots. And that sinkhole, it just appeared under the bridge and swallowed them up."

"Now you just sound crazy. But just so you don't go buggin' other people with this crap, look: stuff happens for no other reason than that's the way the Blue Wheel wobbles, man. That's how the world works. It's like an earthquake. It's gonna happen. We fix what we can and we move on."

Ha. You got to hand it to him. The boy's hardcore. He can keep a family secret.

I'm smirking, and he's in a huff by the time we get to the gate.

"Look, just put the seal back where you found it, man. You've already gone way overboard with this crap."

I look at him, and his whole face has a flashing green glow from the indicator on the dashboard. The boy's prob'ly green with envy on the inside too. His sketching can't compare to this thing. We're turnin' into the apartment complex with the first raindrops spritzin' the windshield. Benet's long black town car is in the driveway, and all the lights are off in the house.

Fifteen

"Shh, listen."

Somethin' more serious eclipsed our argument in the car. The entire house is dark 'cept for a sliver of lamplight coming out Moms' room. There's a conversation going on in there, but that's not Ma Campbell's voice. It's Benet's. I whip around to Frico in the dark.

"Dammit! First he's in the kitchen, now he made it to her bedroom? What? Where's Ma?"

"Keep your voice down. Ma Campbell's in our room again. She got so mad at Momma, she's not sleepin' anywhere near her."

A few words slip out into the kitchen.

"She's talking to him about that fire in the Tapas food truck. He's gonna buy one for Bo's. Cool truck. Benet has more money than he knows what to do with. But why'd she wanna be in business with him?"

"I don't know and I don't care any more, Skid. I just want to go away far from here for a long time, maybe for good. So focus. Go get your old wallet and gimme back that seal, before you forget."

You know, sometimes, even with all his screwed-up ways, I admire my brother. But then, he always goes and says something that just ticks you the *hell* off. I don't need him reminding me about the seal every other minute. Not to mention the fact that he's going a thousand miles away to school in New York City. Damn. It's a lot to deal with. He's cutting his hair and shavin' and liftin' dumb-bells and practisin' the "I'm goin' to college" look in the mirror. Every day he's reading his fartsy freshman brochures and whatever else came in the mail: glossy magazines with pictures of students sitting around on green grass with books open, as if anybody really studies like that. I was there when he pulled out the acceptance letter, for heavenssake. I remember how it crackled, loud and crispy, like when they open a letter in a movie. I was happy for him, but I couldn't smile, cos the sketcher's been much too happy to erase himself from New O'lins. All the time I heard him talking about becoming a great artist or a movie director I'd say to myself: "Poor little Pinocchio wants to be a normal boy like everybody else, and that's a fairy tale." But I'm not too normal myself these days, I reckon.

"Oh, shit," Frico brings me back to the present tense.

I don't need for him to explain why he whispered that, cos all of a sudden I can hear it too. Love songs. Can you believe it? Frickin' love songs, man. The greatest romantic hits are now comin' through the damn walls. Seems like Mr and Mrs Mattis are making up again. And they're going all out this time. Mattis prob'ly got Moms' and other people's hoodoo advance money and went out and got a brand-new stereo system. Saw it inside his apartment the other night, still in the bubble wrap. Well, now it's on full blast, playin' his love-music mixtape – and I wish we had thicker walls, cos Mariah Carey is setting the mood for two other old people right now.

Suddenly there's less talking in Mom's bedroom, and Mattis is starting a different rhythm with his headboard against our bedroom wall again. Frico says he doesn't care, but you should see him walking around the kitchen, right now, anxious as hell. This is not good. Rain is rappin' on the windows now. Sheet lightning outside again. All these romantic atmospherics are just makin' it worse. And when that rain starts pitter-pattering harder on the roof and the Eurythmics' 'Sweet Dreams' comes on, my brother starts switching on all the lights in the house, cos now this is a frickin' emergency. But it seems that, as far as Valerie Beaumont is concerned, we're still out on the road with the car. She doesn't notice a thing. 'Cept that Aaron Neville and Linda Ronstadt are now belting out 'Don't Know Much' through the walls. Damn. Well, look. All this time I was really tryin' to keep calm. But listen. Once the Righteous Brothers start bellowing out the first verse of the 'Unchained Melody', you got to do somethin', cos that song is about time passing and people hungerin' for each other and all that. So I just say: "Hell no, that's enough." I run outside with my wallet, drop to my belly real quick, and I send that hoodoo folk-magic seal slidin' straight up under Mattis's front door, while Fricozoid is runnin' behind me hollerin' "No!" Well, too late. While he's tusslin' with me in the corridor, there's a bright silver flash like it's broad daylight and then a loud *pop* that makes your ears whistle. Now the whole complex is pitch-black and dead, dead quiet.

Well, after the light-and-power people came and put the electricity back on, they said they had more work to do in the area.

"Took out half the Boulevard, that lightning storm."

But now that they're gone, everybody who came out of their apartments with flashlights and umbrellas are just standing around in the drizzle, blinking a bit and talking in their own language. It's the Tower of Babel out here. Many of them, they know English, but we don't know whatever it is *they're* speaking. That sucks, cos they know this and they're enjoying it. Well, thank God Claire is out here, interpreting again. They're all discussing her uncle for some reason, like they believe his loud sound system has something to do with the power outage:

"*Malaka.*" (*Jerk-off.*)

"*Que? Quien? Ese tipo?*" (*What? Who? That guy?*)

It doesn't help that the Mattises seem to be still inside finishing their domestic business by candlelight while everybody else is checkin' out the repair work. Claire says the lights didn't come back on in their apartment: "Larry Lou is coming to look at it."

Benet walks off to his car and drives out. Frico is looking at me as usual. He's livid – and he's not the only one. Moms comes out into the corridor, then wheels back inside so fast she leaves one slipper behind. She comes back out and starts pounding on Mattis's door. For what? Could be anything: the bedroom noise, the power failure – or she wants her money back cos his hoodoo ain't working. Who knows. One thing's for certain: the fun and games are over.

People trail off through doors, waggin' their tongues and draggin' their languages back inside with them. I go to get the car keys from Frico. Claire and I run through the rain and sit in the Tercel. Ignition. Music.

Red glow from the dashboard. Rain drummin' on the car roof and snakin' down the windshield. Electric lights from the pool area splinter through the drops, leaving water shadows on Claire's face. Larry Lou in blue overalls is walkin' back from the apartment scratching his chin like he really knows what the hell happened. Everybody's gone now. She smells like cookies, this girl. I think it's what she sprays in her hair. Women are so wonderful, no lie. Her hair is up. You can tell she washed it earlier today. She had her eyebrows done. Mascara's on her lashes too. In her ears, gold hoops catch the light: huge halos at the side of her head. Got them for her birthday, she says. Only wears them on special occasions. I reckon I'm seeing something happenin' that I've heard about all my life: if a girl likes you, the next time you see her, she'll be in her best earrings, with make-up on, and her hair done up differently.

She tells me I'm being boring by not askin' her out yet. Wants to go somewhere tonight. Maybe we could take the car and see a movie, or just go downtown and walk along the sea wall. I'm wasting time thinking about money and how to approach asking Valerie Beaumont when, without permission, Claire leans over and kisses me, full on. Four seconds at least, and she bites my lip a little bit when she's pulling away. Better than the first time. Strawberry chapstick too, I think. And there's a taste of cigarette in the kiss, of course. I don't mind. To be honest, I'm really bad at makin' the first move. She makes me feel comfortable and brand new. Like after you take a shower in the middle of a hot day and the scent of the soap is still on your skin. She takes my chin and turns my head. Dancing eyes searchin' my face for all the feelings comin' to the surface. I swear she sees everything, this girl. And when I look at her, I don't know where the hell I am any more, or what time it is. Struck stupid by San Tai magic. And her voice... oh, man. Now we're whisperin' between smooches.

"What're you looking at?"

"A gorgeous girl."

"Stop. I'm just a tomboy under all this make-up and stuff."

"I wasn't lookin' at your make-up and stuff."

(*You got to say that or a girl will think you're shallow.*)

"What? You don't like my make-up and stuff?"

(*Correction. You're dead, no matter what you say.*)

"You're gorgeous all the time."

"That's better, you little liar. Anyway, what happened just now, Terence? Do you think—"

"Say it. Do I think I have something to do with all this? Yep."

"Oh."

"Look around. You can see for yourself what happened."

Now she's holding my face with both her hands. You can smell that her fingers are always close to fire.

"Terence. That's crazy. I mean, you heard what my uncle said. Nobody believes that stuff about people being skids."

"He's bluffing. He prob'ly just doesn't know how to handle me finding out about it. It all made sense today. And something tells me you believe it, even halfway."

"What? That you can pull a hurricane onto the island or cause an earthquake? *Psssh*. I should believe you're some kind of zombie or somethin'?"

"Nah. Zombies are supposed to be a Haiti thing. Don't go confusin' voodoo with hoodoo or skids with zombies now."

Claire is looking straight ahead. One of her curls escapes and twirls down her forehead like a spring. She puffs air out the side of her mouth, and the spring swings back on top of her head.

"OK, what?"

"It doesn't make any sense, Terence. If you could really do all the crap you believe you can do, why would your mother need more conjurations to protect you, huh?"

Almost on cue, Mattis appears beside the car in a yellow plastic raincoat. I jump. He's rapping real loud on the window. When Claire rolls it down, her uncle bends slowly and sticks his head inside the vehicle. Water drips off the peak of the raincoat hoodie. He looks past her and over to me in the driver's seat. He's talkin' as if I'm not even there.

"Claire, lissen to me, eh? Get out of this car right now."

"Uncle, you OK?"

He pushes back the hood and wags his finger in her face so fast it looks like Play-Doh.

"Claire, lissen to me! It's not safe to be around Terence any more. Get out of this car right now."

"Uncle Mattis, slow down—"

"Slow down? Get out! None of us are safe, eh? Come now!"

That guy opens the door like it's still his car. He snatches his niece out of the shotgun seat by the arm. She's standing up to him. They argue. He pulls the hood back over his head and I can't see his face any more. She's arguing with a raincoat or Death dressed in yellow. Her hair is sparklin' in the rain, and her make-up turns into black tears streamin' down her cheeks. I can no longer hear their voices. Only the swamp turned up loud in my head: the slow-bubblin' bayou, the chanting crickets, the goat bleating, the roar of flames from underground gas, and the hiss of the earth like a sinkhole sucking down my entire life.

Frico has two bags packed when I get in. He's leaving right after my birthday. His eyes are closed, but I know he's awake, cos his foot is keeping time with whatever is coming through his Walkman.

I pull a headphone off his ear, while rubbin' rain from my hair with a towel.

"Sorry, man. Really sorry about the seal and everything."

He puts the earphones back on, and the words come out louder than normal.

"None of it is really your fault, man. But that doesn't help none."

"I'm gonna get it back."

"You can't. I checked a'ready."

"Whadya mean? I can just go over there and get it right now."

"I tried, Terence. Mattis said he didn't see it. Can't see anything in the dark, cos the power to his apartment is still off. Bad wiring. Maybe he's lyin', I don't know. Maybe he sold it, Skid."

"Yeah, he's got clients round the clock."

I sit on the bed. He snatches off the headphones and turns his face to the wall. I reckon he's watching the droplets gather on the glass or listenin' to the heavy run-off from the roof that makes the rain sound worse than it really is. There's a shadow of a plant by the window, a broad leaf, nodding under the downpour. An abandoned spider web hangs over it, full of water diamonds.

Haunting headlights of passin' cars drag window shapes along the wall. The whole scene is sending me to sleep, when a blackbird, late for its nest, swoops down through the power lines of Hayne Boulevard and flies smack into the window. And all that's left is the fading flutter of wings from the ground, and a few feathers sticking to the goddamn glass.

Sixteen

When you can't find your car where you *know* you left it, it's an out-of-body experience. Yeah. The Tercel is gone.

It would have been easier to bear on a dry day, cos at least I wouldn't have to see where the rain marked out the shape of it on the parking space. I'm the last one outside, barefoot and still half asleep – hollered out of my sleep by Valerie Beaumont after she came out and couldn't find her car. Frico and Moms are interrogating me about the missing car:

"Where're the keys I gave you, man?"

"Did you lock the car, Terence?"

"Who was in there with you? Claire?"

Ma Campbell hobbles up. She has to get a word in, out of left field as usual.

"He sold it. Terence sold that car to buy drugs. Anything that ain't nailed down, these junkies they sellin' it. I see that girl he been canoodling with. Looks like a junkie for sure."

Now Moms is so frustrated she goes back into her room, to avoid grabbing my neck, I guess. I feel stupid. The skid is in full effect. Everything is crumbling. Or this is a really bad dream. I sit down on the bricks and hold my head. This is the spot where Mattis stood and screamed at Claire to get out of the car last night. The car that's no longer there. He finally believes those old folk tales. And he's right. Nothing is safe. I almost want to touch the space to see if the Tercel is there but just invisible. The other cars in the parking area sit there looking dumb, like they never saw anything. Police come. Benet follows, obviously summoned to the goddamn rescue by Moms. He mills around with the cops. They know him. They ask me a couple of questions.

Who else was on the premises last night.

What time did the power go out.

Where exactly was the car parked.

Who was sitting where.

What were we doing in the car.

They wake up Larry Lou, but he has nothing to report, 'cept that he saw Mattis screamin' into the vehicle last night. They don't ask him much more after that, cos his breath must be teetering on roadkill by now. Benet tells them about Claire, and they go to Mattis's apartment. He's leaning out his door half-naked, shakin', gesticulating and telling them about how he lost his stereo last night, like they're from frickin' RadioShack. I don't think he brought my name up. The cops roll out. Benet is still here rubbing Moms' shoulders in the kitchen. He takes out his cellular phone and makes a few calls. Mrs Thorpe arrives at the house in her Terravan. It's the last few days before back-to-school, so I decide to go get ready for Bo's when my mother tells me I'm fired, right there in front of Benet. Well, what she actually said was "No, Skid Beaumont, never mind. It's fine" – but she might as well have told me I'd lost my lousy job. Mrs Thorpe and another church sister will help her out from now on. One will go to the food cart, and the other will stay with Ma Campbell for a couple of hours each day.

So yeah, I got laid off. And in that instant Moms said "Skid, it's fine", the name became a splinter under my skin. When I was growin' up it was cool. Set me apart at school. I used to walk around hollerin' out "Skid!" – just to advertise the name for no reason. I even called myself "DJ Skid" and "Skid Fresh". Now I just hate the damn thing.

Anyway, I feel real foolish about the car. So I escape to the roof to look out over the lake. If you think the swamp is hot, try the city around summer, even after some rain. My cold drink goes warm by the time I get it out the fridge. There's no bayou to cool off in and a busted pool is an abomination on a hot day, believe me. So I'm watching cars go up and down Hayne Boulevard and I'm hoping that after a while they'll hypnotize me out of these feelings.

Footsteps on the roof tiles. I don't even look around, cos this guy is just up here to rub it in.

"How's it goin', little bro?"

I'm looking dead ahead, and he's behind me. I play deaf, and he answers himself.

"Hmm, not good, I reckon."

I turn around a bit and force myself to answer. "This skid thing is a real curse."

He chuckles and shakes his head like I'm pathetic. His half-laugh came from under a sad smile.

"Anyway... here."

He's holdin' out one of those water bottles with a carrying strap on it.

"Lemonade. Thought you'd need to cool down, man."

"Damn right."

It tastes off, like the lemons are old. Frico isn't known for his kitchen skills.

"Really sucks about the car, Terence."

"I could have sworn I locked it up, man."

"Don't worry about it, happens to me sometimes. I forget, I mean."

Pause. Sip. A truck rumbles past on the Boulevard.

"Maybe whatever you and Claire were doing in the car caused some really bad luck."

"I wish. The skid is in full effect, man."

Pause. I know the silence from him is a big, fat *ignore* of the last thing I said.

"Gonna miss that car, though," he says too soon after a big gulp. He coughs. Serves him right.

"Frico Beaumont's gonna miss that car? Thought you said it was a shopping basket with a key."

He cleared his throat. "Yeah it was. But it was OK."

"Even with the egg-nog paint job? And the egg-nog vinyl seats?"

"Even with the egg-nog stuff. And I thought one time *you* said it belongs in a junkyard."

"Well, this whole apartment complex is close to junkyard status, so it used to fit right in."

"Ha, I guess. Anyway, Momma's pretty pissed right now, but she'll be awright. That's what insurance is about. Just don't get on her nerves, man. When I'm gone off to school y'all will have extra space. Use it. Avoid her and Benet sometimes."

Gulp. I'd rather not talk about him leaving. Another mouthful of bad lemonade. Choose another topic.

"Benet. What does she want with Benet? It's beginning to look like more than a business partnership."

"Asked myself the same question. I guess you and me, we don't know what it's like to be forty years old and lonely."

"Hm."

"But if you keep waiting around for Mai, you just might." He says that with a laugh in his voice.

I laugh as well, cos he's right. If my ex-girlfriend had run off with some Frenchy lover boy with long hair and a palmful of poetry it wouldn't have been so bad. But Mai's involved with God now – and that's a different kind of going steady.

Meanwhile, this thing developing between Claire and me, it's too complicated, not to mention the fact that she's from San Tai.

I don't know, but something inside of me wants to avoid that place and all I've heard of it. But if I watch too many of those San Tainos tourist ads on TV, I'll want to go there tomorrow. You'd think the whole place is one big beach and everybody's a damn coconut vendor with really white teeth.

Anyway, I can't tell if it's the heat up here or too much thinking in my head, but I don't feel so good right now. Frico has to be helping me off this roof. We're leaving the water bottle up here too. At the edge of the roof I pause, cos I see Ma Campbell out under the sugar-maple tree with that young church-sister lady. So even though I'm feeling a little off balance, I stick my hands up to the sky and I scream like the Prayer Warriors: "You young boys and the *indiscipline*!" Well, Ma, she just looks up at me and says something about drugs, drugs, drugs.

So I'm finally down and back inside the house and the world is wobblin' side to side now. I'm laughing, cos everything is suddenly funny, especially this whole thing about taking air in through your nose and then letting it out again. Frico is laughing too. This is not one of his sad laughs, this is *crazy* laughin'. He's tryin' to turn on the TV with the portable telephone for godssakes. Ma Campbell comes in and starts mumblin' to herself about callin' the police to come back and get us. That's when I look past her and think I can see Frico's "lemonade" on the kitchen table beside Pa's urn. *Mescal*. That's a kind of tequila – yeah, the one with the dead worm in it. Half the liquid in the bottle's gone, so the worm has either his head or his ass stickin' up above the liquor surface – I can't tell which is which right now – but it's so funny for some reason. Frico sees me eyein' the bottle.

"Hey, Terence, Skid." He's laughing tears and slurring. "Remember – remember that time? That time with that slug? That slug you gave me in a cup? Under that milk, remember?"

I think I'm more sober than he is right now.

"Yeah, classic trick, man. One of my best."

He sticks his hand out and rocks it from side to side.

"Nyaah. I wouldn't say *best*... but it was a damn good trick, that trick. Well, look. After that I tried to get you ta, um, drink a Coke and eat Mentos at the same time, ya know. That would be like a bubble bomb in your mouth. Probably blow your lips off. But you didn't take the bait. So now, how did you like your worm lemonade today, huh? Your worm-in-a-bottle, tequila lemonade, huh? Payback, as they say, my brother, is a bitch."

His revenge is damn juvenile, not very creative and highly insensitive, considering the timing. But it's funny as hell. That mescal tastes like shampoo to me, so you shouldn't worry about me becoming an alcoholic.

Now, I'm laughing and crying, cos I'm tipsy and I'm worried about the skid and I feel bad about the car and I miss my brother even before he's out the door and off to college. He's laughing at my sadness, cos he doesn't know what else to do. Meanwhile he's still trying to turn on the TV with the portable telephone receiver. Suddenly I'm sleepy in the middle of the day. He puts his hand on my head and ruffles it.

"You need a haircut, little bro. Go to sleep. When you wake up we'll go get one."

He finally turns on the tube. We catch a commercial. It's one those beverage ads: teenagers running onto the beach with surfboards to catch a wave that's the same colour as the drink, and they're all happy because they have no pimples or skids or stolen cars to think about. All they have to do for thirty seconds is sip the cold drink and say "ahhh" out loud for no reason. Like anybody really wipes a dirty bottle across his forehead in real life. The only thing worse than a commercial is the news, man. Cos that's like somebody went out and gathered all of the worst stories in the world and packaged them up real pretty, so that everybody everywhere can all feel bad at the same time. My head is throbbing with that stupid jingle, and Frico makes it worse when he starts to sing the damn thing. Then he gets serious. And right before I disappear into the confusion he says: "By the way – Happy Birthday, Terence."

PART THREE

Seventeen

On the bus to the barber's, everybody's talking about it. James "Couyon" Jackson is out of prison.

"He's fixin' to bust that case wide open!" My head. I wish that guy wouldn't shout.

"He got off?"

"Not yet, but bet your ass he's out on bond," says another dude with a really dry, leathery lip. "That murderer got some strong hoodoo working for him in the swamps, you bes' believe that!"

"I hear his old man wanted to kill him early. Woulda spared us his gang and their robbin' and killin'." That's from a lady who looks like she'd beat her kids if they as much as burp.

I knew it. That car disappearing means something. Moms rushin' to work spells with Mattis *means* something. Frico looks happy that he's leaving all this behind tomorrow. I don't have that kinda luxury.

If James is free, sooner or later I'm gonna come face to face again with the most notorious scoundrel in south-east Louisiana. And if I remember correctly the last time we met, we didn't part on good terms. My head is heavy again while I'm listenin' to the people in the bus. Funny how folks always hear only the first part of the news, then run off to get the "real details" from the street. Well, they jawed on and on about James and his gang, but Lord knows I didn't catch all of it. Just when I thought I was settling into the city, I realize I'm gonna need a slang dictionary to understand most of these people. For example, there's this girl with one of those cell phones talkin' "Yat" in the bus. Yat is one of our local dialects – long story. Anyway, she's goin' on about James Jackson to someone on the other end and, apart from the thick accent, you know that sometimes hearing only one side of a conversation is much worse than sufferin' through the whole mess.

"Aww-huh? Say whaaat? Where y'all at? Ya'll just saw him? Who dat? Where?"

So in one minute flat, the driver, he gets real annoyed and tells her we all don't need to hear her second-hand speech so loudly. Well, he was right on time, cos I'm still hearing everything like I'm at the bottom of an ocean of mescal. Trus' me, that stuff gets into your head and stays there.

But look, I'm not mad at Frico for spiking my lemonade. Of course he could get into a heap o' trouble for that, cos he's eighteen and I'm technically still a kid. (I could use that against him some day – remind me.) But he prob'ly figured that with that stolen car on my shoulders I needed some kind of *coup de grâce*. (Look it up, man. Like Pa said: I ain't got the taam taday.) Today, I'm going to do something to pick my spirits up, cos so far this birthday's been like a funeral. Today I'll begin to look like a real New O'lins city boy. I'm cutting off my top knot. Or at least the hair I used to pull into a Taino top knot.

So I'm sitting in this antique barber's chair ready to lop the whole thing off, when Frico tells the guy to close-crop just the sides of my head and put three stripes in it. Well, it's not shaping up to be a bad haircut, but the conversation between the barbers – man. Classic crap. I mean, to the point where, right beside the red-white-and-blue barber pole, they should have a sign in front of that place:

NOTICE: WE CUT HAIR & WEAVE BULL

Of course, they're talking about the headline of the day: "James Jackson Verdict Overturned. Out on Bond until New Trial Date Set." But the *lies* in between the facts! Maan. Beside security guards and taxi drivers, barbers are the biggest gossips, I swear to ya. My haircut is taking a hell of a long time, not because I have a jungle on top of my head, but because these barbers, Omar and Garfield, they have to pause and turn off their clippers and try to outdo each other's rubbish every ten seconds.

"So, Omar, where do you reckon Couyon Jackson is right now?"

"Hell, I don't know. Do I look like one of his gangsters to you?"

"Matter of fact, you do!"

"Anyway, even if he was right here in one o' these chairs gettin' hisself a haircut, I reckon we couldn't tell."

"Whatchoo mean we couldn't tell?"

"Well, they say he's different. Heard he got that plastic surgery."

"C'mon, now. That boy ain't got no money for no plastic surgery."

"You don't know nothin'. He's been hidin' loot for years, so he's richer than all of us right now. How do you think he put up that bail bond?"

"So you mean nobody can tell it's him?"

"I heard you gotta look behind his ear for a mark. Looks like he got a wallop back there when he was younger."

"Well, I'd like to give him a wallop if he ever dared walk in here and sit in my chair, believe me. I swear I'd gag and bound him with this electrical cord and shave him to the skull and throw him back in that prison myself."

Now, look. You can't just walk out of a barber chair when you feel like it, especially with your head half-shaved and with those clippings down the back of your neck and hangin' off your forehead. It's not a good look. So these barbers, they know they got you hostage, the bastards. So I got to sit there and listen to how James also has a protection tattoo – that's why he was set free – and how he's bulletproof and wanted to go to war, but they wouldn't let him into Fort Polk even though he "aced the military-entrance test". *Aced a test?* Maan, they must be talking about *another* James Jackson. Especially when I hear them say that James Jackson has ninja training, cos last time the cops went into the swamp, they caught everybody except him. All the police saw was a puff of smoke and – whoosh – he was nowhere to be found. They say the cops chased him for weeks and he was the one who turned himself in.

Now I'm so embarrassed I don't even want to see the look on *my* face in the mirror while these morons are talking. But Frico, he has his hair cut already, so he's sitting and listenin' to these guys and enjoying their version of life while pretending to read those magazines that are as old as the solar system. He's lookin' at me in the mirror, trying to make me laugh out loud, especially at the part where they say James's mother is the "sweetest lady in all of Louisiana".

Well, Frico pays the guys (a shocker for me). It wasn't much anyways. We walk out into the city and all we need is theme music, man. We are city boys, fresh from the barbers, and you can't tell me that we aren't in our own music video. The whole world is brighter. I'm admirin' myself in a jewellery-store window. Somebody scratched the word "Smiley" into the sidewalk when the cement was still wet. Even with all that's happened today, that's me right now. Smiley.

I love the city, man. Especially with some dude doing street art with coloured chalk. Summer's been "held over" or something, cos lots of kids are out on the sidewalk across from a Walgreens. There's a car with the doors open, and the sound system is cranking out a beat. Makes you feel invincible when you walk past it and it hits your chest. Five girls are around the car doing the "bounce". It's a pretty simple dance. For girls though. The best part is, you tip up on your toes and think of a sentence. Then when that beat kicks in you just write that sentence in the air – with your butt. In cursive. It's educational, I swear.

So I'm enjoying the sights when I figure out that we're actually somewhere near the intersection of Lake Forest and Bullard. I can smell the food. San Tainos and Hispanic food fighting in mid-air. That means we're close to Bo's. Well, before I can find my bearings, I see it: a big, super-sized food truck, parked where our tiny food cart used to be. It's so huge it's dwarfing even the Tapas truck. We pass by people and cut through a long line, and when we're coming around the Tapas truck, Frico – who's in front of me – suddenly lets out a whoop.

That's when I notice that the huge food truck is *brand new*, and right across the side of it there's a fancy logo and a familiar name in blazin' red and yellow:

BCK

BO'S CARIBBEAN KITCHEN

"GET MO' FROM BO'S!"

Frico walks up to the window, and Moms is inside with a grin so wide I'm sure they can see it over there in Tennessee. Everybody's celebrating and clapping and I'm wondering what happened and when and where I was when all this was taking place. Frico designed the logo and the slogan, and Benet went ahead and bought the damn truck straight off the lot and surprised her with it. Cos now they're in business. It's all there: corrugated-steel steps. Stainless steel. Hot plates and a sink with a dish drain and a flat-top griddle and spaces for Sno-Ball syrup bottles. All the decals are on it, and there's that chrome insulation right below the window with criss-cross patterns that make everything look delicious and culinary.

Frico goes up and shakes Benet's hand. Tony and Doug are sitting on plastic chairs beside the truck, eating. Everybody's happy. Moms is counting money and gesticulating to Mrs Thorpe where they can put stuff. Mrs Thorpe looks out and she's waving to me, but all of a sudden I'm in the strange part of my movie, cos something isn't right about all this.

More customers are lining up, even though it's way past lunch-time. People milling around the truck. Lots of people. And me, I'm gettin' so worked up over all this. The back of my ears always get hot first, so I'm wondering if it's the skid coming on. The lines are getting longer. Then I realize that the customers are not customers at all. It's that guacamole Elvis guy with all those girls and the tap-dancin' boys from Bourbon Street. They all turn around to face me and break into song and dance out there in the street like it's the finale of a frickin' musical. And the song they're singin' is a a wicked version of 'Happy Birthday'. And when they say "Happy Birthday, dear Terence" I feel like jumping up and down on the spot. Cos they got me. They all planned the whole thing. They're giving me a wicked open-air roadside tap-dancin' surprise birthday party with balloons and Sno-Balls and music and a cake. And my cake doesn't say "Skid". It says "Terence". I'm pretty amped up, and the day doesn't suck so much any more.

"So the truck is my birthday present?"

"Nice try. The cake is yours. Or should I say *was*. Because it's almost done."

We're rumbling home in the lit stainless-steel corridors of the brand-new Bo's food truck: a seven-by-twelve-foot kitchen on wheels – not including the cockpit. It has that new-truck smell and all the bells and whistles and a marquee light display on the outside, now turned on in the night. Mrs Thorpe embroidered T-shirts with the Bo's logo and everything. Benet's Lincoln is in front of us on Paris Road, but his cellular phone is riding with us. He lent Frico his phone to call Teesha. Frico's got the phone between his right ear and shoulder and he's cleaning out his fingernails as if he doesn't know he's in a food truck. And he's yappin' like he thinks the phone call is free.

"Yeah, brand new. Benet. Yes, *that* Benet. Long story. Datin'? You could say that. Well, I dunno… she's a big girl."

Moms is driving and glancin' at him in the rear-view mirror.

"Wish you wouldn't talk about me while I'm here, Frico."

He's on a small seat at the back of the cockpit.

"This *truck* is a big girl, Teesha, huge. Maybe Momma could help out at the Refuge with all those lunches you guys need."

I see Fricozoid, even on his last day, is way ahead of me in the BCK planning, even though *I* was there at the very beginning. So just to compete, I make some suggestions about the business direction for Bo's.

Of course, I get my suggestions slapped back in my face like a rancid whip-cream pie. "No, don't worry Terence. Tracey's dealing with all that. He has it under control."

"Tracey."

"Yes, *Mr Benet* and I hired some people to help out. That's why we have the T-shirts. Plus, you're officially back at school, young man. And the best hour of the day is lunch."

Silence. Brand-new truck tyres combing asphalt. Now we're passing closed stores with the reflection of the truck playing hide-and-seek in the windows. My mother breaks the silence:

"Just relax. Everything's going to be fine, Terence."

Eighteen

Valerie Beaumont is wearing her best earrings. She has make-up on. And her hair is done differently. It's a school night, the third weekend in September, but we're going out. We're waiting for Benet to get here. He's been to the apartment four times this week. I don't go to sleep until he leaves. And I can't keep going to bed at one in the morning. But deep down I'm beginning to accept the way things are these days. Suddenly Saturday morning is a vacuum and a blender and a pressure cooker whistlin'. Moms is cooking not for Bo's but for Benet. I'm happy she's gotten back into doing that, outside of the food cart – sorry, *truck*. The woman loves experimenting with recipes. You shoulda seen how she missed preparing meals for her husband after he disappeared. She'd make his favourite meal and just sit there looking at it like it was a movie prop or something. Then she'd put it in the fridge and throw it out days later. As we grew up, and the "nest" – as they say – was getting empty, you could see her go from cooking four pounds of rice to two pounds to no pounds at all, especially after the rice-crazy Doug and Tony went to live on their own. Now Frico's gone, and I'm a finicky eater. My mother says that apart from Ma and Mrs Thorpe, all her friends are either dead or two-faced, so she loves to whip up stuff for Benet, who is her only real company these days.

Anyway, tonight she's taking a break. We're going down-town with Benet, in his car, to some place called Agde's. Fancy Restaurant. Three-star. French. He made muffled reservations from his cellular phone while sittin' in our kitchen on Tuesday night. At least that's how it sounded through the door and the darkness. Any minute now he'll turn up in the black Lincoln Town Car. He'll be in white, an '80s bush-jacket suit as usual, tall as a monument, brushin' back his wispy salt-and-pepper hair with his hand, his stone face shaven down to the skin. It's not like you could honestly say Benet's been hit with the ugly stick or nothin', but sometimes I swear that man doesn't remember that he's fifty-late.

I can see the city shining as we slide over Connection Bridge: two steel arms to lift you across the river. From afar, buildings are usually blue, reflecting the sky over New O'lins. But now, right before my eyes, glass and steel become gold bars in the late sunlight, and the Mississippi is a mirror for a minute. Tonight's huge hunter's moon is impatient. Even before the sky turns black, she's a battered Florida grapefruit, frozen over and danglin' off the end of a construction crane.

Downtown New *Orleans* hugs us. This is where the electricity is.

The decor in Agde's is tangerine with thin white stripes. Curtains sweep the floor and go all the way to the ceiling. Rows and rows of tables dressed in tangerine tablecloths, with sparkling wineglasses and more knives and forks than Ma Campbell could capture in a week. We're sitting at a table for four. I imagine the fourth chair would have been for Frico. But he's somewhere in New York City right now. And if I know him, he's found his way around and gotten a coupla friends along the way. Maybe smokin' weed by now, that guy. I'm kidding. Maybe not. I just hate that he's up in a sparkling metropolis without me, while I'm here playing city boy with my fishin' rod and bait still stickin' out my back pocket.

By the way, up to the time we packed his bags into Tony's car, I thought he'd be road-tripping to New York. But the boy was flying. I remember him being very excited on his way to the airport. He was in the front seat gesticulating and he didn't care how close he was coming to tellin' everybody about the skid. His hands were in the air acting out a story for Tony, Doug and Teesha about how when I was two years old he thought my clumsiness was so bad it must have been the work of the Devil. So he baptized me in this ol' tin washtub behind the house. He said he told me before that it was a game. So I was the idiot grinning underwater until my face got pale. But even when my feet started kicking about, Frico in his wisdom reckoned that if people spent so much time in a bathroom washin' their skin, then it should take a longer time to cleanse the soul. Well, it wasn't until my eyes bugged out and I started makin' bubbles through my nose that he figured somethin' was very unholy about the baptism idea. So he pulled me up and slapped the breath back into me.

We were still laughin' when we got to the airport. Then silence fell in the car. Frico Beaumont walked into Armstrong Airport down a corridor that had signs in three languages. Teesha was bawlin'. Like, that was seriously the first time I ever saw her ugly, no lie. Snotty nose running, lips quiverin' and everything. And crying is contagious. So I ground my teeth and breathed deeply to stop my eyes from going crazy. Doug and Tony wanted to grab him by the arms and legs and bounce his butt on the airport floor, but Moms wouldn't allow that kind of "swamp behaviour". She took the time to warn him one more time and then she stuffed something into his pocket. As I watched him walk away, pulling his overstuffed bags behind him, I thought how I was a bruise and my brother was a Band-Aid not big enough to fix it.

So I'm remembering all this while sitting at the table in the restaurant, and I let out sort of a sigh. My mother thinks I'm being cheeky just because Benet is across the table ordering in full French like a show-off. So she kicks me a bit under the table. I'm trying to explain that it's about the washtub-baptism joke and the airport scene when she cuts me off. I didn't mind. It's her night. She looks really nice tonight too, my mother. Her hair is out. She had it done. Yeah. Spent hours at the salon and everything. And maybe it's the chandeliers over our heads, but her eyes are sparkling again. I'd like to think Frico did some makeover sketchin' while she slept. But she's always been pretty on her own. That boy is done with that kind of thing anyhow.

Anyway, she looks a thousand worries younger. She told me that this dinner was Benet's idea as a "belated birthday get-together" for me – but I know better. This is more about Benet and her than about me. This is like we're out on a double date and I forgot to bring *my* girl, man. Classic third-wheel scenario. I'm sure we make a really strange-looking trio, but no one stares and spoils it for us.

Now, Moms is ordering in French. Damn. I forgot she used to work in one of these places when we were living in the swamp. It must have been depressin' to leave this kind of swank and trudge back into the muck every single evening. I look at the menu and wish I took French more seriously. Benet comes to the rescue and orders for me.

I end up with an "entrecôte steak with a creamy Béarnaise sauce" – or whatever. Not bad eating for a guy who used to chow down on swamp rats, I guess. There's a side serving of wild mushrooms, but they smell like wet workboots, even if they *are* three-star. Anyway, I dig in and ignore Tracey and Valerie laughing and trying to impress each other by talking about what kind of wine goes with meat and what goes with fish. Maan, that unfortunate salmon and that poor cow don't care if you're washing them down with red or white wine.

Now Benet, he keeps swishing his glass around. He's droppin' his big nose over the rim of it and sniff-sniffing while the waiter guy stands there with two other bottles waiting. All I can hear is: "Hmm, fruity… slight notes of this and that". Damn. It's just grape juice, man: drink it. What makes all that sniffing and swillin' worse is that I don't think anybody in the world really likes wine. They're all just pretending, trus' me.

Well, Moms keeps smiling and brushing back a bit of her hair when she looks at Benet. That's a giveaway. She likes the guy. Their time in San Tainos before she married Pops comes up, but she doesn't want to talk about that. It's prob'ly too soon after the memorial service. That's fine. I'm sick of hearing about San Tainos too. Anyway, the naked truth, as they say, is that my father intruded on something that Benet and Moms had. A relationship that started a long time ago and far away from here.

Benet changes the subject and talks about his time in the Coast Guard. That's when I learn that Frico and Teesha've been out on his frickin' yacht with him twice this past summer, while I was bustin' my ass over at Bo's. I also figured out that he bought Frico's plane ticket and told him that any time he needed to get back from New York he should just give him a call. That thing Moms stuffed into his pocket was Benet's numbers.

Anyhow, Benet says some interesting things, that guy. And you could hear Moms' version of proper English rubbing off on him. Take for example this wonderful sentence of his: "The scrapyard is the inevitable destination of every ocean-going vessel." Wow. I wrote it down on a paper napkin and I'm keeping it.

Well, after a while their voices get real low, to the point where I want to excuse myself. All I hear is scraps of conversation flutterin' past me. I piece those whispers together and realize that these two ol' people are flirting – in front of me. Trus' me, you don't want to be there when some guy is dropping lovey-dovey lyrics on your ol' lady. He's sittin' right there telling my mother how beautiful she is. C'mon, man.

And if that's not bad enough, soon they start talkin' about ripe bananas, spicy cinnamon, hot chocolate syrup and Caribbean rum. Now I swear I'm going to lose my appetite, and maybe my steak, for godssake. Turns out that they're really talking about dessert, thank God. So Benet hollers out in French and the stuffy-looking waiter guy, he swoops in with a banana flambé. Now, if you've been lucky enough to see a banana flambé, great – I'm not talkin' to you. But if you haven't – here's the short version: butter, sugar, cinnamon powder and ripe bananas, they pop them all in a hot pan beside your table. They add some Caribbean rum and *boom*, there's a fire all over your food. Now, don't panic and show the whole restaurant that you're not sophisticated. That's how flambé's done. It's awesome, really.

Anyway, as soon as those orange-and-blue flames erupt inside the pan, I see my mother's eyes glaze over, cos she's suddenly remembering the colours of the fire that night when the gas came up from underground and the swamp was burning down. Benet doesn't have a clue. He's still talking about sterling-silver napkin holders and the finer points of French desserts while Valerie Beaumont is miles away, stumblin' back through her former life in hell.

I can't bear to watch the lights in her eyes go out again, so I excuse myself and take off to the restroom. Now these Frenchy bathrooms have only one letter on the door, as if writing out the whole word would have cost them more or prob'ly confused the hell out of people. I'm walking into a stall thinkin' that it's really refreshin' not to feel the skid warmin' up behind my ears and my bones rattlin' even with all that schmoozing at the table. There's finally a real sense of things comin' together, and I'm happy about that.

The urinal has a window over it. So if your brain can handle the double duty, you could prob'ly do your business and move to the music in the street at the same time without making a mess. Well, I was doing well with the restroom multi-tasking until I lost my aim, cos some moron who works at the restaurant, the same waiter guy maybe, he pushes his head in through the door behind me and hollers out that my mother needs me right away.

Now, I don't know, maybe I'm getting sleepy or some cinnamon smoke is still in my eyes from the flambé, but when I emerge out of the restroom and come around the corner I can't believe what I'm seeing off in the distance. Against one of the tall curtains, the shadows of my mother and Benet are looming. My mother is still seated at the table. But now she has both hands over her mouth. I walk faster. Benet is down on one knee in front of her. In his hands – a small black box. I'm runnin'. There's a sparkle, a gleam and then a light leaps out of the box and into my mother's eyes. I get there just in time to hear her say "Yes".

Nineteen

Valerie Bernice *Benet*? Over my dead body.

At least that's what my heart is saying. My head knows different. This was fixin' to happen for the longest time – like, say, twenty years. I tried reaching Frico on the phone, but he was out. That's what some dude in the dorm room said. As far as this engagement thing and Tony is concerned, he said he's not Benet's best friend, but Moms' marrying Benet is *her* business. Tony's ready to get married himself, and now that he's no longer with his nerd girlfriend he's prob'ly planning to bring a real skank home to Moms and use the fact that she married Benet as a bargaining chip. Guy's a genius, like I told you.

Now Doug, he's more cryptic about the whole thing. I ask him about it as soon as he blazes up our driveway on a goddamn Kawasaki Ninja. Yeah, the boy actually spent money on a real machine. He ignores my question, whips off his helmet, boots the kickstand and leaps off to go take a lecture from his mother about ridin' so fast. He's growing his hair long again. I tell him he looks Puerto Rican. He tells me I sound stupid. He hangs around for a while watchin' TV and eating our food before he asks me if I want to roll with him to Lake Forest Mall to see the renovations they're doing. My mother throws the both of us a look. Doug is ready with his defence.

"Momma, don't act like you and Pops didn't zip around San Tainos on a Honda 50 like two crazy hippies back in the day. That motorcycle ain't even got space for one, but y'all did it. Don't lie to me, Momma, I've seen the pictures."

"Doug, don't give Terence permission to act like a fool. Furthermore, that was back in the day. That machine you got out there's a monster."

"Yep, don't I know it! More specifically, though, it's a bread-makin' machine. You need that kinda speed to knead the dough!"

Right away the guy shows me that he isn't talkin' 'bout working for a bakery.

He heaves a canvas bag off his shoulder and dumps stacks and stacks of cash on the floor. Damn. I mean *money* – lots of it. So I holler out to heaven and I'm fixin' to dive into the pile and wallow in it like a hog, but he blocks me with one arm and starts countin' those stacks two by two. Each stack is in the thousands. Man, there's got to be close to half a million lying on our kitchen floor. So I'm thinkin': "Dougie did it! Doug finally did it. Just like he said he would. Look at all that!" Then I see that his face doesn't look like the face of a man who hit the jackpot, so I reckon the money ain't his. Must be that Benet buried treasure he was talkin' about. Oh crap. Besides that, Moms just took one glance over her shoulder and then turned back to the goddamn stove, as if makin' tomato sauce was the most excitin' thing in the world.

"Take that money up off my kitchen floor, Dougie, before neighbours peep in and think we robbed a bank."

The wind is crazy, whippin' past you on the back of that thing. Doug is gunnin' the "bread-makin' machine" down Gannon Road, tryin' hard to look for cops through the tears streamin' out of his eyes, cos he gave me his helmet to wear. I can barely hear anythin', cos I dropped the helmet over the hoodie I have on. Yeah, 'Zoid went to New York and left his Lannaman's hoodie, so I'm takin' it for a spin, so to speak. Girls love looking at college guys, so hey. Anyways, I'm hangin' on to the rear safety handles of the Kawasaki till my arms go numb. Keep it loose. Lean when he leans. Hold on tight. Stay alive.

At one point, when we sail past a police cruiser I wonder if Doug's into drugs and robberies and stuff. He talks about money. He just dumped out oodles of it on the floor. But he never mentions workin'. Anyway, that's crazy. He'd never do that stuff. Hell, if he ever heard *I* joined a gang or somethin' he'd go ballistic. I wouldn't join a gang, though. And I guess the only time I can say I ever hit a store was with that manhole cover.

Doug slows down a bit. It's the worst time to do this, but I'm anxious to ask him. I got to do a slow advance on the guy, though. So I clear my throat and holler through the helmet:

"So Doug. Whadya think 'bout all this marriage stuff with Benet and all that?"

"What about it?"

"You agree or not?"

"Not my business, Skid. Like Tony says, your mother's a big girl. Been takin' care of herself before you were born. She says so all the time. And look. If you survive Alrick Beaumont and his ambitions, you survive any damn thing."

"Hmm."

Wind flutterin' up under the helmet. Doug's voice comes through the noise.

"I guess... if you don't want to be Backhoe Benet's stepson, you could always tell her you're runnin' away and never comin' back. Didn't you try somethin' like that one time in the swamp?"

"Run away... psssh. If I tried that these days, she'd prob'ly thank me. Cos she wouldn't have to cook dinner!"

Doug is haw-hawing so hard I'm scared he's gonna lose control and soon enough we'll flip forward and become just two blotches on the asphalt. When we roll into Lake Forest Mall it couldn't be too soon.

Across the parking lot they're putting in a Sears and a cinema. Maybe Claire and I could come here sometimes. Doug goes into a store, and when he gets out he hands me a shoebox.

"Happy belated, and welcome to the city, Skid."

It's a pair of spankin' white Adidas tennis shoes. Superstar Shelltoes. Leather uppers. I check the side to make sure it has three stripes and everything. The guy has a fortune's worth at his house, and I've envied them for ever. But he wears like a size twelve, for godssakes.

Doug switches the ignition and the motorcycle sits under us, grumbling. There's a squawking, and for the first time I see that he's installed the old CB radio onto the motorcycle.

"A brand-new motorbike with outdated Citizen's Band technology. That's tacky, bro."

"Yeah, kinda. But it helps me stay in touch in this business. Old-school kind of cool, man. Just like your tennis shoes."

He revs the engine. But before he sends us flyin' across the parking lot again, I speak up.

"That wasn't Monopoly money, Doug – what's up?"

He was ready for me, almost like he knew I was fixin' to quiz him about all that money. He says this over his shoulder:

"Skid, I had a regular nine-to-five. But every month, by the time there's a full moon, my damn pockets are empty. So I found me something riskier that makes more money."

"Tell me more."

"All you gotta know right now is this: you oughta grab a hold of all those demons from yesterday if they insist on hauntin' ya. Turn them upside down. Shake 'em and take whatever falls from their pockets. That's how I feel."

Doug and his money soundbites. He's not a guy to explain everything all the way down to the rivets, so that's the most you'll get from him. If you ask me, I think that blurb is all about Benet.

Doug holds Benet responsible for messing up Pops' life with ridiculous oil-and-gas business deals and pie-in-the-sky projects. But that kind of thing is debatable. Pops knew what he was doing.

We ran circles around the city for an hour, but it felt like seconds.

He's sittin' in the saddle and walking the motorcycle out to the slope of the driveway.

"By the way, Skid. You heard Couyon's out on bond. I don't like Couyon Jackson. He's the worst and he's damn crazy. So... wouldn't you prefer to live in a house with security cameras and iron gates than out here? This place is wide open."

Now, that's the kind of food for thought that makes your mind gag and throw up a li'le bit.

Kickstand up. Engine roars. Blast-off. And now that Doug is becomin' a dot down Hayne Boulevard, I'm retracing the route in my head and all he said, and I figured out a few things. Doug Beaumont is actually workin' for Benet. Like Frico said, Benet owns a couple of side businesses around New O'lins. That includes the Tapas truck and that floral place that gave Moms a good deal on my father's memorial-service package. Doug is his debt collector. He rides around muscling money out of people who missed their deadline.

"The Bread-Maker can outrun bullets." That's what he told me.

Things are changing. The Bo's food truck now rolls around the city. It's not confined to the intersection of Lake Forest and Bullard any more, especially on Mondays, when some food businesses are closed. Moms is at home more now, doing the books and the "meal design", as she calls her experiments. She has a small team handlin' the truck. Our kitchen at home is now fully painted in honour of that French restaurant downtown, and Moms is slowly getting rid of all the old pieces of furniture. We got a cherry-wood living-room set with coffee-coloured upholstery. Virgin suede, soft as ever. That was right after the exterminator took care of the silverfish. I walked in one day after school and wheeled back outside to make sure I hadn't gone into somebody else's apartment. I'm happy for her, though. Lord knows Moms needed some help in the decor department. That damn beaded kitchen curtain with the fruity fridge magnets wasn't very Nineties at all. We threw stuff out. So much stuff that some competing dumpster divers turned Hayne Boulevard into a racetrack.

The Salvation Army people came for our old sofa, and more importantly, they took my father's workbench that had been stuck under the stairs for a while. I mean *really* stuck. The thing refused to come out from under there, like it knew it was the last piece of Alrick, so it was hangin' on to Valerie for dear life. Well, you shoulda seen Moms crawl up under those apartment stairs outside and get behind that workbench and push with a vengeance until it popped out and the Salvation Army guys nearly fell over under her strength. And she just stood there heaving like she was giving birth. When they loaded that thing onto their flatbed truck and rolled out, trus' me, it might as well have been a coffin. You could see it leaning this way and that way on the back of the truck, tryin' to shake off the weight of all those years. A thing full of memories and mistakes, like the swamp. Anyway, these days Moms falls asleep with a bridal magazine and a book called *First the Flames, Then a Phoenix* by Swami-something-something. Maan, that thing is so read it's got more dog ears than a real dog, believe me. And she's taken one of those new fluorescent highlighters to mark her favourite quotes. Not like she had to. You can hear it all over her language when she's having a heart-to-heart dinnertime talk with Ma Campbell, like she swallowed the whole book:

"For some twenty-one years I've been *feeling my way through a fog* and falling down. But it seems like the fog is liftin'. I've been stumblin' ahead. And I don't mind fallin' *every now and then*, as long as I'm movin' forward."

Meanwhile, Ma Campbell has made herself Moms' unofficial hoodoo guide and protector. Moms can't scratch her skin without Ma Campbell makin' a comment.

"Don't be leavin' your hairbrush too close to no windows now. Cain't be too safe with your weddin' comin' up, Valerie. I wouldn't put it past your noisy neighbour to sabotage your weddin' day. Oh, an' you need to be tellin' me more about your dreams, so I can interpit what's goin' on with you between now and the honeymoon, y'hear me?" Her voice goes to a grumble. "'Specially 'f you start seeing snakes or fishes in those dreams. Cos that'd mean you're pregnant. And then I'd know why you're in such a damn hurry to git married."

Moms is in a hurry to stop smokin'. She's down to three cigarettes a day now. May sound like nothin' to you, but trus' me, that's a miracle. I'm happy for her, even though I don't like hearin' all the details of her new lifestyle. You know how health freaks can get: they need to tell you how they actually drink eight glasses of water every day and how many bowel movements you should have and all that. I say: drink all the water and decaf you want and do your business, but I don't need to hear about your bathroom life.

Anyway, the biggest change on my mother right now is the eight-and-a-half-millimetre Princess-cut diamond on her left hand. The thing looks like a star that fell from space and landed quietly inside the platinum prongs on her finger. So with that kind of property on her hand she had to get a cleaning lady to come by on Thursdays. The place is spotless when the lady leaves.

And Valerie Beaumont, she's purgin' everything. Just yesterday she gives me a box and tells me to throw some old papers out for her. So she hands off this box to me and turns back to her

ROLAND WATSON-GRANT

calculator. I'm standing there goin' through the box with only my eyes and... this stuff? This stuff is golden, man. Precious memories, like they say. She didn't even look up when I left. I hurried out the front and down to the old pool like a stray dog that found leftovers in a lunchbox. I'm diggin' through what she was throwing away. Mostly old greeting cards, some grocery lists and failed recipes, and then... jackpot: some old San Tainos and USA postcards from as far back as *nineteen sixty-frickin'-nine*. Correspondence between Valerie *Thompson* from San Tainos and some young American dude called Alrick B., who was wicked with a pen. I'm sitting there in the pool, imagining the two of them writing smoochie-smoochie postcards back and forth to each other. Ha. The one my pops sent to her had a red-white-and-blue USA rocket on the front with beautiful flames and smoke like clouds crowding around it as it blasts off into space. On the back he wrote:

Who is this woman
who ignites all desires
and sends my spirit soaring?

See you soon
Alrick B.

Oh man. Alrick was a lovey-dovey dude at one point? Man, this is news. I always thought the guy had the emotional responses of a toaster: you had to push to get any kind of reaction. But he used to be a real romantic. Wonder what changed all that? I hear kids can bring a different kind of love into your life that sends all others to the goddamn junkyard, no lie. Anyway, my mother was just as much of a cornball. On the back of a postcard with the pretty San Tai countryside, fresh and green after a shower of rain, she wrote:

From a spot that barely makes the map
Castaway and even more lost in love.
Waiting for you where time can never touch us.

                                          Love,
                                          Valerie T.

Wow. Lyrics. They used to burn the place up. They even had mushy pet names like "B" and "T". Anyway, as soon as I was enjoyin' that little jog through all the wet sugar those two shovelled on each other, the truth came over me. Valerie Beaumont is preparing for her new life. She's busy throwing out her memories of the days before reality – like the skid – came and broke things into pieces. Now, the world as we know it is just one big terrazzo floor full of feelings that you can't sweep up.

It's funny, Frico always said that when a place is Pine-Sol clean, any bad odours you smell must be the inside of your own nose. He's disgusting, that guy. But something *does* stink around here, even with all the newness and freshness that's taking place. It's not something you smell with your nose, though. You feel it. Maybe it's because now that Claire has gone back to school in the city I really haven't heard from Mattis in a hell of a long time. Since his home stereo got killed in the power cut, I've heard him only once over there, pickin' out a Tracy Chapman tune on a box guitar in the dark. It's bad when you start thinkin' your neighbours are prob'ly dead just because they decide to shut the hell up. Truth is, I don't give a rat's ass about that fake *obeah man* or how he feels about me being dangerous or whatever. It's just that he's my only link to Claire. It was a good summer only because of that girl. Even with Mai still hangin' around in my head, I can't forget meeting Claire that night at the pool or her crazy conversion to believin' in hoodoo a little bit. That and her honey-coloured eyes.

I miss the girl, no lie. So when Moms and Ma Campbell, those overnight health freaks, decide to take a long walk along the top of the lake levee across the street, I figure it's time to pay a visit to dear Mr Mattis just to ask him about Claire.

Now look. I'm passing by his apartment and I notice that his little kitchen window has no curtain in it. I step up to the apartment door – and it's *open*. Push the door and it swings free. And – can you believe it? – all I can see is an empty living room. No furniture. No Mattis. No wife. No honey jars, no candles – nothin' but more and more terrazzo floor and the echo of the doorknob hittin' the wall behind it. Those people disappeared. Moved out quietly in the middle of the night. Moms had no clue. Ma Campbell, who sees everything, saw nothing for the first time in for ever. Of course she had to comment:

"I'd like ta be able ta say that man and his wife were prob'ly raptured. But they didn't sound like the heaven-bound type at all."

All the other neighbours don't give a shit. They're actually happy to be rid of that guy, cos the Mexicans, especially, they just break into big smiles when I ask them in broken Spanish what happened to him. Or maybe that's just because I sound funny tryin' to speak their language, even though I'm not so bad with it. Yeah, look, if you think people sound funny when they're tryin' to speak English, try speaking Mandarin or Cantonese to a Chinese person without some serious lessons. You'd sound illiterate to them, most likely. And you bet they'll tell all their friends about it and imitate your bad Chinese behind your back too, just like you do to their bad English. I'm just lettin' you know. I had a Vietnamese girlfriend once, so…

Anyway, the only person who has some kind of explanation for the sudden departure of Mattis is Mr Tracey Backhoe Benet, my soon-to-be stepdad, who rolls into the complex and explains that all the wannabe bad apples are getting out of the city since they heard of James Jackson's return. Hell, Mattis is the one who should be locked up for attempted destruction of our bedroom wall and for reselling useless hoodoo material. Oh, and for takin' my mother's money and not delivering on the protection spell. Guy moved out cos he had no clue how to stop the skid. All that said, I am kinda pissed that I've lost a serious customer after only making the grand total of a lousy forty-two bucks. Matter of fact he still owes me for the last one. And that particular seal should cost double or triple.

Anyway, I've got bigger plans than being just a frickin' hoodoo-seals salesman. I'm thinking to get out of the magic business in about a year or so. Yeah. I could use some money and invest in some new ideas, like city-raised catfish or hydroponic lettuce or somethin'. Hell, I could do all that right now if the apartment-complex owners were nuts enough to give us permission to use the old pool. Damn pool's just sittin' there empty and useless anyway.

Well, I shoulda known that me causing the car to get stolen would come back to inconvenience me sooner or later.

See, since the beginning of September Valerie Beaumont had been swinging by the school to pick me up in the Tercel, now that the Bo's truck is doing business closer to the river. But with the car gone and me takin' extra math classes after school, I pretty much have to find my way home now. Well, good ol' Claire hid from her uncle and left me a romantic letter in that inlet in the pool. It's our new love-letter mailbox. Yup. Real secretive Romeo-and-Juliet-type stuff. Anyway, in her last letter she told me about a short cut on foot that was guaranteed to shave twenty minutes off my walk home.

It's a pleasant walk, especially after summer, when the sky is cold and blue and the sun is becoming useless.

She's genius. And she's a poet, that girl, but she ain't no angel. She's got ulterior motives. That short cut takes me from the outskirts of New O'lins East up through the back of Chalk Park Fair. That's an abandoned amusement park between my house and the Meat Mart. It used to be all the rage in the Sixties. It's still got all the rides in it, even though it's really broken down and torn up. The city authorities always talk about repairing Chalk Park, but it's still just sittin' there suffocating in the bushes off to the side of the road. You can barely see it from the roof, and it doesn't look like much from the street, but it'd make a hell of a nice hangout for lovers.

So you know, Claire and me, we've been meeting there all week. Her uncle would pop his head gasket if he knew, not to mention ol' Valerie Beaumont. But here we are on an after-school make-shift picnic. I'm holding the barbed-wire fence so Claire can slide through. Today we got cotton candy and salty-sweet popcorn just for the fun of it. Now we're hangin' out three days straight, the first people to have fun on these premises in twenty-odd years. We're under a maple sittin' on a concrete bench that we had to dust off quite a bit on Monday. Fall colours are creeping into the trees, even though it's still September. Claire's lyin' down with her head in my lap, lookin' up at gold leaves against that cold blue background. Clear skies are in every direction 'cept for her cigarette and those wispy clouds higher up. They're so thin they look like salty foam on an upside-down sea. On the ground, path-ways curve in and out of crab-apple trees. Abandoned machines wait for riders to return, and old park signs are still shoutin' at those who left long ago.

Tickets! Popcorn! This Way to Carousel! One Token = One Ride

Now Claire's laughin' about that One Ride sign for some twisted reason. I'm lookin' down at her with her curls spread out all around her head when my bones begin to rattle a bit.

"What's wrong?"

I would tell her if I knew. All I know is that the power lines are howling on the Boulevard, metal things clang and yellow leaves scatter down like drops of fire. Claire sits up, and I wonder if she can see the rust climbin' over carousel seats, crustin' on the bumper cars, becoming metal blisters that break open on everything. Vines are grabbin' at the gears and weeds wriggle up between bricks, breaking buildings down. Time, like Pa Campbell said, is swingin' her three swords in this place. The whole amusement park is drowning in brown. This feels like the dream I had about Pa. But it's not. It's real life. And yes, that really is James "Couyon" Jackson comin' around the Ferris wheel, a claw hammer in his right hand.

Run.

I really didn't have to tell her. Claire takes off along one of those paths into the bush. In a second, Louisiana's most notorious criminal is grabbing me by the backpack. I slip out of the bag, but he sweeps my feet from under me with one kick, that bastard. I flip over in the dirt and start walking backwards on my butt and heels, while this guy spins the claw of the hammer towards me.

"I been lookin' for ya, Skid Beaumont."

Voices always surprise me: I never get what I expect. James Jackson's words are icicles. He's in a denim shirt with the collar and the long sleeves buttoned tight, just like a hermit type of killer in a movie. Shaved head. Suede-leather skin stretched tight over a steel frame. He's laughin' like a maniac, and his eyes are wide enough to show white all around the pupils.

"Stop your runnin'. I ain't gonna hurtcha."

I turn around to take off, but my forehead hits metal. It's an old turnstile gate. People used to walk through here to buy tickets. Crowd control. Damn. This thing is so rusty and covered in vines, it doesn't turn any more, and there's a solid iron fence with barbs on top running off on both sides into the bushes. I'm slim enough to squeeze between that turnstile and the fence, but James isn't. So now he's rattling the gate, cos he can't come through, thank Heaven. I think I'll stick around and taunt him now that I got the gate and the fence between us.

"Woah. Easy. Take it easy, ya fat felon. Looks like somebody ate a whole bunch of hush puppies in prison. You're one portly prisoner, my friend. Damn, you let yourself go before they did, didn't ya, James?"

Well, all he's doing is grunting and tryin' to push open a gate that hasn't budged in decades. I keep up the taunting.

"But look, you oughta know, since you're back in town. The Skid Beaumont you met back in the swamp is no more. I'm new and improved. You should try that, you know, improving yourself. Matter of fact, that backpack has a few books that could set you straight if you read 'em. Oh, sorry, you can't read, I forgot. Well read my lips: *go away*. You don't know who you're messing with, so stay away from my family, or else. Wish you'd gotten caught up in between the actual turnstile right now. Lord knows I'd-a taken that hammer of yours and clobbered you stupider than you are now."

Well that guy, he just starts laughin' again from behind those turnstile bars like I just said somethin' funny. Out of the corner of my eye I can see why. While I was running my mouth, I didn't see that there's a big frickin' hole in the goddamn fence, just a few feet farther down. Ol' Couyon saw it before I did. Shit. The guy doesn't even hurry through it. He just goes and walks through and steps towards me real cool, like he's browsing for groceries in a goddamn store. *Well this is it, Skid.* Show time. I'm not running. I imagine the fence and the turnstile falling forward and knocking him out. Nothing happens. Damn, they made fences strong in the Sixties. I try again. But I can't even shake a dry leaf down off a damn tree. I'm dead. The skid's left me like a loose wheel spinnin' off a speedin' wagon. When James reaches down, grabs me by the collar and hauls me to my feet, I figure out why. No hoodoo seal in my pocket: I'm powerless. Either that or James really has a protection tattoo scratched somewhere on his parts.

Twenty

Valerie Beaumont and Tracey Benet are going to have a garden wedding in November. The ceremony and reception will take place at Orange Oaks. That's a plantation house farther down Hayne Boulevard. I've always heard about it, and now that we're here to look around, man – you really can't get classier than this. It's Moms, Benet, Mrs Thorpe, Ma Campbell, Teesha Grey and me. I also told Peter Grant to come along, since Orange Oaks' musicians rehearse on the lawns, so I know he'd go crazy.

And while we're on the topic of "crazy", I think the fact that I'm still here telling you about this garden wedding is strong evidence that I survived James Jackson's claw hammer over in Chalk Park. I'm filling Pete in on the details while we walk into Orange Oaks. You should see his eyes.

"I thought I was a goner, but by the time he was hovering over me with that hammer, I realized I was sittin' in the middle of a junk pile: radios, TVs and some really old computers. This pile is ten feet high. So I'm thinking: "This boy's as far gone as all this garbage." Well, it turns out he'd been taking appliances apart with the claw hammer when he spotted me and Claire.

"*Sacre bleu!*"

"Well, Pete. James is smart, man. He pulled me up, then sat down, real tired, on the lowest Ferris-wheel seat and said: 'Hand me an old radio, Beaumont. I'm breaking up old appliances for the circuit motherboards.' Turns out you can find little pieces of gold in old electronics and sell 'em. It's frickin' genius. I shoulda known this a long time ago."

"Actually, I heard about that before. But you got to break up a ton of that shit to get two ounces of gold, so your boy is still stupid."

Sometimes I don't know why I waste good ideas on Peter Grant. I think "Couyon" is on to something with his gold-salvaging idea. I'd be happy to grab a hammer and break up appliances with the guy, but you gotta be real skilful.

James used to work at an oyster supplier, for heavenssake. If you can shuck oysters and clams and scallops without leaving shell all over the meat, you can handle a stupid radio, trus' me. So yeah, I'd work with him if he wasn't a guy going back to stand trial. Or if he wasn't the kind of business partner that might go berserk when you least expect it. I swear you could go into business with him today and tomorrow morning he's heading off to Port Royal to become a pirate or some other crap. Anyway, Peter Grant is feeling all pompous till I pull a fat wad of cash from my pocket. I could hear his smirk fall off and hit the frickin' dirt.

"This is what James gave me, man. This is the money he made from the whole thing."

"*Sacre*... that must be like a thousand bucks in there!"

"Three hundred. Mostly ones. But it's still a lot of money to make from junk."

We're walking up the cut-stone path, past a gushin' fountain with carved lions that greets you halfway to the plantation house. Peter is so floored by me pulling out Couyon's cash that he isn't even hearing the music or enjoying the scene. Fancy fold-out chairs are already fannin' out like white wings across the green, so you can see where the guests will be seated. Just by walking into this place, you can tell Benet knows what Valerie Beaumont likes. Birds are everywhere at Orange Oaks, and you should see Valerie Beaumont's face when they release white doves just to show her what it will look like on her wedding day. She loves it, but then she says she doesn't like the idea of the birds bein' locked up, so she's going with fireworks instead.

Now I should tell you that wad of cash from Couyon is for his mother, so she can "buy something nice to wear". He took it from his pocket and bopped me on the head with it while warning me: "Make cert'in my momma gits it, or else." And I will most definitely make sure Ma Campbell gets it. Just as soon as she tells me where our goddamn knives and forks are. I'm tired of eating with plastic like I'm at a cheap church barbecue.

Well, Benet and Moms are on the steps of the Orange Oaks house where all the "I dos" will be said. In my head, I'm looking back at all the plans for the wedding, and I realize that Tracey Benet he's got *more* than money. He's got taste. You got to hand it to him, the man knows the finer things, even though he behaves so damn hillbilly all the time.

Anyway, he pulled out all the stops. A wedding planner in a suit showed up at the house to talk over the plans for the ceremony and reception with Moms. She's using crispy words like "itinerary" and "checklist" and "contingency". I only caught the end of it when I got home from Chalk Park one evening. They'd kept at it all day, I heard, while I was at school trying to convince some dudes that I wasn't goin' to become a jerk because of Benet's money. Yeah, word gets around real quick. The speed of light can't compare to gossip in these parts – especially gossip about a millionaire marrying your ol' lady. That's how people are. And then some of them (even in the bridal party), they'll come to your wedding to criticize the bride's dress, eat more than their share of the food and pray that your marriage is a disaster. Well for the time being everybody's excited, cos we're about to see the reception area.

Now look. I can't stand the idea of white canvas tents at a wedding. No sir. When I get married to Claire, we won't have tents at our reception. A wedding is not a camping trip or a circus.

Moms and Benet won't do tents neither. Those two are having their reception in style: under this grand ol' terrace that comes out from the right wing of the house. It's got a fancy trellis over it with cast-iron columns and just the right amount of rust to make 'em look classic. A solid cut-stone floor is under your feet. Over your head there are vines with evening sky and early stars peeking through the canopy. A balcony hangs over the trellis, so you can go up a spiral staircase and get a better view of Lake Pontchartrain across the street. Standing there looking down a gentle slope towards the water, you could get the impression that there is no Hayne Boulevard, no train tracks, no levees or fences standing between the property and the lake. Like you could run down that grassy slope screamin' and plunge right into Pontchartrain if you felt like it. Well, wait till you see the head table.

While the wedding planner is reeling off the menu (tasty words like "braised" and "drizzled" flyin' all over the place), I wander off to the front of the terrace. The first thing that hits you at the head table is the chairs with real silk tie-backs covering them completely. On the back of each one, all the silk comes together in a ruffle that makes you think of butter: fresh and creamy. Maan, those chairs are so well dressed they look like guests who arrived too damn early and have to sit around waitin' patiently for the bride.

Then, right above the head table, Japanese blossoms hang down in soft clusters, some prob'ly two feet long. You stand under those lavender blooms and they're like a downpour on pause. You'd love if they would shower all over your head. But only the perfume washes off on the breeze, a scent that makes you feel like everything will be OK with the world now and for ever. The wind picks up, and I feel a thrill, almost like those shivering flowers are connected to my feelings by an invisible string. I see why she wanted them at her wedding. She told me something more too.

"Wisteria represents longevity, Terence. It blooms even if you abuse it."

These things mean a lot to her. The wedding planner managed to get green orchids and white calla lilies and some other things I can't pronounce. Those are for Moms' bouquet. I'm sure everything has a meaning, but to hell with it. They're pretty, and that's it for me.

Ma Campbell comes in with Mrs Thorpe. I tell Mrs Thorpe to guard the forks. Benet cleaned up nice: shave, manicure and all. No hair dye, though, that would be cheesy for him, cos his greys are too obvious. Even with the silvering hair, he's looking more like he used to in those San Tainos photos Pa Campbell showed me. And even if it was years ago, I don't have a chance to forget all about that island and the history of Moms and Benet. Cos the Orange Oaks people they put up a gallery of those 1960s San Tai pictures of Moms and Benet to celebrate their "long and lasting love". I don't know whose idea it was to put up all those ol' photos, anyway. It's awkward. Especially the one with Benet and Moms on the beach and my father's shadow, just his shadow, sliding into the photograph – leaning in from the left, cos he was the one taking the damn shot. I know that silhouette anywhere.

Now here it was, hauntin' them.

Well, some Orange Oaks attendants they take Benet upstairs to a lounge while some others take Moms to a back room to look at the dress. Before long she comes out on a platform in the middle of the room like it's a fashion show. And the women, they all start weeping for joy and fanning their eyes with their hands. Wow. Valerie Beaumont is beautiful. Prettier than ever. And my father, wherever he is, he didn't deserve this woman. She's an angel. Teesha takes pictures. I stick my tongue to the top of my mouth, cos I feel that familiar heat in my eyes again. No, I'm not crying. It's just pride pouring out over my eyelids.

Who knows, maybe the heat in my eyes is from all the sparkles going off on her dress. Cos right now she's glitterin' and we're all cheerin' like it's the wedding already.

"Yay, Valerie!"

I wish Mrs Thorpe would stop all that yellin'. She's excited for Moms, though. Even Ma Campbell, the worst critic in the world, is smiling. The Orange Oaks people realize it's a pre-celebration complete with cryin' and huggin', so they bring a box of Kleenex and complimentary champagne. Moms walks the runway like a star. And that dress is glitterin' like they rolled the woman in sugar. Twice. She's a princess. She says the dress has sheer gloves that come up all the way over her elbows, but she didn't try them on.

"You really shouldn't put on your full wedding outfit before the big day." Now I see why she wanted to lose her "water weight" before the wedding.

Well, some attendants behind me are debating whether or not the bride should be "marrying in white", but that's just envy talkin'. You only get a few chances to be Cinderella before that glass slipper can't fit your diabetic foot. So they really should leave my mother alone. Anyway, I decide not to turn around and say anything to them, cos Terence Beaumont is really trying to keep calm today.

Those green-eyed people at Orange Oaks are the least. Ma Campbell was on to something when she started up about protecting Moms before the wedding. The Prayer Warriors are back. Frankincense smoke is gonna stick to the walls for days after this. Turns out there's somethin' else goin' on inside our house. The Warriors say another "presence" has come into our apartment. Now, I'm not the first guy to shout "ghost", but something's definitely going on. You wake up at night just in time to catch some movement with the corner of your eye – shadows without a light source. Little sounds goin' off all night in the house. I also tried blamin' Ma Campbell for taking my old sneakers and leavin' them on the roof in the rain, but her specialty is silverware. She might be a damn banshee, but she can't climb up to the roof.

Well, here's the fun part. Two nights ago somethin' solid bumped into me in the kitchen, the same way a bully would swing himself and bounce your shoulder in the corridor at school. Well, at first Moms was being her usual self. She didn't believe what I said (just because *I* said it) until she went to sleep and she and Ma Campbell woke up next morning, completely flipped. Yeah, creepy. Their bodies were turned around: heads pointing towards the bottom of the bed and their feet propped up on their pillows.

It also doesn't help that Larry Lou keeps sayin' he's seen strange lights goin' off in our kitchen when we're asleep at night, even though any bulb that actually works is a frickin' strange light for Larry Lou.

Well, one night we did see a light, and when we all got up to investigate we found the little kitchen table set with all the tarnished knives and forks Ma Campbell hid from us a while back. Again, Moms thought Ma was messin' around, but we couldn't explain the four big ol' bayou stones in the bathtub and the telephone directory torn clean in half. That's when Valerie Beaumont got on the phone and dialled up the Prayer Warriors herself. Well, it's been an all-night vigil and we're tired. When the ladies leave, Moms sits down with a cigarette again. She says Broadway and Squash are still up in our kitchen. The whole place smells depressing and muggy.

"Terence, I need to do something. I've been getting dreams about Tracey's sons. In the dreams, they say—"

"They say the mausoleum in Lafayette Cemetery is cracked open and they can't rest in peace whenever it rains. Yeah, I know".

"Well, how do you know that now?"

"Your other son he used to eavesdrop on your conversations before he went to New York."

"Anyway, I dreamt it, like it happened right in front of me. And you know I don't like ignorin' dreams. Something must be done."

"Well, how 'bout… they fix the tomb over in Lafayette?"

"They did that already. Took a while, and cost Tracey a lot of money, because those grave-robbers really went wild on it a few months back. The thing looks like they used jackhammers. But now something needs to be done to fix the spiritual side o' things. So, since Ma's finally decided to sprinkle Pa's ashes in the swamp, I asked Tracey if he'd mind if I did some simple rituals at that sinkhole where they died, you know, at the same time."

"Rituals? Isn't that like… hoodoo? Isn't that like talking to the dead? Thought you were done with that stuff. 'Specially after Mattis up and left with your money."

(*Truth is, come hell or high waters, I just want to keep her and Benet out of where I get my money from, even though Lord knows the apartment could do without smelling like mud and mildew.*)

"It's just prayers and candles and singing songs, Terence. Nothing special. It's not even hoodoo per se. It's just the least we can do to let those spirits leave us in peace."

Well, Valerie Beaumont sees my face all blank. She sighs and turns away. I hurry up and tell her it's OK if she wants to do all that hoodoo stuff, but I'm gonna have to be there with her and Benet. Truth is, I want to keep an eye on things. Well, you shoulda seen the woman spin around towards me so fast she almost gave herself whiplash.

"Hell no, Terence! For heavenssake, stay outta that place. I'm gonna ask you to avoid that swamp from now on, y'hear me? I already spoke to Teesha about gettin' someone to take your place at the Refuge."

"You did what?"

"Terence Beaumont. If you never listened to your mother before, you need to listen now. Avoid that swamp. Please. It's not safe on so many levels. I hear the sinkhole is behavin' like a monster now. It tore itself open and swallowed up quite a few acres. The damn thing is stretchin' out under all that open water. And it's not done yet. I'm only doin' this for Pa Campbell and those two boys."

"Who'd you hear all that from, Moms?"

"Does it matter, boy? The *news*, for godssakes! They tell people to avoid the far-south-east end of the swamp."

"So why don't you, then? I get why you'd do this for Pa Campbell... but Broadway and Squash? Why?"

"You mean apart from gettin' things back to normal around here?"

And with that Valerie Beaumont becomes the tour guide on my one-way guilt trip.

"You shouldn't dare ask that question. But if you have no conscience left, Terence Beaumont, then lemme tell ya. We do what we do because we're decent people tryin' to make a difference."

(*Oh, Jeez. Bring in the violins and dim the lights, for godssakes.*)

"You grew up in some backwaters, Terence. The wilderness. And as long as you live, you should remember that we survived cos all that water was not as thick as blood. So that's how we got by: protectin' ourselves while helpin' other people out. Doesn't matter who they are. It's called 'decency'. It's what separates us from other people. Like the kind of animals who would tear down a cemetery gate and desecrate the final resting place of someone else's family."

Twenty-One

"Couyon" Jackson lives inside the old ticket booth over at Chalk Park Fair. He's been there since shortly after they released him from prison. He says it's OK and the toilet and plumbin' in one of the restrooms still work by some miracle, so he's good for now. He's got it all planned out: the roller-coaster is his lookout point. The carousel is his rainy-weather shed. The Ferris wheel is the dining area, and he lights a fire on the old mini-locomotive tracks when he's got somethin' to cook. Lake Pontchartrain is right across the street if he wants to take a dip. But he'd rather not be seen and jeopardize the secrecy of his hideout for something as trivial as a bath, so the guy reeks to highest heaven.

"Why don't you try gettin' a place? I know you make a bit of cash."

He's swinging in the lowest seat of the old Ferris wheel when I say this. I'm crouching on a tree stump watching him dig into Moms' Tupperware container with some BCK oxtail stew I stole. Dirty rice is fallin' out the side of his mouth. One single grain hangs on for dear life. Now it's riding the edge of his bottom lip when he talks. Can't take my eyes off it.

"Ha. Don't think I ain't tried. But folks ain't big on handin' out second chances these days. Prodigal comes home – whoopee. Any kind of excitement cools off real quick, and it's back to real life. I tried makin' myself at home in the city and in that swamp where y'all used to live."

"Woah, that wouldn't work out. Been there. The swamp went to hell."

"Well, I didn't mind the state of the place. It just got a little too crowded for me. Then I tried a few halfway houses. Got chased away from those homeless shelters by *homeless* people. Can you imagine what woulda happened if I wasn't a decent citizen?"

He laughs at his own joke. I feel sorry for him and his lonely rice grain.

"Hm… Sorry about the plastic fork by the way."

"That's OK, Beaumont. At least it's a fork. This stuff tastes like Mrs Thorpe's cookin'."

"Yup."

"Good. I'm glad it's not yours. I hear your mother actually let you help out over at that food truck y'all got. If I was her, no sir, I wouldn't let you anywhere near the damn food. Last time I ate somethin' you cooked, you tried to assassinate me with salt, as I remember."

I want to go back to talkin' about forks, but all that's left to say about that is how his mother took all our flatware. And you never know: Couyon might not find it funny.

"Only thing that's better than this lady's cookin' is her heart, God bless her. She's been kind to me since I got back out here."

"Well, maybe she'd let you stay there?"

"Naw, naw, you crazy? Couldn't do that to the poor lady. Ol' James Jackson's gonna bounce back. Give him time. James Jackson's not homeless, no sir. He's just on his way home. And along the way, I'll forgive myself and my old man before I expect people ta forgive me for what I been doin' since the third grade. By the way, you coulda reminded me to say grace."

"Sorry, you just dug right in. It's OK, man, I understand."

"OK? No it's *not* OK. And look, I'm only halfway through. Theah's still food in this bowl to be thankful for, ya goddamn heathen. So let's go. Close your eyes."

Now, to tell the truth, I'm not about to take my eyes off him, even though I dared to come back in here with food for this felon. But my powers have gone dead without the hoodoo seal and all that, so I can't take any more chances. So I bow my head real low and I'm watchin' his shadow on the ground shiftin' over the autumn carpet of red and yellow leaves. He's off and ramblin' a long prayer like a parson blessin' a four-course meal for fifty really patient people. Of course he had to bring up the fact that I stole the food to bring to him and I need forgiveness, so God should "blot out the methods by which the meal was acquired" and "bless Beaumont's good intentions instead".

"Help young Beaumont to be honest with hisself. Help him to see his transgressions and let him blame no one for the faults inside hisself. Most of all, may all the mighty hosts of heaven hold back his pilf'ring hands from my mother's money. Cos Lord, you know I do not like prison, and this little guy has his whole life ahead of him. Aaaay-men."

I raise my head – and from the looks of it, he had his eyes open the whole time, watchin' to see how I reacted to him mentioning his money. Now this hobo he has his tongue chasin' rice inside his cheek. He stops just to hit me with the question.

"You gave Ma the money, Beaumont?"

"Yeah, yeah, sure, c'mon."

"OK, don't play with me, Beaumont. That's hard-gotten cash. Plus I been tryin' ta get that money to you for months."

"Months?"

Damn right. I sent some of my boys ta find ya. They say you ran into Lafayette Cemetery screamin' like a girl."

"What? That was you?"

"Not me. Those were my boys. Hired help, really. They had the money for Ma Campbell and everythin'."

"No, they had a baseball bat, a big ol' rock and a goddamn belt buckle. They tried to *kill* me and everything!"

"What? I told 'em not to bother with all the extra-curriculary activities. They need ta work on that. Single-parent kids all of 'em. You know, no father figure like us. But they say some spooky shit was happenin' in Lafayette that night, so they left in a hurry."

"They shoulda told you the truth. I chased them outta there."

"Not what I heard, but – never mind."

Cannot *believe* Couyon sent those morons.

"So, anyway, when are ya gonna see your mother?"

And I *really* cannot believe that just came out of my mouth. But I guess I got caught up in his story. I mean, since runnin' into him last week, I've figured out some things about him. And while I'm not ready to see him over at my house, Lord knows he needs a break – or at least some decent food every now and then.

Well, soon as I mention Ma Campbell, a big ol' smile stretches across his face and my eyes got real warm and misty to see it, no lie. There's a love between mothers and their boys – you can't explain it. Sometimes, I swear, daddies need to stop competing, cos man – mommies and their sons? Only the Good Lord's got more love than that.

He looks down into the empty Tupperware and starts up a beat with the fork.

"I cain't let my mama see me like this."

"She'd love to see you. And for what it's worth, she's been prayin' for ya, man."

"Whaddya mean 'for what it's worth'? My momma's prayers musta kept me alive. I been shot at so many times."

"You been shot at, man?"

"Heheh – hell, yeah. You surprised? Nearly every day. Got so used to it – 'twas like my alarm clock. *Pow*. Good mornin' James Jackson. Ha. Some folks over in Atchafalaya still like the idea of

'Wanted, Dead or Alive or Dead', so they came out blastin' every-thing: rifles, pistols, BB guns – fishin' harpoons for godssakes. And that's *after* they welcomed me in as a stranger and gave me crawfish and potaters and a place ta sleep. Then in the mo'ning, my god-damned moustache had grown back overnight, so they recognized me. Woke up to five nozzles up my nose and a boot on my chest. Lit outta there without my legs touchin' ground. That was the first day of the hunt. Got worse. I swear I've slept under water at least twice with only my nostrils out. I'm so serious right now."

The guy should get a job entertaining people. You should hear some of the things he's tellin' me he's learnt – words of wisdom really: "Never rob a food truck. It can come after ya."

Clouds cover the sun.

"Gonna see Ma soon, Beaumont... I just got one final thing ta do. Som'taams you wake up in the middle of the night and realize your garbage stinks and you have ta get up and throw it out or you cain't sleep. Gonna take a long bath, freshen up and come see her."

"Yeah, cos I ain't taking her over here, James."

What I meant to say was: ol' Ma Campbell is a handful, but I can see he's thinkin' otherwise.

"What wrong with here? I live in ol' Chalk Park Fair, man. This place was the greatest show in the galaxy for a kid back in my day. Fats Domino played here, for godssakes. Never mind that I didn't get to see him play."

"Why not?"

"Well, for one thing, the city was segregated back then. Chalk Park was built for black folks. Folks would get anxious and warn my old man not to come around here. But he loved it. Operated one these machines for a few months too, just for the fun of it. When I was five, he used to tell me about Chalk Park Fair all the time, like he was a kid."

"And he didn't take you here, not once?"

"Never."

He looks around at the rides, and there's such a gleam in his eyes you'd think all of them are freshly painted and ready to run again. He's coverin' the Tupperware container so tightly you know he's just findin' something to do with his hands.

"No, sir. No, sir."

He keeps saying that under his breath. And when he looks up again, you can see he's far away.

"I remember the night I left. I was a kid back in the swamp. Pa Campbell went into the city to do some errands. Before he left he said: 'James, tell your mother to make you wash up and get some clothes on. Cos when I get back, me an' my stepson, we're headin' out to the Fair!' But day turned to night, and I'm sitting there in my good clothes on a cinder block out in the middle of the yard, watchin' the path that leads into the swamp from the train tracks, wondering if something happened to my Pa. Well, when he finally comes down the slope, staggerin', I'm so glad to see him, I don't even remember the Fair. Well, he just stops and hollers out: 'Ellie! Why's this boy drudging his good clothes out in the yard, huh? Get those clothes off, boy!' I turn to get inside and he says: 'Nah, right here, strip'. He puts the whisky in his left hand and pulls off his leather belt with his right. And just when the mosquitoes start comin' down, he pours that whiskey on my head and starts puttin' on those licks. I'm cold, that whiskey's in my wounds. Those mosquitoes keep dive-bombin' till they're are drunk on blood. My best clothes are in the mud and my mother is cryin' for me in the house. She locked him out, cos she knows she's next. Pa fell asleep on the porch with that belt in one hand and the bottle in the other. After that, I decided I was either going to be a corpse or a runaway."

"That's one sad story, James. I just don't know Pa to be like that, though, ya know."

"Well, wake up and smell the counterfeit, my friend. Do you ever wonder why I'm heah in this abandoned place keepin' company with half the rats in New Awlins, Beaumont? Cos this is where all my night dreams took place. These days I get up with the seven-o'clock traffic on Hayne Boulevard and I listen to 'Ouisiana waking up, everything creakin' under the weight o' the sunlight. And I try to remember what I dreamt. Nothin'. I don't dream any more. But when I was a kid... *ooowee*. I used to go to bed and run around in this amusement park all by myself at night: no gates, no guards, all the rides, no rules and no one told me to come on down from this Ferris wheel. I'd wake up and Ma would git me ready to go. And I waited and waited, while this place was broke down bit by bit, then all the excitement just evap'rated. Too late in the day to love now."

"You still talkin' about Chalk Park – or Pa?"

"You a psycholotrist now, Beaumont? You think I'm mourning over Lobo Campbell? Look, you don't know Lobo Campbell. You knew some sweet ol' guy who used to show you how to fish and tell you fancy Caribbean stories. You got the saint. I knew Satan hisself."

Oh shit. Captain Morgan's comin' out.

"See Beaumont, you got the best out of him. Me? I got a heavy hand, almost every day. Cos that brand o' whiskey he drank, that stuff used to have lead in it. So he's comin' straight from Copper Still Bar to beat up on me, and then my old lady. Why do you think she's half deaf? Now you tell me he's in an urn on your kitchen table. Haw! I bet he loves it in there. Was locked up in a bottle his whole damn life."

"He said he was sorry, though. Told Ma Campbell to tell you."

James jumps up so suddenly the Ferris-wheel seat is still swingin'. He steps over and points the plastic fork in my face.

"Shut the hell up! I heard all that crap. The man was dryin' up in the desert and he wasted time tellin' more lies. He said he was sorry a million taams in his life! All of 'em was a goddamn echo in an empty bottle. None of those apol'gies lasted a whole night. The only thing permanent is all those marks from a good five years of bein' whipped with a switch. I still got 'em all over, from my toes to my ears!"

Couyon is poppin' press studs and rolling up his shirtsleeves. The sun is explodin' over his shoulder, so I can't see his face any more. But his arms are shredded. I look away.

"Lobo Campbell could've saved his sorrys and given hisself one more breath in his life! And you can keep your memories. Cos I got mine. Now git outta here – you're beginnin' to git on my damn nerves, you and your goddamn plastic bucket."

I snatch up Moms' container and I'm reversing along a path towards the barbed-wire fence till I think it's safe enough to turn my back to him.

But maan, he's following me through the trees and hollerin' after me.

"Bring a plate and silverware next time! Think I'm a hooligan just cos I been in prison? Matter of fact I'm improved, just like you. I can read now, you li'le *Tupperware*-carryin' bastard. And who'd you borrow that *Lannaman's* hoodie from? Everybody knows you'd never get into that college!"

I'm crunching leaves under my foot and headin' back up Hayne Boulevard feeling like the empty container is packed with all the heavy stuff James Jackson just told me. He didn't have to be like that. I'm just happy he didn't shank me with the stem of that damn fork. He's ungrateful. But you know, I'm not even really mad at him. What Pa did to James was messed up, man.

Well, Claire meets me by the old pool. I stare into her honey eyes for a minute and that girl is medicine for me. She wants to know what happened over there. She's a little worried, so I tell her a version of it. But there's no way I'm tellin' Moms about meetin' James over at Chalk Park. 'Specially since I know now that that crazy bum is the real reason she wanted a protection spell for me. Funny, Ma Campbell was prayin' for his release from prison, while Valerie Beaumont was tryin' to keep him in there. Well, Heaven cancelled both orders. None of that stuff worked on either side. Far as I'm concerned, he's still in prison in his head – and sooner or later he's gonna turn up at our house, whether we like it or not. And Heaven help us with whatever personality he shows up wearin' that day.

Twenty-Two

I found Mattis by accident. Peter Grant was going on about how somebody must have jinxed the Saints' football season. So I tell him he doesn't know jack about jinxes. He says he does. He even knows that guy who sells all kinds of "slammin' hoodoo stuff" in the French Market. Soon as he says it, I know that's got to be Mattis he's talkin' about, cos apart from the description (big porcupine-looking guy), no *genu-wine* conjurer is gonna be caught dead in the French Market. They got all good stuff, really nice stuff. But it's *tourist* stuff. They got what they call "voodoo rag dolls" with limp arms and stitches for smiles and pins stuck in 'em and all that cute stuff. C'mon, seriously. So I ask Peter to take me there, hopin' to Heaven it's really Mattis, and whaddya know. He's over in a corner booth with his hairy self, fallin' asleep instead of hawking his pseudo-hoodoo-voodoo material. I walk up and tap him on the leg.

"I hear you got magic seals for sale."

He leaps up off the stool and damn near breaks his neck tryin' to abandon the booth. I tell him I'm gonna wreck the whole damn place if he doesn't stay put.

He sits down. This skid thing could be put to good use. It makes people listen to ya. Peter is amazed by all he's seeing, cos he doesn't have a clue. He just thinks this big burly guy must be an idiot for taking orders from the likes of me. I've never told him my family's magic history, and I sure ain't gonna start now. He wouldn't believe me if I told him I'm some kind of folk-magic Frankenstein monster, compliments of my old man's poor conjurin' skills. Well, as soon as Peter walks away to give us some privacy, I'm all over the guy with questions.

"Where'd you go, man? Didn't we have a deal? Where's my mother's money? Where's Claire?"

(*Had to add that last one to keep him off Claire's tracks.*)

Well, the guy starts speaking San Tai patois, the worst kind.

I roll over my eyeballs, and I guess he just saw the white of my eyes, so his language skills improve.

"Anybody with common sense would want to avoid you, Terence. You're a magnet for trouble right now."

"Is that what you told Claire? She even missed my birthday."

"Yeah, well, happy birthday, but I can't help you with nothin'."

"You can pay me for that last seal I slid under your door."

"Oh you mean the hoodoo seal that dragged a bolt of lightning through my window and split open my mattress? Look, lemme tell you somethin'. That lightning busted open the bed and barely missed me and the missus, eh? The scorch mark is still on the bedroom floor… so *you* should be payin' *me* for damages! Well, my friend, I was so busy packing my shit to leave I can't tell you exactly where your seal is."

"You didn't sell it?"

"No. Enough went on that night for me to know I had to flee that apartment like it was Sodom!"

"So where is it?"

"Look, you threw your property away. If you want me to help you retrieve it, you need to pay me, eh?"

"Pay you… you owe me and my mother, man."

Truth is, after the skid failed the first time I ran into Couyon in Chalk Park, I'd pay a hundred bucks to get my seal back. But I can't look too enthusiastic. So I walk off a bit like I'm leaving. But you can see the guy couldn't care less.

"OK, how much, how much?"

He grabs my money and shoves it deep into his pocket without countin' it. Now he's wearing a big ol' smirk.

"Your magic seal should be in the same place you left it. Look, I got customers to take care of now, eh? You done?"

"That's not true. I went over there, looked around the empty apartment. Didn't see it."

"That floor is terrazzo, my friend. You might want to look around a bit, eh? And why do you even want it back? You know what these things are. I told you it's an angel-signature seal. The hosts of heaven, they take offence when you use their names for your own greed. They'll tear the whole earth up searchin' for their signature when they're trying to redeem their name from those who abuse it, eh? Terrible things happen. I've seen them with my own two eyes in San Tainos. Giants tramping round the narrow cobblestone streets in the dead of night, searchin'. You know them by their height and their faces, eh? Bronze faces, still burning from burstin' in through our atmosphere. No mouth, only goggly eyes with throbbin' lights like dyin' coals. Some parts of 'em are made of metal, so they rattle when they walk around draggin' those wings behind them. And they know where their names have been. It's like those hoodoo seals leave a smell on your hands and a mark on your soul. And those mighty warriors, they'll turn things upside down till they find it, eh? So all that upheaval is what people call 'bad luck' and freak accidents and such. You bring it on yourself. Nobody puts it on ya. So you shouldn't even be askin' back for that kinda thing. Take my advice. Leave trouble alone."

"Yeah, you can say anything now that you got my money."

"You paid for the *information*. I just gave you some advice… for *free*."

"You're lousy, man… you and your angel stories. And you look like a… a horse-hair brush."

"Horse-hair what? Listen to me, Skid. I can still *smell* my nose hairs, OK? Everything got singed by *lightnin'*, eh? Do what you want. But I'm not interested in whatever brand of hoodoo you or your modda's into. And separate and apart from that, I told you already, I do not want you around my niece, eh?"

When I'm walking out with Peter, Mattis is callin' after me with no respect for privacy.

"Oh, one more thing: why do you care about your modda's down payment? Ain't your family fixin' to be rich soon? I hear she's marryin' that natural-gas guy. She can do a lot more once she gets a-hold of him that way. Marriage is a sly form o' magic, y'know."

Twenty-Three

Well, even though I couldn't find the hoodoo seal when I got back home, one thing is clear: the skid is back to work and worse than ever. Yeah. Benet asked Larry Lou to take a look at the faulty wiring over at the empty Mattis apartment before the whole damn complex goes up in smoke. Well, one minute Larry is tramping around on the roof and the next second all you see is a shadow fallin' past my bedroom window. After the thud we run outside and, while ducking the sparks showerin' from the roof, we figure it out: Larry Lou went and got himself electrocuted. Fell nearly twenty feet, poor guy. Third-degree burns. But he's not dead. One of the Mexican dudes told us he was outside watching Larry on the roof. He said Larry fixed the wiring and stepped back like the Lord did on the last day of creation to check out his work. He shook his head and grinned and looked down and showed the guy a thumbs-up sign. That's when he lost his balance and held on to a high-tension cable comin' in off the street. When the electricity grabbed him and wouldn't let go, Larry just kept lookin' into the guy's eyes like he was beggin' for help that he knew no one could give him. The guy said he called out to Santa Muerte in his heart, and the cable for some miraculous reason just slapped Larry down on the roof tiles and then flung him off like it was the Devil's tail itself. Larry still looked like he was grinning on the ground when we got out there. But that's because his lips were burnt backwards up over his teeth. You can hear the pop and crackle over your head and the power line hummin' like a proud predator that has just struck. The smoke smells.

I swear I've become the curse of this place. And to tell the truth, it's not like the skid doesn't warn me before this stuff happens. See, I dream like my ol' lady, and one night, even before runnin' into Mattis in the French Market, I had two of 'em. It's like we were in the French Quarter, where they got these tall red-brick apartments, and I just kept lookin' at this one particular seven-storey buildin' cos it had a bright-red fire escape zigzaggin' all the way down the side of it and touchin' the ground, like a lightnin' bolt. In the other dream it was raining, and I saw a strip of lightning come down out of a black cloud in slow motion and slide into the Mattis apartment and curl up in there like a miserable old sky snake in hiding. And Mattis? That guy doesn't even realize that all his talk about angels only confirms the things I've seen. Anyway, Benet's payin' for Larry Lou's hospital bills, which is a lot, I hear. He's got to feel guilty for sendin' the guy up there like he owns the place, and lettin' him almost lose his life. But that's Benet. Mr Take Charge. And I guess that's not always a bad thing.

Now, just this month, October, Moms quit cigarettes completely after seein' Larry on the ground with smoke comin' out the sleeves and pockets of his blue overalls. Should have stopped a long time ago.

She gets irritable every now and then when she doesn't have a smoke. But, like Pa always said, there's no power on earth like a woman who has made up her mind. But the real miracle happened today, on the first Sunday of October 1990. Man, you shoulda been there. Everybody in the city prob'ly knew *something* was up this morning. You could feel the energy in the air. And it wasn't just because the Saints would be playin' Atlanta. In the apartment complex, everybody knocked on each other's door and popped in for a few minutes to say what they thought they heard. At church, before the service, people moved from group to group in the parking lot, whisperin' among themselves.

Well, that's a normal day at church, anyway: gossip to begin with, and then the gospel. But when the preacher ended the sermon with an altar call and we saw that the back pew was full of reporters, we knew this was no ordinary service. People went up for prayers, then back to their seats. The preacher disappeared behind some large burgundy drapes hangin' right behind the platform. The guy on the organ played hymns with his eyes closed. Then came the drama. Suddenly people started standing up and screamin' in the pews. One woman stood up in the aisle and waved her arms really wild. In other words, everybody in the building was behaving a bit like Ma Campbell.

Meanwhile Ma had made her way to the podium with the help of a deacon and Moms. And the frail little ol' lady, she stood there, in a brand-new dress, shaking a tambourine lightly. The organ dude, he played softly, and all the reporters started snapping pictures of Ma standing there. I felt like I was the only one who didn't know something. Moms is on the platform beside Ma Campbell, but it's the ol' lady that's the focus, even with sparks goin' off on Moms' engagement ring as she adjusted the microphone for her. The organist stopped playing, people quieted down and Ma, she spoke so sweetly, quoting ol' St Luke, you wouldn't believe it was the same woman who robbed us of all our silver the first day she came back to Louisiana.

"For my son was dead, and is alive again – was lost, and is found."

Well, when she said that the whole place got into a frenzy, and you wondered if people were just reacting to each other or afraid that the mother of the most notorious criminal in the state was on the platform. That's when the lights went out and in the darkness camera flashes were going off like crazy. Up front, behind the platform, the large burgundy drapes were parting. And when the fluorescent lights came on the baptismal pool was in full view. Deacons stood around like guards. Down inside the pool, Pastor Fields and two more church elders stood on both sides of a familiar-lookin' man in a white baptismal robe.

It's Couyon Jackson.

Then they hollered out to heaven and dipped him quick before he changed his mind. And when he came up out of the water, they held a microphone in front of him. And all he said was: "Destiny is whatever a man is doin' when he dies. Nothin's set in steel. Who said a man cain't change? Ay-men!" And about six men lifted him and carried him off into the vestry.

Well look, man. Even with that "set in steel" mistake, that place turned *upside down*. People hollerin', cryin' and singin' and beatin' the church benches, and Ma Campbell's face was shining bright. They took about ten minutes to quiet down that congregation that had gone from terror to tears.

Now, I was feeling good about ol' James changing his life all of a sudden and all that, even though I must admit that at one point way in the back of my head I went "pshhh", cos I know his mind still does whatever it wants to do on any given day. Maybe tomorrow he'll wake up sober and freak out when he finds himself on the straight and narrow. But he seems good for it. Even though I know he still drinks like a deep-water fish. Got that from his old man. And from where I was sitting, I could see he still had on that silver-and-turquoise ring he stole from Pa back in the swamp. If that thing was even gold-*plated*, he'd have sold it by now.

Go ahead. I guess you can imagine the newspaper headlines since the baptism. Any headline or story about James "Couyon" Jackson that you can imagine: it did happen or it will eventually. I heard that apart from scraping gold from discarded appliances, James is making a fortune from all kinds of contributions, cos some people really believe the man's changed. Mrs Thorpe invites him to travel with her and the minister across the lake. She even takes him into her kitchen for food and drinks. And that boy can eat. Hell, he even drove up to our Bo's truck and cleaned out the whole sandwich supply. People crowded around the Terravan like he's some kind of celebrity. James couldn't even get out of the vehicle, I heard. Well, the guy deserves a chance, I guess. But don't tell that to Valerie Beaumont. She trusts James just about as much as you can trust a hungry gator to take you more than halfway across a bayou on his back. Matter of fact, Mrs Thorpe and Moms are not on speakin' terms, except for business. Seems Moms doesn't like the fact that Mrs Thorpe is building an extra room onto her house so James can get a decent place to stay till the trial.

He helped build the room, and it looks darn good. Good for James. He got some religion, told the authorities he has a new address, and now he'll get to see his mother more often. And nobody's calling him "Couyon" any more, except Doug. Doug Beaumont has had a permanent smirk on his face since the baptism.

"Skid, I don't care what anybody says. I'm not impressed. He's tryin' to win a case. So you call me the minute you see ol' Couyon on Hayne Boulevard, OK?"

"Well, too late for that now, Dougie." Well, that's what I want to tell him.

Instead I say, "When're you gonna stop callin' the guy *Couyon*?"

"When he's no longer a damn crazy fool."

I'm sure James was hoping that name would start and end with Pa Campbell. He's come a long way with it on his back. The boy needs to take some meds though, for real.

We're in Mrs Thorpe's kitchen. Ma came with Benet to visit her son for the third time this week. I came along for the ride. And when you go around to Mrs Thorpe's, she thinks she needs to defend her decision even if you never said a word.

"Somebody's got to help him make the most of what's left of his life. He never had much to begin with."

Another time she brings cookin' into it when she really wants the point to sink in.

"Terence, do you know how to tell for certain that a cake is ready?"

"No ma'am I don't. Moms knows, though."

"I didn't ask you about your mother, boy. I as'ed you if *you* know. No, you don't. So listen."

You know, I swear old teachers are all haunted by the classroom. They gotta find somebody to teach somethin' or their heads will just explode. Out of the oven she pulls a tin almost like it's a cookin' show, and she was bakin' something the whole time just to make her point. The crust swellin' over the top looks crispy-gold, like Louisiana autumn sky. She drops it on the table top and blows at her fingers.

"Now this is how you know if a cake is ready."

She grabs a butter knife and punctures the crust. Steam slips out, and the whole world smells delicious right now.

"If you stick a knife into the middle of it, and it comes out clean, then it's ready. But if it comes out with crumbs all over it, then it's got a little ways to go."

OK, so I just got a lesson in the culinary arts, but I missed her point. So I guess I got a stupid look on my face standing there. She sighs and plunks the knife into her sink.

"People wonder why I took James Jackson into my house. Well, somebody's gonna have to help him come out clean. There's no other way or he'll just keep going back into prison and getting out crummy. That's if he ever gets out for good."

"Well, that's nice of you, Mrs Thorpe."

She looks at me like she knows I'm trying to cut her off.

"Well, thank you. But if you've got both hands stretched out to help people, you got none to pat yourself on the back with. That boy sits in my kitchen and talks to me at night. He says, 'Mrs Thorpe, I don't sleep well, but it's OK, cos I dream with my eyes wide open. I see myself takin' care of my mother. Maybe even a grandchild to put a smile on her face.' Give us all a second chance to be family."

Old people go a far way to make a minor point. And only Pa Campbell could make deep, sentimental things like that sound real funny. But Pa Campbell couldn't bake a plain cake like Mrs Thorpe, so she's off the hook. Anyway, James is not here today. You'd think living here means he no longer hangs around Chalk Park, cos he's got clean sheets and a room for himself. But it doesn't. He still calls Chalk Park his "workshop", and he certainly seems more comfortable there than at Mrs Thorpe's, no lie. Part of the reason is people like Doug, who make it clear that they are no fans of Couyon Jackson. And to be honest, I think that kind of negative thinkin' has infected me just a bit. Last time I sat on the roof and looked over Chalk Park, I knew he was there cos of some barely visible smoke breakin' through the trees. When I went over there luggin' more oxtail stew (for sale this time), he told me not to come into "his place" unannounced. The nerve. I listened to this guy scoldin' me through the food in his damn mouth and felt happy I didn't enhance the food-delivery service by taking him a decent plate and silverware, cos the hooligan ain't worth it.

Furthermore, imagine Skid Beaumont shufflin' along Hayne Boulevard with a trash bag full of clattering flatware over his shoulder. What am I supposed to tell a cop who swoops down to ask me where I'm goin' and what's in the damn bag?

Anyway, like I was sayin', James is making me believe that he's hiding somethin'. So, all the time he's eating and scolding me and talking 'bout this and that, my eyes are all over the place, lookin' behind this ride and that shed, trying to spot somethin' to confirm he's up to no good. Somethin' like, say, a 1981 Toyota Tercel that just evaporated out of our goddamn parking lot. But this bastard won't let me out of his sight. Every time I try to get by him or wander away, he's on to me.

"Hey James, gonna take a leak."

"The restroom's right behind me. You're goin' the wrong way."

"Hey James, need to see those other rides up close."

"They're all broken. Nothin' to see. Siddown."

To make matters worse, now he's been asking me for all kinds of random stuff.

"Beaumont, I need an Igloo cold container, you got any ol' Igloo cold container?"

"Naw, I don't. There's no such thing as an old Igloo. People use that stuff until it falls apart, man."

"What about salt? Can you get a few pounds from your kitchen for me? Simple table salt. Help a neighbour out."

"Naw man, it's not my kitchen. I don't own anything, 'specially serious stuff like table salt. And nobody ever has 'extra salt', man. People buy what they need and no more."

"OK. Charcoal? How about some charcoal? It's fall. I know you got charcoal."

"Jeez. You think we live in Ohio?"

You know what? Doug's right. Never mind this guy's baptism. I am not messing with him any more. Next he's gonna need a frickin' sofa bed. Treatin' me like his damn butler. Matter of fact, this is the last time I'm comin' over here, even though he looks like he's got other plans. Cos now he's tellin' me he wants me to take him books to read, starting today.

"You got fifteen minutes. It'll be dark soon. Don't let me come an' get 'em." That bastard knows Moms still doesn't want him at her house, so he's twisting my arm.

So I get back to the apartment and go into Moms' room, and there're a couple bridal magazines open on her bed. She's looking at wedding gowns.

"Isn't it too early for that?"

"Huh?"

"The dress. Choosin' one. It's too early."

"No. Can you find Teesha for me? She hasn't called me much since Frico left, and I'm a little worried."

"I'll find her for you, no problems."

"Thanks, I need her help with pickin' the dress. We're movin' the wedding forward."

"Really?" I slump down on the bed. "Backhoe's pressuring you?"

"Actually, it's my idea."

"So what's all the rush? I mean, I know you've known him for years, but…"

The woman looks at me over those new fancy reading glasses she's gotten since she turned forty. It's that look that tells you you're getting on her nerves. She pulls it out every now and then when she wants to scare you into silence.

"Terence, did I raise y'all by myself these past couple o' years?"

"Yes ma'am."

"Do you think I done gone and lost my mind?"

"No ma'am."

"Do you think Mr Benet needs to swoop down and save me?"

"No, not at all ma'am."

"Did anyone ever tell you that I can't take care of myself?"

"No. The opposite. But I see how you look at him, especially at that restaurant. You like that man."

"Well, that man was talking about San Tainos and the past. Maybe I was remembering another man."

"Maybe."

"Well, there's a lot more going on here than you understand, Terence. A whole lot more. Now that your brothers live on their own and Frico's goin' away for a while, it's not easy for me. Many nights I go to sleep wishin' I could just gather all of you under my wings like a hen and stare down all your worries as if you're all still babies. Cos it's still a dangerous world even when your babies turn into men."

"Deep. I don't follow, Valerie Beaumont."

"A mother will do anything to keep her children safe. One day you'll get it. But for now, just trus' me on this."

Damn. Everybody's too deep these days.

The only thing I know for certain right now is that that bastard James Jackson is gonna get a kick out of this bridal magazine I'm bringin' him. Or maybe I'll get kicked in the teeth. Whatever the result, I think I'm fixin' to issue him a goddamn library card and charge him fees and fines in addition to money for the food. See how he'd like that.

Twenty-Four

We wake up one late-October morning and there are skulls in the old pool. Our Mexican neighbours drained out the green puddle and whitewashed the inside. Then they painted the cartoony-looking skulls along the inside edges. Big grinning skulls with black teeth and wide holes for eyes. By nightfall the eyes are glowing sky-blue and the pool is overflowing with candles and fluffy orange flowers. Marigolds, I think. You can smell them from inside the apartment when the wind cuts through on its way to the lake. Think I'll hang out by the pool and speak Spanglish for a bit.

"*Son ofrendas del Día de Muertos*. It happens *en seben* days," says a woman sticking flowers into white styrofoam. She looks a little surprised that I'm asking her what all this is for. You can see her eyebrows raised in horror. She must be an annoying supervisor in one of those office buildings downtown, I'm sure. One of those people who glance up at the clock or tap their watch when you're late. I just wanted to make conversation, though.

Of course I know what the Mexican Day of the Dead is, and I prob'ly glimpsed it when we lived in the swamp and came over into the city. Every year people take time to remember and honour their family members who died. At the end of October you can see people whitewashin' New O'lins cemeteries and buildin' displays with so many colours it makes you dizzy. But there's nothin' dead about Día de Muertos. Hell, I've never seen our old pool look this *alive*. You're walkin' down the steps towards a deep garden full of flames and flowers. Everybody's millin' around and talkin'. Some guys slap dominoes onto a rickety table by the poolside and sing along with a rusty transistor radio. They seem pretty happy about all this preparation. Even our other neighbours who aren't Mexican are comin' around. Some are helpin'. Others are just plain envious, you can see it. Some pull curtains aside and look down from inside their apartments, but they won't come out, the bastards.

Valerie Beaumont is one of those who stay inside. Her reasons are prob'ly different, though. You know her beliefs about talkin' to the dead. Or maybe she's more afraid of all the sweets and chocolate skulls that are laid out on long tables beside the pool. The woman could go into diabetic shock just walkin' past all that sugar. Poor lady pricks her fingers everyday, and even her wedding shoes can't be too tight and fancy on account of that diabetes.

So anyway, the Mexicans they decided to start celebratin' seven days early and they invite everybody to get involved. That's cool with me. Something tells me they wouldn't have done it if Mattis was still here. Even with all the spookiness that's happenin' inside our house, there's a good feelin' in the air since Mattis took off and James got converted. People feel safer at night.

Soon Benet rolls up. He steps out of his Town Car and launches himself across the courtyard and down the steps to the pool. He pats me on the shoulder, hovers over some people playing dominoes, then goes over to light a candle before a statue of the Blessed Virgin that they just set down at the edge of the pool. For a hell of a long time, he stays there with his head bowed. The man is remembering his sons. I'm full of guilt right now. I go stand beside him, like a hypocrite, and light a candle at the altar. I'm thinkin' about Broadway and Squash and Pa Campbell and Belly, even though I'm not Catholic or anything. Belly is my cousin from Georgia who died, if I didn't tell you before now.

Benet and I go to check on Moms. When I get in, someone's wearing out a violin in a corny scene of an old movie that Moms was prob'ly watchin' when we barged in. You know those black-and-white movies with lots of smoke and a lonely street lamp? Yeah. And it just has to have a greasy-haired handsome guy in it, grabbin' up some girl by the shoulders and kissing the hell out her while she looks him in the eyes. I can't stand seein' a girl look so helpless. It's distressing. The women I know would prob'ly punch you in the nuts if you tried that, trus' me.

Anyway, I go into the bedroom that I now share with Ma Campbell, and she's permanently taken over Frico's bed. She says Moms' room is more haunted than mine. What's haunting me is the damn hoodoo talismans that she's been planting all over the place. They're taped to the ceiling over my bed, tied to the doorknob, stuck under my pillow. I know the ol' lady does hocus-pocus over me while I'm sleeping. But while I'm awake it's the frankincense that's killin' me, not to mention the mumblings under her breath. I listen close, and she's talking about me stealing her money. I didn't, really. I just *borrowed* from the wad James gave me. Don't judge me, man. You know I had to pay Mattis for information on where to find my hoodoo seal. Well, it seems James told his mother that the money he sent was more than two hundred and fifty bucks. So I'm really hoping his conversion is for real, or I just might have to send him to hell myself. Yeah. Cos I finally found the seal again. It was in the guardhouse, left there by the poor soul who picked it up from the terrazzo floor in Mattis's apartment. Guess who? Larry frickin' Lou. And the rest is misery.

Well I go back outside to avoid the incense and Ma creeping me out from the other side of the room.

I'm takin' this picture I have of Mai out to the altar to pray for her too, even though Mai, she's not dead or anything. I just want to feel closer to her, I guess. Now, it's not even a good shot of Mai. Frico prob'ly took it on the day the Lam Lee Hahn family was moving out of the swamp. Mai is sitting on the hood of the Mitsubishi Montero with one fuzzy hand stretched out towards the camera and the other one half-covering her face. Her mouth is frozen open in a "no". It's the kind of shot you laugh at and then throw it out when you get back the reel from Kinko's or wherever. But I like it, cos it's not posed. Y'see, people are more than just poses. Somebody actually *happens* in front of you, a li'le bit at a time. That's why your pictures never do you justice, even if you're pretty. Cos it's just one frame out of a million moves. That doesn't mean I hate photos. Matter of fact it's nice that you can snap off a little piece of life and keep it fresh for all time. Anyway, like I was sayin', Mai looks like herself in this photo: bossy and cute as ever. Furthermore, in the picture I can see things the way they were in the swamp: before we broke up, before the swamp was burnin', before the water came and covered everythin' over. So I put the photo on the altar and, under candlelight, she is so alive I know I have to see her again.

The Land Rover rolls up to 113 Meadowvale, off Gregorian Boulevard. You wouldn't believe it's a convent. The place looks like a hacienda – one of those old Spanish estates you'd expect to see in some foreign country. It has a belfry and everything, and there's a whitewashed wall with brown bricks runnin' like a border along the top of it. A low archway curves over a wooden gate. Blue and white tiles follow the arch with letters that spell out "Meadowvale". A corny box buzzer is attached to the little wooden gate – and that's the only thing that spoils the whole classic look of the place.

Teesha pushes the buzzer once and we wait like that little handwritten sign says we should. I'm trying to look over the wall while Teesha's asking about Frico.

"Do you think he found friends in New York already?"

"Oh yeah, no doubt."

I know she wants to ask if I think Fricozoid would cheat on her or something. But I'm not goin' there. That's just like giving advice. Last thing I want to do is give anybody advice about their love life. That's one sure way to be a cockroach tryin' to stop a waterfowl fight.

Anyway, a serious-looking Sister opens up to us. Right away, Teesha straight up lies to the woman of God, telling her she wants information about becoming a nun (she's not even Catholic for godssakes). Says she was "inspired by a friend of hers who is currently a postulant on these premises". Good speech. Well, I'm so caught off guard by Teesha's lies I can't come up with anythin' half as good when the nun asks me my business here. And "I'm with her" just doesn't cut it. The Sister tells me I'll have to wait in the gardens while she has a word with Teesha. Strict rules apply in this place.

The nun turns and heads towards a hundred steps with huge clay planters on both sides. A series of archways every few steps makes you feel like you're in a hall of mirrors. You can tell that Mai is here by all the juicy bougainvillea blooms pourin' out of the planters and drippin' off the archways. The nun speaks without turning around.

"So, your friend, the postulant, what's her name again?"

Now Teesha is off guard. I'm tryin' to motion to her, but her back is turned and she's so deep in her lie, walkin' piously beside the nun, she doesn't see me wavin' like the ocean in a damn storm.

"Oh, uhm, Sister Mai," she says, with the confidence of a fool who doesn't know that Mai might not yet be called a *sister* and that she's using her American name.

The nun stops on a landing of the steps and turns her whole body towards us.

"Francine!" I holler out.

"Wait here."

I sit down on a bench by the steps and watch the nun and the liar walking up the stairs. From the looks of it, there's no way ol' Teesha Grey's goin' to pull this off. The plan is for her to get Mai to take her on a "tour of the premises". This tour will conveniently take her past where I'm sittin', and then – well, to tell you the truth, I don't know what will happen then. This girl hasn't seen or heard from me in over a year, and I don't know what to expect from an ex-girlfriend who signs off her letters with a blessin' instead of Xs and Os.

You can see postulants in their pre-nun uniforms hurrying past, carryin' cloth and candles. They're preparin' for All Saints' Day, which happens around the same time as the Day of the Dead. They look at me and giggle. When girls are in a group you can never tell if they're laughin' at your haircut or admirin' you. Doesn't matter. They're all spoken for anyway.

The convent is spotless. Every inch swept clean, includin' the corners where the stucco walls meet. Plaster statues pray inside alcoves. Beneath their feet, water pours out into concrete cisterns. The trickle is giving me the urge to pee. So I look away and, when I look back, at the top of one flight of stairs is Mai. I'm suddenly nervous. My bones rattle. This is supposed to be a blessed place. Maybe the skid will keep quiet. Mai makes the sign of the cross and walks down the stairs towards me. I would recognize that awkward walk and bright face anywhere, even under a nun's habit and layers and layers of clothes. Teesha walks behind her, not wanting to interfere in the moment. Just before she reaches up to me, my ex-girlfriend looks off, as if she's thinkin' of what to say to a stranger. Small talk.

Hi.

Hi, Mai... Francine. How are you?

I am blessed. You?

I'm good. So how are you?

I said I'm bless-ed.

Yes you did.

How's your mother?

She's gettin' married.

That's really nice...

Birds chirping. Over my head, a jet plane is pulling white wool across the blue, stitchin' up the sky. Our conversation crashed into a pause. Or we're sitting suspended on those three dots at the end of a broken sentence, waiting for more words. A nun laughs out from afar. Deep down you can tell that Mai has been happy. She's been keepin' busy. Her hands are wrinkly from workin' in water, maybe planting lilies. I took her away from what she was doin', obviously. I'm botherin' her. She looks at me, and then the worst thing happens. I feel nothin'. Absolutely nothin'. 'Cept maybe the discomforting thought that I shouldn't be here standin' in front of her. We both know this is a funeral. Some blossoms sweep across the cement. There's somethin' about flowers scuttlin' about on concrete that makes me feel so lonesome, no lie. Maybe it's cos they're fallen, but still too pretty to look like litter, so it's kind of sad, I don't know. They turn into a tiny whirlwind and whip around her feet before breakin' up and shufflin' off in different directions like the jet plane's white thread now unravelling above my head. Mai breaks the silence.

"I wrote to you."

"I know."

"I broke the rules to do that."

"Sorry."

"Say hi to your mother. Tell her I'm happy for her. And Terence—"

"Huh?"

"You shouldn't barge in here again like this, OK? It's not safe for any of us."

"OK."

I swear, loneliness can make you long for somebody until they're back in front of you. That's when you see that you only missed your memories of them. Cos they're not the same person you knew at all. Whatever we had back in the swamp is over on every level. Mai, she's different now, gone for good. And what does she mean by "not safe for any of us"? I wouldn't be surprised if Fricozoid told her to avoid me, just like Claire's hairy uncle.

"Terence, go. Now."

Almost on cue, the nun who let us in appears in an archway. She's in a huff, marchin' down the steps. One arm ratchets out like a switchblade and points in the direction of the gate.

"Out!" is all she says.

Teesha quickly walks down the steps. I follow. When we get through the wooden gate, Teesha keeps walkin' towards the Land Rover, but I turn around to face the mad nun.

"Sorry."

"Shush!"

"I didn't mean—"

"Shush! Shush! Just go."

Truth is, I'm only buyin' time to take one last look over her shoulder at Mai. Mai, both hands in front of her, all ten fingers clasped. The flowers regroup around her feet just before my view is blocked by the slam of a weathered gate, inches from my nose. And there's that last picture of my ex, still standin' on the steps, posin'.

Twenty-Five

We're movin' the smaller things first. That will make the final move after the wedding easier. Yeah, it's a few days before Halloween and we're haulin' stuff to the Benet mansion. Now this is uptown. This is New *Orleans*. By the east wing I can see the Mississippi sweeping around a curve and, by the west, glass buildings glistenin' in the financial district. Everythin' feels so close together. Like you're inside a hug. Trees. The river. The Connection Bridge. The Superdome. Even the traffic doesn't bother me, cos for the first time we're part of *the city*. Valerie Beaumont keeps lookin' outside every time an ambulance or a cop car goes by. She's tired of seein' red. But I guess once you live in the city, you're always under some kind of siege. I don't mind the ruckus, but still, as we head back to Hayne Boulevard and the view fades away, I keep feelin' that something's missin' – or you could say "amiss". You know, it's maybe that kind of feelin' my mother says she gets when she sees a really stand-out pair of shoes in a store window. Once she takes it home and tries it on with every piece of clothes in the closet and dances around in it a little bit, she just puts it down and starts feelin' really pissed off. Cos suddenly that pair of heels just doesn't look the same way it did in that store window, without the "sale" sign above it, and it's not surrounded by all the colours of the other things you couldn't afford. The only thing outstandin' at that point is the goddamn price, man.

We got into the city, but I feel like we've paid too much to get there. And I don't mean payin' too much in money. Nah.

We're payin' for it in *pride*. I feel like the real Beaumont dream failed with our father, and here we are, dragged along by Benet.

Now don't get me wrong. I know he was my mother's first love or whatever you want to call it. I know they were together in San Tainos before my father forced himself into the picture. And I can see that my mother had gotten her business started and was buildin' it before Benet even appeared. But maybe it's all the sudden changes: the dinners, the mansion. The slick wardrobe includin' the crisp white suit I'm gettin' measured for right now at the same Orange Oaks haute-couture wedding parlour. All this stuff is great, but at the same time I'm nervous. Like we're all changin' too soon – and it makes me feel false. "Faux" like Larry Lou.

(*But maan, you should see me in that suit. Boo-yah.*)

Mr Terence Beaumont, new and improved. Classy: like a top model or a real slick businessman, no lie. "You're all grown up, Terence," I tell myself, tuggin' at my fancy suit in the mirror.

Moms is havin' her own troubles. Maybe bridal blues. After all, her rush wedding is in a week. Yeah, it's that soon. Or maybe she's sittin' over there watching me try on the suit and wonderin' why her boys grew up so fast. And how she wished we didn't have to do it without our old man.

I like sneakin' into the back of her mind by listenin' to the songs she sings to herself. You should try that sometime. The songs people sing under their breath can tell you what they're thinkin'. Today she's singin' oldies. Helen Reddy this time. Now, if you ever hear your forty-year-old mother crankin' out a tune by Helen Reddy, she's prob'ly thinkin' about your pops and the old days. Well, she sees me across the room and turns the song into a hum, like I need to hear the words to recognize it. She knows it too, cos she looks a little embarrassed. So she speaks up about nothing.

"The tailor says he needs to adjust the pants on that white suit, Skid."

While he's re-measurin', I hear him ask Benet, who walked into the parlour sippin' a wine cooler, if the "other suit will be the same size". Benet nods, and Moms is smilin' at me. So I'm gettin' two suits. Cool. But I'm growin' out of my clothes so fast I'm not sure that's such a good idea. The two white suits suddenly make more sense when we swing into Armstrong Airport afterwards and Frico Beaumont steps out from the terminal with a bag behind him. He's smilin' and I'm bear-huggin' the guy like he wasn't gone a mere couple of weeks. He says he got special permission to leave school.

"I'm shootin' a short film about Halloween, Day of the Dead and All Saints' Day. I convinced them the best place to see all three is New O'lins. Just consider it early Thanksgivin', even though I need to be back in a few days." The boy is a genius. He put on a few pounds, so I know we're heading back to the tailor's soon.

Back home he's askin' me to fill him in while he's in front of the bathroom mirror. I give him only the things I don't have to explain, cos too much has happened and I don't want to talk to him while he's diggin' into his nose with a tissue. He pulls the tissue out and it's as black as charcoal.

"What the hell? You OK, man?"

"Uh-huh, you should see inside my ears. That's New York City for ya. Soot and dust. The whole place gets up your nose. I love it there, though. Here."

He pushes the tissue towards me and I back away.

"Suit yourself. Don't ever say I never brought you back anything."

He did bring me back something, though. He dipped into his bag and brought out this rusty metal sign, so old you could hardly see the top half of it. But the bottom half was yellow and written in bold black letters as clear as day:

FALLOUT SHELTER

"That's a black-and-yellow radiation symbol at the top. I pried it off a buildin' close to George Washington Bridge. Not even sure if that was legal, so don't tell anyone, but that sign is so cool. Those places were for people to hide underground just in case there was a nuclear-missile attack. Thought it would look good in your room. Lord knows in here looks like somethin' hit it since I left. Tidy up, boy."

"Thanks." The boy is weird for strippin' a buildin'. But the sign *is* pretty cool.

He's paler than I remember. New York City soakin' into his skin. But he's more excited than I've ever seen him. He shows me a picture he took lookin' down at Broadway. Taxis turned it into a yellow brick road. Rivers of people rushin' across it.

"You have to get movin' in the direction of the river or you get washed away, man. That's New York City."

The boy found a new kind of magic, you can tell. Even though he's cool and everythin', I feel a li'le bit like I'm talkin' to an alien, especially when video-camera equipment comes out of his bags and he's yappin' about filters and stuff, technical terms leapin' out of him like a foreign language.

Anyway, it's almost nightfall, and he just saw the pool full of flowers out back. So now he's racin' out there to set up a tripod. When he starts shootin', I'm his assistant, whether I like it or not. My hands are tired from movin' around the tripod. But now he's doin' a playback on the camera. And when I see that digital timer runnin' and there's time-lapse footage – wow. You can see the day coolin' into blue night, and the pool explodin' into candles. Life-size shadows from plaster saints shiver against the back wall.

Frico is looking at the camera screen, rewinding again and again. He knows there's somethin' caught on tape. But he hasn't heard about Broadway and Squash hopping around the premises. Poor guy. New O'lins spirits are now too quick for his New York eyes.

Twenty-Six

Shoulda kept my damn mouth shut. But no. I just had to come in and tell Moms about what I saw on Frico's camera.

She gives me the verdict.

"I should've known. Those spirits love that pool. Herbert and Orville had a Taino mother, so they need tribal burial rites. I need to do something similar in the swamp."

Ma gets in the middle of it.

"Well, I remember Lobo sayin' that a loong taam ago. You shoulda known better. And call Benet. He needs to hear this."

So now, because of me, my mother is out doin' an ancient ritual dance around the ol' pool. Now that's not city behaviour. I'm thinkin' about runnin' back inside and crawlin' up under the bed, but the neighbours love it. The older Mexican men, they were fixin' to stay up late and slam more dominoes onto that ol' table anyhow. That Mexican lady I spoke to the first day they painted the pool, she's tellin' me her greatest-grandfolks were Mayan.

"Spirits, dey looove deep places. My ancestors are here tonight as well."

She lights more candles so we can see Valerie Beaumont in full flight. Moms' put on all her amulets and bracelets and let down her hair. Now she's walkin' around the pool playin' a *güiro*. That's a curved piece of wood that sounds like a washboard when you scrape it with a stick. Yeah, super low-tech, I know, but it makes a good rhythm for the song she's singin' about Atabey. That's a Taino goddess who rules all waters in the world, I think. I guess that would include the swamps and the sinkhole.

223

Well Moms she goes down into the pool among the marigolds and turns in all directions of the compass with four feathers in her hand, and I feel all tingly for some reason. Then some neighbours start comin' to their windows complaining about the noise from the damn *güiro* and the dominoes, so we leave a coupla chunks of guava on the altar for the spirits to snack on. Taino ghosts love that stuff.

On All Saints' mornin', Moms wakes up with her two big toes tied together. There's a spot of Four Thieves oil on her forehead and a strip of red cloth around her wedding finger. Not the spirits this time. It's Ma Campbell's version of a protection spell. She struggles to get up.

"Don't get all bent outta shape now, Valerie. This is for the cem'tery. Lots of things walk round in the cem'tery. I found a double yolk in my breakfast egg this mo'nin'. Definite sign this wedding's gonna happen. Cain't nobody or no spirit nowhere try to spoil it now."

We're going to the cemetery to lay wreaths on the tombs of our ancestors. It's a beautiful All Saints' Day ritual. I'm lookin' forward to it, especially since I hear my father's name is on a plaque in Lafayette Cemetery now. Maybe this'll help me accept that he's gone. After All Saints' Day they're going to move it to a graveyard closer to where he was actually born.

Anyway, Benet picks me up from school in the Town Car. You should see silly kids pointing and making a big deal out of it. Soon as I fasten my seatbelt, Benet is tryin' to pick my brain. He's very soft-spoken today: trying to be all fatherly I guess, asking me if I had lunch and how it was. Damn. I'm sixteen years old. Lunch is not a topic. Poor guy's so out of practice. Then he gets to his point.

"Yer mother and I have always made a great team, Terence."

Damn. Five minutes in the car and I get "the chair". I swear, the passenger seat is where adults strap you in and torture you with all their memories and expectations.

"OK."

"Yessir, next year makes, let's see now... *twenty-two* years ago I first laid eyes on her. Sweet lady. Think yer mother's gorgeous now? Wow, back in the day—"

(*Whoa. I'm really not gonna have this conversation with this guy.*)

"So whose idea was it to get married now?"

"Heh heh. Well, to be honest, Terry, if things had played out the way they should've, yer mother and I woulda been married decades ago – but the Lord knows best. Maybe I woulda just fallen under her spell and gone off in my head like yer father did instead of buildin' my businesses, y'know. There's a certain power a woman has over a man once yew give 'em a ring, remember that. Heh heh. 'Specially a mystery woman like yer mother. But even then, the things we can achieve together. I don't expect yew to understand that stuff."

And that's another thing about talking to a guy like Benet. He's an upstager. Yeah. One of those rich guys who needs to put down what you just said with a response that's supposed to be even more revealing or more clever or whatever. Watch out for any guy whose responses to you end with "I don't expect you to understand" or begin with crap like "The bigger picture is" or "The truth is" – as if you were talkin' small-time crap the whole time before he chipped in with some ancient wisdom. I mean, I respect the guy enough already. He doesn't need to rub it in.

Anyway, he's still goin' on about how he *adores* my mother and how she looks out for him and even got him to brave up and go surgically remove the ganglion on his wrist. This is definitely gettin' awkward, so I mess with the radio a bit and start tellin' him about all the new video games and CDs (the Town Car has a cassette player, for godsakes), and he's really fascinated with this stuff. Thank God. Cos Lord knows that beats talkin' about his damn ganglion.

He takes the long route, and that's OK. These days New O'lins has some pretty modern packagin', but in the middle of the city it's still mostly French stuffing. We pull up to a lily-white buildin' with a large clock on the façade being held high up in the air by a goddess-lookin' lady loungin' on a fancy chair. Gold trim and Roman numerals, massive double columns and curled concrete decorations everywhere. Benet says it's Beaux-Arts architecture. I think he just pulled up out front so I could see the swank of the building. That's Benet. He's a skilful kind of show-off. Now we're entering the building from the back, on Poydras Street. Around here is nothin' like the front. You wouldn't even know it's the same building. We slide into underground parking with concrete columns and a reserved space with Benet's name on it and everything.

"My office is on the seventh floor. Small enough operation, but it's got ambition. We're makin' a quick stop."

Now, outside looks like it's a two-hundred-year-old design, but inside is not what you'd expect. Modern. Marble tiles everywhere, and even the security guard's desk is real posh. He calls Backhoe "sir" and touches the peak of his cap and all that. The elevator has glass at the back, so you can see the parking lot and people gettin' smaller as you go up. You prob'ly want to take the stairs after lunch. The receptionist fixes her hair and bats her eyelids and gives him a bunch of "While You Were out" messages. He hands them off to me and tells me to read 'em while we're walkin' down a corridor with cubicles on both sides and people mindin' their own business or busy on phones.

Now, if you missed the gold-leaf sign on the glass door out front, don't you worry. There's no way you're gonna forget where you are. "EARNEST-BENET" takes up the full length of a white wall behind the cubicles. That's no less than forty feet. And the stainless-steel block letters are six feet high.

"Recently renovated. My daddy opened these offices back in the day. I ain't half the man my father was, Ter'nce, but I'm workin' on it."

He throws open some deep-stained wooden doors at the end of the corridor with more drama than was necessary, but I see why. Wow. There's a meeting room with a high ceiling back here. The massive table's the same colour as the door. And it rolls out all the way back to the window overlookin' traffic. High-back leather chairs with headrests are gathered around the table. Genuine leather too. You can smell them. All of a sudden I feel strange and small in my Chuck Taylors, dowdy windbreaker and half-dirty Levi's. This office is all suit-and-tie, even if Benet is in a plaid shirt and slacks. He runs the damn place.

"Take a seat, Terence."

I don't have the balls to walk another inch in this place, so I grab the first chair to my left.

"Good choice. Yew just sat at the head of the meeting table, Terry. That's the boss's seat. Uh-huh. That's what I like about yew. Yew know what yew want, son. So while yew're sittin' there, why don't yew go ahead and tell *me* what to do."

He laughs out and claps his hands.

"Go on. This meetin' is called to order. Read those messages yew got there for me."

So now I'm feeling like a part of a school play, and the leather chair is squeakin' under my butt, but look, maybe Tracey Benet isn't playing a game. Maybe he wants to see if I'm a take-charge kind of guy. So I shuffle through the messages in front of me and

I tell him that the meeting with DipaGas is on Tuesday and he's going to the Pennsylvania-Mississippi Gas Conference on the ninth of next month. He nods like he's never heard this before, like he's actually taking instructions from me.

"See? My poor sons would never fit into that chair. Got spoilt by their mother. She taught them early that life is full of fun and games and all yew need to be is a rich man's son. Then she left 'em there in the swamp with just me. But yew know 'bout struggle, don't ya, Terry? I saw yew grow up."

I don't know what to say, so I look at the messages again. The hyphen between "EARNEST" and "BENET" is actually a sideways blue flame.

"I'm an old lion with dull teeth. But yew and yer brothers are young and quick 'n' ambitious. And we'll be fam'ly soon. And I know y'all have what it takes. See that guy?"

He points to a sepia photo on the wall.

"That there is William 'the Furnace' Earnest. My daddy saw the fire in him when he opened this natural-gas business back in the day. Believed in him so much he put his name first. Most people think 'Earnest-Benet' is a fam'ly name. That's what they'll think about 'Beaumont-Benet' years from now. Yessir. I'm thinkin' of changing the company name. Ol' Earnest has long gone to glory and has gotten his reward both here and in the Hereafter.

"Speakin' of which, Terence. We gotta go take care of some fam'ly business now."

On our way out he stops by this big map of the whole Gulf of Mexico with red push pins stuck in it all the way from Texas to Mississippi.

"Know what those pins are Terence? Those are oil rigs. Know how many of 'em I own? Zero. But I want my own – one or two, or a few."

Back in the car Benet is goin' on about "urban decay" and how we need to be "preserving the Beaux-Arts and neo-classical buildings of the South". He says his house in the city has a mix of both styles.

"While I was livin' in the swamp, I took my time to build it. Got the best designers too. Yew been there, Terence. From the get-go, the chief builder, he told me: 'Mr Benet, we're gonna build yew an entrance hall that looks like the White House! And the rest of the mansion will be wrapped in a façade that looks like somebody carved the whole thing outta white-chocolate frostin'.'"

Interesting. And to be honest, I really would give a shit if my stomach wasn't grumblin' louder than his architecture lecture. Benet suggests we go get *bánh mì* at Dong Phoung Bakery, but that's all the way on the other side of town, in Little Vietnam. We'd never make it back in time for layin' wreaths in Lafayette. Plus we picked up Claire at the hair salon, and I don't think it's appropriate to take her somewhere that still gives me butterflies in my gut. Yeah, still. I thought I was over that Vietnamese wanna-be nun. But I'm not. I swear next January I'll still be sittin' on my roof, watchin' the Year of the Goat fireworks goin' off over Little Vietnam. They'll be too far away for me to hear, but I'm sure I'll still feel explosions in my chest.

Anyway, we stop at Jill Cunningham's Café on St Charles instead, near to Lafayette Cemetery. Benet's plate of rice and beans reminds me of swamp mud, so I order a chilli dog. Claire is being dainty. She gets a mahi-mahi, as if eating a simple sandwich wouldn't go with her wicked-hot hairdo. So we're seated upstairs overlookin' the street with a balcony so full of French filigree it could make you dizzy if you looked too long. I'm halfway through my hot dog when Benet starts up again with stuff so boring I start noddin' off. Now look. I don't know 'bout anybody else. But once I'm fallin' asleep and my lower jaw drops down – my eyes are gonna flicker open real quick. It's kinda like that light in the refrigerator and how it works with the door? Yeah. Anyway, Benet must have seen me slippin' away, and when adults know they're puttin' you to sleep they save themselves by gettin' all up in your love life.

"Sooo, Ter'nce…"

(*Fridge light.*)

"…Yew two are an item these days, huh?" He's pointin' at me and Claire with his fork.

Claire laughs. He's scratchin' his beard. It makes me think of one of those shredded-wheat cereals. Claire frowns a little bit.

"An *item*, Mr Benet? That sounds like something you pick up at the grocery store."

"Sorry, Claire. I see the light in both y'all eyes, though. Young love. Ter'nce, I knew yer old man when he was just a bit older than yew are right now, when he had that light. He got interested in good ol' San Tainos more than I did. He was crazy for yer mother and all that hocus-pocus. Tried all his life to impress her by learning hoodoo. Made more mistakes than magic, I'll tell ya that! Matter of fact, one day he came over the train tracks to me for money after y'all were born so he could go to the island to buy authentic stuff like seals and talismans. He was so *obsessed* with it! Anyhow, can't blame the guy. That's how he stole yer mother from me. Heh heh. Betrayed me, that bastard. But that's bygones. To the future!"

He raises his glass of whatever and we say cheers with him so as not to make him feel bad. He's so awkward. And when he's making a point, his bushy eyebrows go so far up on his forehead it makes *your* eyebrows feel weird. But look. Never mind me calling Benet corny or whatever. I'm thinkin' about the future, like he said. I'm thinkin' about Beaumont-Benet. I'm eighteen next year. A man now. A *business*man. But Bo's ain't my kind of business. After a while that deep freeze gets to ya. And me goin' back and forth into the swamp for magic seals? Well, that was beginnin' to feel like sleepwalkin' and draggin' things back from a dream. So maybe it's time to try something else. Diversify, like I've been plannin'. So from here on out I'm gonna imagine myself successful – like Tracey Backhoe Benet. Natural-gas royalty by the time I'm thirty. Hell, screw thirty – by twenty-five. I ain't got the taam. Tracey Benet has been hinting at mentoring me all evenin'. He's lookin' for new blood, so this is my shot. My pops would be proud. Or pissed. And that's my dilemma right there.

Over by the Mississippi docks, the robot cranes are winking in sequence. Streetcars screech on St Charles Street. The electric smell reminds me that Claire hasn't even tried lighting up a cig in front of Benet. She respects him so much it's ridiculous. Calls him "Mr Benet" and everything, you heard her. Her mother worked with Benet on a dredging project back in the day. And she has no idea her daughter's blazin' a ten-pack every two days. Poor girl gets jittery at the table until she "goes to the little girls' room" and comes back with the smoke lingerin' in her clothes.

Jill Cunningham walks over with the bill. She looks good for her age, even behind the Sophia Loren vintage glasses. Benet leans back in the plastic chair. He grabs a napkin, wipes his hands and mouth in a hurry.

"Jill!"

While those two adults do the absolutely necessary small talk and double-kiss and mandatory business chat, I lean over to Claire.

"So... how do you stop it?"

"Tried many times, Terence. It's not easy."

She looks a little sheepish, cos she thinks I'm talking about her smoking.

"No, babe. I mean... the skid".

"The what? The skid?" *Pause.* "Are we still goin' on about that?"

"Shh. Yeah, accordin' to those San Tai folk tales, how do people, you know, turn back a bad spell. Can they?"

She actually says the word "Sigh", which is another way women say "You poor thing you", which is unfair, cos I've never gotten on her case about her habit. I'm just lookin' for help with what haunts me. Furthermore, I'm thinkin' about the both of us. See, just this evening I got to thinkin' that maybe I can find a "correction" for this hoodoo-magic mistake. I'm thinkin' about me and Claire and the future. I don't want the past hangin' around.

She looks off towards the street like she'd rather not discuss nonsense like this.

"OK, Terence. When my uncle gets back, I'll ask him. He went down to San Tainos for two weeks."

"Oh, he did?"

"On vacation, he says."

"I was wondering how you decided to come with us out here."

"Yeah, my big bad uncle is away. You got lucky"

"Anyways. Don't people have to actually *work* to take a vacation?"

"That's what I told him. But I think it has more to do with working than taking a break. He makes loads off hoodoo in San Tai tourist areas."

"Yeah, he's a touristy kind of guy. Thought he was makin' money in the French Market."

"He was, but it's not safe for him any more. He said something about too many morons swarming the place."

I tune in to Benet and Jill Cunningham again.

"So how's business, Jill, ol' girl?"

"Just happy to be serving the likes of you again, Cap'n Benet. It's been a spell. Say hi to Mrs Benet for me?"

"Oh it's been a spell awright. Me an' Mrs Benet parted company a while back. We're divorced now."

"Oh I'm so sorry, I didn't—"

"Doesn't matter. I'm happy, she's happy with some guy richer than me over in Shreveport. Gives me motivation to be a better man. And I'm workin' on it. Right, Terry?"

People around the city, they like this guy. Even though I hate how he harps on my old man's mistakes, I like his future plans in general.

We're prob'ly the last ones to get to the cemetery today. All the whitewashing has been done, and Lafayette No. 1 is gleamin' under the sun. We're all here, even though Doug looks like he'd rather be somewhere else. I guess it's awkward working for someone who turns up at family gatherings. Tony starts up with his nonsense about tying my hands and feet while we're in the graveyard just in case a light breeze comes along and scares me away. He doesn't have a clue what I've seen in this place.

A jazz funeral procession enters – a file of black and gold umbrellas, brass bands and purple sashes dancing in through the entrance. Frico's shootin' the scene with his hand-held camera, and Teesha's running behind him for a change. I've never been to the cemetery on All Saints' Day, so it's very interestin' to watch people roam the corridors, bringin' fresh flowers "for the bones" as they say. Moms is smiling at all the wreaths they're layin'. Along the east end of the graveyard are the wall vaults. They've turned the entire wall of tombs into a fence of flowers. When you see all that kinda beauty, you can't even think of what's behind it. I thought All Saints' Day would be sad, but it's not. Even when we see the plaque with Alrick Beaumont's name on it, I feel nothing – nothing bad, at least. I just wish there was something more to honour the memory of a man who was a genius most of the time. Well, Mrs Thorpe has it figured out. She brings the Terravan around to Washington Avenue. It's packed with yellow helium balloons that all say: "Alrick".

We gather along a walkway away from the trees and hold the balloons up while Mrs Thorpe says a prayer. Let go together on the count of three. Those balloons climb and become a rash against the sky. I can't stop lookin' until they vanish. Now all I can see are those ripples that appear in front of your eyes when you stare at somethin' for too long. Trees hang over and sigh as we exit the graveyard. That broken monument is still there. They leant the pieces up against a wall, and I feel bad about it. I hear it's been here since nineteen thirty-three.

Teesha comes over and hugs me around my upper arm and rubs it in the way that says: "Sorry about your dad". That's a big improvement to slappin' me silly. Plus she smells good.

Towards the entrance, something's holding up the people traffic. We can't get past. As the line shuffles closer, we can hear preaching.

"Whitewashed! Whitewashed! Some o' y'all are covered over like these tombs heah. Me? My life is an open book. James Jackson, prisoner, convict, criminal, mental patient – call me what you want, but I'm not hidin' any more."

People are actually stopping to hear James out. It's kind of awkward for all of us, cos apart from Ma Campbell, I'm sure nobody wants to be singled out by a criminal-turned-street-preacher in a graveyard with a flask of liquor in his hand. The preaching gets into high gear as we get closer.

"I got nothin' to hide. I've been the worst there is. Been to hell and back. Anybody ever been beaten with a hickory stick? You've been to hell! Anybody ever worked on a corn farm? You've been to hell! Cos look. At harvest time on a corn farm, when they're heavin' all that grain into the bins and all that dust is swirlin' in the air – if you as much as *think* about lightin' up a cigarette, you're gonna have a flash fire. And a flash fire is over in a split second, but it burns as hot as hell. And you know you're in trouble when you're seventeen and you go through a flash fire in a corn bin in the middle of winter and you survive but your skin is peelin' off o' ya. And you know you got a home in Louisiana. But you can't go back theah for salvation. Not in any season. Cos your old man, he's got a hickory stick soaked in salt water waitin' for your flash-fire skin. And in every direction it's still a long walk home through deep frost and bitter cold and you cain't figure out the first step. So what do you do? You commit a crime, so that you can get roughed up and then cared for, and you just hope that a hospital or a prison's got heat, even though you've had enough for four winters."

Man, he's got some people weepin'. Others just look at the ground and pass by. I'm with that second group. Last thing I want—

"Beaumont!"

Doesn't matter if there are five people with that last name around, I know James is talkin' to me specifically.

"Whitewashed, Beaumont. I told you. Hidin' skeletons under their coats!"

I dip through the crowd and make it to the gate, but not before he starts quoting Scripture about fathers not provoking children to wrath. That's how you know he's fixin' to go on and on about what Pa Campbell did to him in the swamp. I'm so grateful when the Lafayette security guards walk up and stop the anti-Pa preachin'. I feel bad for the guy, and I don't mean to be insensitive but, like Benet says, it's all bygones, man.

Closer to the gate, Frico's showin' me the last of the All Saints' Day footage he got earlier. That boy went back to that Meadowvale convent and got *access* to the place by himself.

Yeah. No kidding. He even made that old leathery nun laugh out loud on camera and tell him that he could come back *any time* and bring friends. Damn. He even got five minutes' footage of my ex-girlfriend, in her postulant clothes, talking about All Saints' Day and the mercy of the Blessed Virgin. Wow. The boy's got personality. And besides the hoodoo sketchin', that's a power by itself.

Somebody across the street from Lafayette Cemetery is playing the old tune, 'Oh, When the Saints', very slowly on a steel guitar. Now that song is so old and dusty, but on that steel guitar it slices into your soul, man. Clouds crowd over the graveyard, and the monuments are all turnin' bronze in that final flash of sun. People light candles even though it's still daytime. We pass by the newly repaired tomb of Broadway and Squash. Doug is on the side of the pathway towards the tomb, so he walks with Benet to go to light a candle. Benet comes back smiling, but with a tear in his eye.

Twenty-Seven

Now that he's done shootin' his documentary and wowing the clergy, Frico Beaumont can get back to being a super-jerk. No, really. You should hear this guy hoggin' all the conversations since we left the cemetery. I guess part of it is that he feels in charge, since he's the one who got Benet to let us hang out at his mansion for a while. Yeah. When Moms and Benet were heading back to Hayne Boulevard, Frico joked about house-sitting for Benet for a few hours. Well, the man leant his head and ducked into his Town Car and came back out with his house keys and a remote control for the electronic gate, just like that. Moms protested from the passenger seat.

"Tracey. Four teenagers in a big house, at night – what's the idea?"

"C'mon Valerie. They're respons'ble enough. Plus it's only fer a few hours."

"All kids these days need is one minute."

"Well, you don't sound like yew trust yer own kids, Valerie."

"Oh, Tracey, I trust 'em. But the Devil is busy these days, so only under the condition that y'all behave."

"Yew heard the lady. Behave yerselves."

Benet winks and Frico turns on the charm.

"Of course, Momma. I'll keep these slackers in check."

Soon as the Town Car hits the highway, the boy is plannin' a "New York-style rooftop-pool party", complete with Jack Daniel's jello shots and strip poker. I swear Valerie Beaumont's boy is gonna become a bum before graduation.

Well, we meet up with Peter Grant and Suzy. They were walkin'
along the sea wall as usual – and of course, being full-fledged
bourgeois bums themselves, they just *love* Frico's idea.

"*Magnifique!*"

If those two idiots could think in English for two seconds, they'd
figure out they're only being invited cos Teesha's mom took the
Land Rover, so we need Peter's car. Frico Beaumont is evil.

So finally, after rolling around town to grab drinks and games,
CDs and bikinis, we're up on Benet's pool deck cannonballing
into the pool. Now this is sweet. The pool deck is actually
elevated, so you can view the premises below you, washed in
fluorescent light. And as far as your eyes can see, it's all Benet
property. The place is huge. Lush lawns and brick walkways roll
up to black-and-white chequered floors, and up winding staircases
you'll find huge double-doored bedrooms. But Benet locked all of
'em. And that was a smart thing to do cos, trus' me, those jello
shots are gonna take a while to set, and six teenagers got time
to kill. Crank up the music. Shuffle the deck.

I leave them playin' strip poker by the swim-up bar. I know I'm
tipsy when Peter and Suzy begin to sound sensible.

So I take a break and doggie-paddle with much difficulty over
to Claire, who's on a pool chair, hammered from havin' too many
jello shots. Trus' me, she's literally over the freakin' moon when
I launch out of the pool and slosh over to her. The conversation
is classic.

"Hiii, Terence. Will you look at that? Wow."

She's wiping her whole hand across the Milky Way as if it's
right there under her fingers.

"Looks like black marble, doesn't it?"

"Kind of. Wanna hear what I think it looks like?"

"Can't wait. Go ahead, Terence Beaumont."

I turn some cogwheels in my head for a few seconds, then clear my throat.

"Pixie dust wasted on God's glass floor.
Sparkles pasted onto night.
The fading trail from the Great Conjure –
Lovely, hovering, lingerin' lights."

"Wow. *God's glass floor*, that's great."

"I roll out a wicked verse, and that's all you say? Damn!"

"Terence, baby, you should write that stuff down."

(*Funny. Soon as you say something out of your soul, people suggest you write it down. Well, that's like tryin' to keep a house cat in a damn cage. It's just wrong.*)

"Nah, I don't think so. I told my mother something like what I just said when I was about thirteen or so."

"At thirteen? That's so cute. What did she say?

"She said, 'Stop playin' with the Lord, boy.'"

I don't know if it's the shots, but Claire can't stop cacklin', even when I try to talk seriously about my feelings on Moms and her old-time religion.

"I swear Claire, older folks never get that kind of stuff."

"Oh man. Hilarious. You get all cosmic and shit and your mother says, 'Stop playin' with the Lord, boy!'"

"But seriously, I mean, how is that 'playin' with God'?"

She starts imitating my mother, cigarette between fingers and all: "God's glass floor my ass. Boy, shuddup. Terence, I don't give one crap about your blasphemous poetry, man! Go do the dishes or your homework. Come on out here playin' with Almighty God. Tellin' me God has a glass floor. I swear if I ever said that to my mother back in the day in San Tainos, I wouldn't live to tell the tale. Glass floor. Pssssh."

I'm not even offended that my girl is ridiculin' me cos, to be honest, it *is* funny. Best way to beat being the butt of the joke is to join in.

"Write it down, huh? Yeah, right. I write that stuff down and a few years from now some guy and his girl will be sittin' on the edge of some old pool readin' my journal and laughin' like hell."

Well, it looks like ol' Fricozoid can't stand when people laugh out loud outside his comedic presence. So he swims over from the strip-poker game that has obviously gone boring. Of course we're stiflin' giggles by now.

"Wha's so funny?"

"Nothin' you wanna know 'bout, 'Zoid. Poetry. Swimmin' pools. Boring stuff."

"Yeah, sounds pretty boring," he says with a sneer.

Claire bursts out with another whisky laugh that ends in a wheeze. I have to stop her from rollin' off the pool chair. Now Peter and Suzy and Teesha come crowding over as well. Frico's got his audience back, so he heaves a wave out of the pool and splashes me and my girl with his half-drunk self. Well, it's gettin' tense, cos nobody like to see siblings having a stare-down contest.

Now you should see this guy parading in the pool. I swear, too much alcohol is like a goddamn microscope that you turn on yourself and then tell everybody to come take a close look at how crappy you really are. Confidence is one thing, but 'Zoid's so full of himself for all the wrong reasons. I mean, to be honest, if we should go out in a group, girls are gonna look at Frico first, no lie. It's not that he's better-lookin' than anybody else, but you know, he's got this artsy-fartsy hairstyle goin' on, and girls go for that stuff. But talk to the guy for two minutes and you'll prob'ly see he's got as much flavour as a frickin' cardboard cake. I'm serious.

"Got somethin' you wanna say, Skid?"

"Don't splash my girl, dude."

"Your *other* girl, you mean."

Damn. It just got awkward, as if big bubbles came up from underneath somebody in the middle of the pool.

Claire is staring – no, *glaring* – at me, cos this whole time I haven't mentioned Mai even once to her.

'Zoid might as well have shared the whole story about Mai right there and then, cos that would have been much better. Him droppin' that one statement and then backstrokin' away just opens up all kinds of questions.

It's OK though. I'm plannin' the last laugh right now. When this guy is back in NYC freezing his ass off, I'll prob'ly give him a call just to let him know I'm swimmin' around the pool in warm weather, all by myself while he needs to take off three layers just to take a piss.

Anyway, that's strange. Soon as I think about making a call, the phone inside the entrance hall just starts ringin' off the hook. And that's what stops a major Skid-Frico fight from goin' down in front of everybody. Frico traipses inside to answer it, like he's the man of the house who's tired of havin' to answer the phone all the time.

It's Benet on the line. I think he's just checkin' in on us. But when Frico stays on the phone for over two minutes, switching the receiver from ear to ear, we all start gatherin' round. My mother and Benet are all the way in the swamp doing All Saints' Night rituals, and there's an emergency.

Twenty-Eight

Ma Campbell is very upset that Moms and Benet left Pa Campbell's urn in the house on Hayne Boulevard.

It's a bad sign, she says. The poor ol' lady must be ready to cry now. She's been working hard on lettin' go of her husband. I'll miss Pa Campbell, but I agree with her. That thing's been sittin' beside our salt-'n'-pepper shakers for much too long.

Well, as soon as I hear Benet rambling on the other end, I can tell that him and Valerie Beaumont are deep in the L-Island swamp. You can hear the crickets comin' through the phone so loud Benet has to shout:

"Frico, dammit. I left the urn. Yer mother's gonna kill me. She asked me to make sure I had it and I plumb forgot. Ma Campbell must be havin' kittens. Valerie!"

He's tryin' to talk to her, but I reckon Moms is in a trance by now, prob'ly off by herself, up on the train tracks, throwin' flowers and spices down into the sinkhole. Benet gives up on her. I have my ear against the back of the receiver.

"She's far away and deep into what she's doin', Frico. We hafta fix this. I need yer help."

He says somethin' else to Frico, then the call goes dead. I'm surprised he even got through to us on that cellular-phone gadget in the first place.

Well, I didn't think it would, but just the mention of the word "swamp" gives me the creeps. 'Specially at night. 'Specially since Valerie Beaumont opened her eyes wide and warned me never to go back there. But Benet needs us to take Pa's ashes as close as we can and he'll meet us. I must be the only coward, cos everybody wants to go, including Claire.

"Hell, it's All Saints' Night, babe! We'll be all right. I hear the angels are out in droves!"

That's when I know they're all pissin' drunk. So imagine six people crammed into Peter's car flyin' over Connection Bridge and zipping up Hayne Boulevard. We only fit because Suzy's in Peter's lap in the back, and you can't tell them apart until Peter borrows his lips back from her so he can start whining about the goddamn gas.

"This trip is gonna cost me."

Really? You wouldn't believe this is the guy who just got free shots and a swim-up bar with a frickin' view. Some people. I wish it would cost him. We're all tired of travelling clown-car-style anyways, so we're only too happy to turn into the apartment, grab the urn and switch vehicles.

What I'm not happy about is all this rushing. I wish we had more time, so I could at least find my swamp boots under the kitchen counter or somethin'. I still got on those white tennis shoes Doug bought me for godssakes, but we got to move. We can't fail Ma or Pa. And Heaven knows I don't like the idea of Moms waiting too long for us in that hellhole. You never know what that swamp will do, I swear.

"All you young people goin' out there this time o' night?"

Mrs Thorpe takes a break from tending to Ma Campbell to bless everybody goin' on the "treacherous journey". Good ol' Mrs Thorpe's prayers must have messed up that strip-poker game back at the mansion, no doubt.

Now we're walkin' out to the Terravan.

"So who's driving?" I'm the only one who wants to know.

"Whoever is in the driver's seat, Skid," says Frico. "It's that type of vehicle."

Everybody's cacklin'. Good one, bro. Haw-haw. He's just excited to have one more adventure in the South to show off to his fartsy New York friends, this guy.

Well, he climbs into the cockpit and mucks around a bit, cos he has no clue where what is, as usual. The headlights flash when he's searching for the indicator and, of course, the wipers are wavin' around for no reason.

People sit in pairs, cos those jello shots haven't worn off yet and everybody's feelin' mushy. Almost to the back of the bus, it's me and Claire. Two seats before us is Le Frrentch Couple, already joined at the lips, and up front, Frico and Teesha Grey are havin' the time of their lives.

"All aboard, strap yourselves in, we're about to sail! Ladies and gentlemen, we're heading into the beautiful, balmy, south-eastern Louisiana coast on a quick night cruise. I'm Frico, your Captain, and I'd like to thank you for choosing us. Hope to see you next time you travel."

Wish he would just shut up and drive, but everybody thinks the guy is hilarious.

Now I like adventure, but I think it's prob'ly best to drive the well-known route at night. But Frico says Benet suggests it's better to head south on Paris Road and keep going until we get to a dirt road beside a levee, where he'll take the urn from us. Frico makes a quick stop at the Meat Mart down the road for snacks and an air freshener. OK, I get the air-freshener part (the van reeks), but snacks? Right now? Seriously?

I hop out with Mr Responsible just to make sure he gets back into the Terravan real quick. The Meat Mart has an auto-accessories section towards the back (yes, *auto accessories*, believe it). You can get steering-wheel covers, rims, WD-40 and everything. On our way to the cash register, we hit the snacks aisle, and the Meat Mart guy he comes out and plops down a "Caution: Wet

Floor" sign in the aisle. Poor guy is dead certain there's bound to be an accident once he sees the likes of me and Peter anywhere.

Back in the Terravan, we need the air-freshener more than ever. Frico's passing around the worst things in the goddamn world: pork rinds, liquorice sticks, salt-'n'-vinegar chips. Real dorm-room-type shit.

I mean people are eating it, even without dip, cos they're starving. But trus' me, the only thing more tasteless than that stuff is the interior of the Terravan. Check this out: a fake-wood formica dashboard, worn-out corduroy seat covers and some sad, sad linoleum covering the floor. This van is a trip, so to speak. It's like Mrs Thorpe bought it off some 1970s wanna-be rock star who said "screw it" and went back to his job pumpin' gas when he couldn't sell his demo tape even to himself. The thing needs remodelling or at least a good interior wash. Well, we're heading east again and I'm thinkin' I should've left my wallet with the seal at home, cos the skid just started up I think. That's triple trouble. My bones are rattlin' and the Terravan is already wobbly with Frico at the wheel. To make matters worse, Teesha is sittin' beside him in extra-short denim shorts pulled up over her bikini. The thing is cut so high up you can see half her pockets, I swear to you.

I know we should have searched for those damn hip boots.

Soon as we get back on Hayne, we run into a sudden fog, hangin' over the road like sheer-white laundry. The backed-up traffic is blazin' brake lights through the mist. There's bound to be a drizzle and a bit of mud by the time we get to the dirt road. And I'm the one holding Pa's urn, so guess who's gonna have to get out to slop through the mud while Frico sits in the driver's seat and gives Benet the frickin' traffic report?

On the bright side, we're all OK, and Pa's urn is still right-side up with the lid on tight, even with Frico navigatin' corners that are not on the map. Up ahead, the whole place suddenly blazes bright red. Police safety flares. Cherry flames fizzin' like Alka-Seltzer and thick white smoke bubblin' up into the air. Now that just makes me sick to my stomach, cos it means there's been an accident or somethin'. Frico adjusts the rear-view mirror so you can only see his eyes in the waverin' red glow.

"OK, children. Looks like we're delayed on the tarmac. Stay inside and make sure you're covered. It's chilly out."

Well, it's true that we got more time to kill. People start pulling off the road. Frico does the same. When he finally stops twisting the steering wheel, the Terravan is so drunk-parked you really can't tell which way is east or west, but it's OK as long as we're off the road. The fog is comin' down low. Up front, Frico and Teesha Grey start lip-lockin'. It's his final night here, so hey, I don't blame 'em. In other news, Peter Grant and Suzy Wilson have not looked up at the world since we left the Meat Mart. They're hot and heavy and heading for a heap o' trouble. But I ain't got time to watch people. I'm sure Claire's got some stunts of her own she wants to try. Nope. Not at all. Claire is *sleepin'*. Maybe she's still bent outta shape about that "other girl" comment that Frico conveniently made in the pool. So she ran off with ol' Jack Daniel's. I'm fading too, so whatever.

Frico cuts the engine and the headlamps go off. The soft shoulder of the road rolls off into the bushes. Pitch-black bushes. So dark you can almost feel the shadow stickin' to your face when you look out the window. I'm nodding off thinking: "This is hell right here, only slightly redecorated." I wake up in the night, still groggy. The traffic's moved on and the fog is lifting. There's music. At first I think it's the radio. But the tune is comin' from outside the van. I sit up to see silhouettes in the front seat. Frico Beaumont is huggin' his girl with one arm and sketchin' on the fogged up windshield with his other hand, the way kids do in a rainstorm when they can't go outside to play. And my brother, he's drawing an outline of something across the street. We couldn't see it at first with all the fog, but it turns out we're right across from the amusement park. And lo and behold, Frico Beaumont is sketching it as it was back in the day. Chalk Park Fair, not broken down but repaired and beautiful. Teesha's oohing and ahing as he's tracing the whole scene over the ruins and the bushes so you can see what the place used to look like with its walkways and hedges, the ticket stand and a big-mouth clown that's really one hell of a garbage can right at the entrance. Over the treetops, a full Ferris wheel, flooded with light, is slowly turning and twinklin' above and through the trees. The van is full of the flicker from red jelly-bean bulbs and ice-blue blinkers that sparkle all over Chalk Park. Inside the gates, a happy man is on a loudspeaker saying "Come on out" – and I can almost smell the popcorn and hotdogs floatin' over the road. You feel the creak and rumble of the machines in your chest, and the lights are dazzlin' my eyes right now.

There's a face at the window of the Terravan. I'm halfway outta my skin before I see that it's James. Now, everybody's wakin' up to see James Jackson's face behind frosted windows, lookin' in on us like we're live lobsters at a goddamn seafood joint. I can't hear the guy, but I can safely assume he wants us to open the Terravan door. Yup. The pistol in his hand tap-tappin' at the glass confirms it. So while I'm busy thinkin' James has gone from preaching in the cemetery to finally flippin' his lid – and Frico needs to get us away from here – Peter Grant reaches across his girlfriend's lap and pops open the door, just like that, explaining:

"Where I come from, you never say no to a nozzle."

James orders Frico and Teesha out of the front. He lays down flat on the floor of the vehicle.

"James, what's up man?" I don't know why I'm whispering.

"Shh. Shuddup, Beaumont. E'rybody just keep quiet, please. It's gonna be a'right now."

He might as well have told the girls to count to three and then all holler to high heaven, cos that's what they're doin', over and over. Peter's the loudest. And you should see the terror on Frico's face. This is something he can't fix, especially with his head still full of whiskey jelly.

Well, James is up off the linoleum, and it's a van full of terrified teens that he takes off with down Hayne Boulevard. In the rear-view mirror, Chalk Park Fair is cold and old and dead again, and the only red and blue bulbs are the ones on three patrol cars rolling after us.

"Are you outta your frickin' mind, James? What's this?"

He's wild right now. I've seen him mad, happy, nostalgic, sad or just plain crazy. But I don't know the face in the mirror. This is Outlaw James running for his life.

Now he's goin' into a chant above the screamin' and shoutin' in the van.

"Shamsiel deliver me. Psalms of David, protect my life. Many are they that rise against me. The wicked bend their bows, they make ready their arrows upon the string. Selah."

"James! Lissen, man. Don't do whatever the hell you're up to."

"Siddown, e'rybody!"

He's wavin' the pistol around, so we all get horizontal.

"And close y'all eyes while I'm prayin', for godsakes!"

He's *scared*. I reckon ol' Chalk Park Fair comin' to life would frighten the wits out of anybody.

So *stay calm, Terence*. Talk him out of whatever this is.

"Where'd you get that, Jim?" I'm talking with my face pressin' against corduroy.

He's shoutin' over his shoulder.

"Wouldn't believe me if I told ya. Those people at the Meat Mart wouldn't let me buy a bowie knife to protect myself tonight, so let's just say I got this gun on the street instead. We're goin' back theah right now. I reckon they'll have a change o' heart. And I won't have to turn over a few shelves this taam. 'Suriel, Ariel: protect my life.'"

It's funny how everybody in the van is cussin' at the criminal while he's calling on angels. And he's got good reason. We won't make the Meat Mart. The parking lot is littered with patrol cars from James's earlier visit. So we're all flung to the side in a sudden U-turn. The Terravan stops in the middle of the street. A giant dust cloud with a hunchback hurries off into the dark.

"Get out. All of ya. Close the door behind ya."

Frico and Teesha are out first. Peter and Suzy fight for third and fourth place. Claire and I are tumblin' out of the van when I grab the urn. I don't think we're making the swamp tonight either.

"Leave it, Beaumont. You've had it long enough."

"James, c'mon. Get out."

He's lookin' at me in the mirror with his tired eyes flashing red and blue.

"Tonight my name *is* Couyon. Cos I did somethin' really, really stupid. Made mistakes all my life, Beaumont, but this one was the worst."

"Well, we all make 'em – James."

"Get out, Beaumont. I ain't got the taam for this!"

Claire drags me off the van step. His cussin' gets muffled when I close the door. Then it's completely swallowed up by screechin' tyres.

Twenty-Nine

Usually, by this time of morning, sunlight would be pullin' the black blanket up off the planet. But it's overcast. Across the lake there's only a shred of blue between dirty clouds that look like dust bunnies swept up into a corner of the sky. They found Mrs Thorpe's van in the lake. I haven't taken ten breaths since the divers went in to get it. Now, a wrecker is crankin' up steel cables and draggin' it onto land. The thing groans when it breaks the surface. Green water and grey mud rush out through the front windows. The windshield is bashed in. There's no one inside.

Now, if you think James kidnappin' us, ditching the van in the lake and takin' off is all that happened last night, look, there's more. Matter of fact, last night must have been the worst All Saints' Night in history.

Last night, Doug fell off the Bread-Maker at seventy miles an hour and broke both arms.

Last night the cops found Peter Grant's car abandoned under the overpass along Paris Road.

Last night Larry Lou died in the hospital.

Last night a satellite got dizzy and fell from frickin' space. It broke up over the Gulf. A chunk the size of half a schoolbus slammed into the swamp and set some trees on fire.

All that fog over the city was actually smog.

"Shoulda known, Valerie. Felt it comin'." Ma Campbell hasn't stopped talkin' since we got back. She does that when she's nervous. Even if James escaped, he's got a gun. That means he's goin' back to prison when they catch him. To make things worse, he's the one who hot-wired Peter Grant's car. He was makin' a scene at the Meat Mart down the street until they called the cops. So he came up Hayne Boulevard and snatched the car, but didn't get far before patrol cars were all over him on Paris Road. So he ran up on us in the Terravan, cos he needed another vehicle. Chose the worst one, though. If you're tipsy and terrified and not too familiar with the Terravan you just might put it in reverse before you floor it. And instead of zoomin' into Chalk Park, that minibus is gonna shoot across Hayne Boulevard, ride up the levee, jump the train tracks and end up in the damn lake.

Moms is fiddlin' with a brand-new ten-pack. You can hear the cellophane wrapper, the box top flippin' open, the tap-tap-tap on the table and the crackle of the fire over the tip of the first one she's had in a long time. There's somethin' comforting about that suffocating smoke. I guess it's because it feels like your mind. Deep down, my mother knows somethin' else happened last night. Something bigger. Valerie Beaumont, of all people, she knows things don't just happen like that. Ma Campbell knows it too.

"That blackbird at your window every mo'nin' for months was a warnin'. Darkness was comin'. You did nothin' about it, Valerie, 'cept to consult a hoodoo *obeah man* who ran off with your money. I had Prayer Warriors up in heah and begged you ta do somethin' more. But you couldn't be bothered."

That hit Moms hard, even though she has a thick skin. You see the vertical crease in her forehead deepen.

"I should have never let those kids stay by themselves las' night. I should have stood up to Tracey. He always tries to be so damn cool with the kids, like he's nineteen."

"Don't you blame no one but yousself, Valerie. Everything was fine until y'all discovered you left the urn. *You* left Pa's ashes, Val. Pa was always theah for you. And in the end you left him heah. When his remains was the first reason that made you want to go into the swamp to do rituals. You say Benet was in charge of takin' them? Well, the man has four businesses to run. How in the hell is he goin' ta remember the ashes of an old man?"

Truth is, Valerie Beaumont couldn't control a damn thing that happened last night even if she wanted to. At first I thought Mattis was just being dramatic. But so many things do not happen at the same time. Maybe last night's pandemonium comes down to a credit-card-size hoodoo seal I've been carryin' round in my wallet for months. The same seal I flung into the lake this morning after they dredged up the Terravan. Maybe one of James's angels *did* touch down in Louisiana last night. Maybe he hitched a ride on the back of that satellite and hopped off runnin' like mad. Maybe he slowed himself down suddenly with all six wings, cos somethin' else caught his eye. Maybe he got caught up searchin' for somethin' else.

That gown is gonna smell like smoke. Valerie Beaumont is puffing like a frickin' dragon on the mornin' of her wedding. Maybe she feels guilty. I think it's too soon to be having any kind of festivities, what with James missin' and three vehicles wrecked and Doug's limbs locked inside white plaster, makin' him look like a half-mummy. The feelin' that there's something's wrong is a bit like that smog still hangin' over the city. You can survive it, but it seeps into everything. You can ignore it, but it's inside you. Anyway, wedding-wise, we only have today to do it.

The wedding planner is like a drill sergeant. That lady waits for the second hand on her watch to hit the hour. And at 8 a.m. sharp, as planned, she claps her hands and calls the bridal party together on the lawns of Orange Oaks. The only thing she needs now is a whistle and camouflage fatigues. Doug has to sit this one out. My two other brothers and Peter Grant march with their girlfriends, and me gettin' to walk up the aisle with Claire somehow makes us official. So even though I have to overhear Tony Beaumont talkin' about the fallin' satellite fifty times over (it's called Retiro 5D68) and sometimes I have to be Doug's back-scratcher, I think I'm goin' to enjoy the ceremony. All this is about Moms anyway. The minister is here. She takes her position on the steps of the plantation house and opens that little wedding book they carry all the time, as if they haven't said these things a hundred thousand times.

Her glasses have no rims: you can hardly see 'em. She fits right in with the setting. Everything is so white and fresh, and the chairs fanning out on the green are filled with about two hundred people who took the time to put on make-up and perfume and neckties to come see my mother and Benet get hitched, even under the circumstances. Benet walks out and takes his place between the girls and boys of the lavender-and-white bridal party. He cleaned up real nice. My mother and the wedding planner got him to wear a suit for once instead of the communist-leader-style bush jackets he's always in. We're all lined up on both sides of the steps at the end of the walkway that's now carpeted with snow velvet: a white road for the arrival of the bride. Birds add to the background sounds. Live music. Some of the lilies are still dewy, and Claire, beside me, she smells like spices and vanilla. Behind us the lake sparkles at the end of the rollin' slope. And you can tell it's fall. When we got up this morning, the sugar-maple tree at the apartments had gone from gold to pumpkin to blazin' red. Now it's a frozen fire: a burning bush in the middle of our courtyard. The leaves over at Orange Oaks are doin' the same kind of slow sizzle.

It's perfect.

Speaking of burn, the only problem is, you just can't ignore the wisps of ash floatin' down from the sky all over Orange Oaks, softly settling on white suits and getting' caught up in women's hair. We know it's all from the swamp and that satellite. We've kinda gotten used to it. But suddenly it's becoming a frickin' black-powder shower. Just when Valerie Beaumont appears at the other end of the path with Mrs Thorpe, who is the giveaway "father", the breeze picks up. Ashes start slappin' on to people's clothes instead of touchin' down quietly. The lilies shudder and people hold on to their hats. More black wisps, looking almost like hair, crash into the white carpet and start rollin' up the aisle.

A cold breeze sweeps up the slope from Lake Pontchartrain. It's the kind of breeze that comes in just before the rain, moist and full of loneliness and the smell of sprinkled earth. It's one of those that pounce on you so suddenly it makes you look in the direction it came from. Now everybody's rubbernecking. And a ripple is goin' through the crowd. Cos lo and behold, while we were watchin' the bride, a big, soggy rain cloud crawled in and parked itself over the waters of Lake Pontchartrain, right across from Orange Oaks. Everybody's watching this monster of a black cloud when in about ten seconds the thing grows a tail. Yes, I'm not kiddin'. Something huge is trailing down out of the cloud. People start walkin' out of their chairs to get a closer look. Then everybody gets excited. I don't blame them. Cos right away water starts leapin' up off the surface of the lake to meet that thing coming down out of the cloud. Everybody's seeing this thing, but no one moves until someone in the back shouts "Waterspout!" and all hell breaks loose.

Meanwhile the poor wedding planner is clapping her hands to restore order, but it's over. The water from the lake and the cloud, they meet in the middle and form a massive white column, all the way up to heaven. It's standing still, almost asleep, but look: everybody's calling their kids' names and searchin' for their purses right now, cos that brand-new waterspout looks like it's fixin' to leap over the train tracks, hop across the street and slither up the slope towards us. People howl. Cos all of a sudden raindrops are everywhere, cold as ice, ridin' sideways on blasts of air. The waterspout grows fatter and you can hear the wind comin' off of it, like ghouls caught up in the power lines down below. Rollin' up the slope the wind becomes a damn whip, curling around plants and rootin' up some tents in the far corner of the lawn, leaving them flapping around. It swoops into the reception area underneath the trellis and yanks the tablecloth, flingin' crystalware to the floor. People start to leave. It's my mother's wedding, but I can't blame 'em. When those waterspouts come that close, they like to grab on to the shoreline. And if they climb onto land they become frickin' tornadoes. Rain-frosted French windows slam on hinges. Wisteria flowers shower down from the trellis, sprinklin' people who gathered to watch from the cut-stone floor. Now everybody's runnin' in heels and slappin' at themselves – like those blossoms just became a swarm of purple bees.

Now look, the size of this waterspout is officially *awesome*. So I walk out into the wind to get a closer view of it. The thing is standing still, waiting at the edge of the lake. Frico is beside me, crouching, his camera clicking on rapid. It's something to see, really: a pillar holding up the sky. This ain't your everyday waterspout. No sir. It's wobblin' now. When it leans in, the head-winds get serious, rattling the cast-iron trellis and turning tables over. Then, in the middle of the heavy breeze, my mother shows up beside me, calmly as if taking a stroll on a Sunday. The wind is ragin' up the slope, but her wedding dress is not movin'. She claps her hands and keeps clappin' 'em until, off in the distance, that giant white column standin' on the water just breaks in two. You can hear it fallin' back into the Lake. Now the rain is comin' down harder, but the breeze ceases and that cloud crawls away with a bobtail behind it.

Thirty

All the wedding guests are gone. Half of them were well-wishers whose wishes didn't work, and the others left when the food blew away. Claire is sittin' on the Orange Oaks steps, crying. I tried to calm her a dozen times. It's my fault. I mean, maybe I shoulda waited until after the wedding to ditch that seal in Lake Pontchartrain. I shoulda seen it comin'. But you know, after they dragged out Mrs Thorpe's van and I stood there thinkin' about all that happened the night before, man! That thing just started feeling like it weighed a ton in my wallet.

So I walked to the edge of the landing with the seal in my hand. And, to tell you the truth, I hesitated a bit, but then I saw myself. Yep. I looked straight down into the water below me and I saw my ol' selfish self. The flatfish came early this fall and they've stirred up the mud in the lake, so there was a perfect reflection on the surface. And lemme tell you something: if there were more mirrors in the world this planet would prob'ly be a more honest place. You can prob'ly pull the wool over somebody's eyes, but it's hard to look at yourself and do the wrong thing, man. I guess that's why they got big mirrors in department stores for shoplifters. That's why, back in the day, when Valerie Beaumont figured I was lying, she'd put a brand-new fluorescent bulb in the bathroom and tell me to go stand in the mirror and tell her the lie again. So I did the right thing. I flung the seal sideways across the surface. It bounced twice, then cut the water like a circular saw and disappeared.

Claire is calm enough to talk now.

"I just can't imagine what it's like to have your day ruined like this."

"I need to talk to your uncle."

"Did you hear what I said, Terence? And can you be a bit more respectful? This was your mother's moment."

"Yeah. I heard you. That's why I need to talk to your uncle."

"He's in San Tai, I told you. What does he have to do with anything?"

"After they found the Terravan in the lake, I threw away the hoodoo seal."

"You say you threw away the seal? I thought you did that a long time ago."

"Yeah, long story, honey. Anyway I threw it away *again*. Guess where?"

(Sniff. Sigh.) "I don't know, Terence. Tell me."

"In the lake." I pause for her to connect the dots. She's not in the mood.

"OK, you threw it in the lake, so what?"

"Did you see that waterspout today? That was no ordinary waterspout. They don't even come that close to shore. Don't laugh, but my guess is that something big was prob'ly troublin' the water out there just now."

"Something big? What are you talking—"

"Warrior angels, Claire. Reapers, like your uncle said, whippin' up the water and searchin' for somethin' with their names on it. Ain't you ever read about the pool at Bethesda?"

"Oh good Lord. Lord, have mercy. You've gone damn crazy with this hoodoo thing. I should have left that diary alone. What was I thinking reading it to my uncle? I started this whole thing!"

"Claire. Your uncle is a genius. He was sayin' these things don't stop until they take apart the whole world. Look at all that's been happenin'. Don't you see it? You cannot hide from them. You heard him. That's why he says you should stay away from me."

"Yes, he's a genius. And you're a skid. And that waterspout was actually a friggin' elevator sucking the damn hoodoo seal up to heaven – right, Terence?

"Yes."

"No. The only thing we know for sure is that you're being a moron. I'll give you my uncle's number in San Tai anyway. That's if you dare call him long distance from your mother's phone. But please don't do it when I'm at your house. There's nothin' more annoying than the sound of two idiots exchanging ignorance. By the way, your mother's ready."

Moms is in the Town Car. She's not even breathing, I swear. Benet is trying to cheer her up. He's sayin' they'll clean up and dry off the chairs and they'll ask everybody to come back tomorrow, even if he has to pay twice.

She glarin' at him.

"Take me home, Tracey – to *my* house."

It's been three days now, and everything is beginning to itch like a stale bruise. Doug won't tell me about falling off the Bread-Maker (I'm sure it'll be a funny story once he can take a leak by himself again). Meanwhile Peter Grant is pissed with the whole world, especially me, cos Couyon happened to steal his car from where I live. Anyway, the worst thing is that Moms retreated. Yeah. Moms feels so embarrassed about the wedding wreck that she packed a few things, told Tony to come watch over me and went to stay with our Aunt Bevlene on Honey Drop Drive. Now, that's so close to the swamp you can smell it. That's how desperate Valerie Beaumont is right now. I call her and she doesn't want to answer any questions. She just gives me a list of the same instructions over and over again.

Food is in the fridge.

Take the edible wedding souvenirs out of the freezer.

Put them in the sink.
Turn off the lights at night.
Wash up. (I don't like rats in the house.)
Bar soap is under the bathroom sink.
Stay in the house. Lock up.
Remember to rotate the key twice in the front door.

Meanwhile, maybe it's my mind or just the light in Louisiana this time of year that's playin' tricks with my eyes, but the wedding dress standin' in the living room is beginnin' to yellow. Go into the closet and the white suits Frico and I were supposed to wear look the same way around the edges too. Claire doesn't think so. She says I have too much time on my hands after school and too much mind space to waste.

"Soon you'll tell me the wedding dress on the mannequin looks like a headless lady."

Oh dammit. I wish she hadn't said that. Now everytime I step out of my room the wedding dress on the mannequin really does look like a headless lady. It's haunting the place now, and I wish I could call Orange Oaks and tell them to come pick up the dress and our clothes until Cinderella Beaumont decides to get crackin' with her wedding again. Well, Benet gets that done. He swings by, followed by the Orange Oaks van (they call it a "shuttle", but it's just a creaky ol' panel van). They take the dress and the suits and load them into the back. The suits and the dress are just hanging and standin' in the otherwise empty space like people who lost their way and ended up livin' with us for a while. The Orange Oaks guys pull down the panel door. *Rattle. Slam. Click.*

Now, I can just imagine those clothes rocking back and forth when the van rolls along the long lonesome driveway into Orange Oaks and some guy called Stephen or Miles will take them all out and talk to the wedding planner by phone and she will prob'ly be very upset. And they'll park those clothes in a back room under plastic, while the three-tier wedding cake takes up space in the fridge behind them. And all the time that icing will be crackin' like the plaster tombs under the sun out at Lafayette.

Anyway, Benet came to the house yesterday, and we went to Jill Cunningham's with Claire again. He wants to know how to get Moms out of her funk, but I don't give domestic advice. Trying to be anybody's cupid is stupid, man.

"She won't talk to me, Ter'nce."

The guy looks like he's about to cry. He can't even eat what's in front of him.

"Yes, I know. Doesn't say much on the phone to me either."

"Well, I miss her, and I'm worried about the weddin'. Is she sayin' anything about it?"

"Naw, not partic'larly. She talks a lot about locking up at night and turning the key twice in the door."

"As well yew should – James being back on the loose is nothin' to turn a blind eye to. Everybody's gone back inside their houses at night. I was rootin' for that connivin' bastard."

"I guess. I'm sure Ma can't wait to know his whereabouts."

"Oh, the whole Louisiana cain't wait. Ol' James turned out to be a wolf in white wool – but still, I'm so sorry for his mother. I know what it is to lose two sons at the same time. Still hurts me to the core, like it happened yesterday. One day yew're still a daddy and by nightfall yew just ain't. Hurts like *hell*. So it's gotta hurt a mother a whole lot more than that. That baby boy came from her flesh, you know. I'm gonna send prayers, cos she's walkin' through the fire right now."

Claire's playin' with her food. "Sounds like the police knows he's dead."

"No, they don't. They'll jus' keep on searchin'. They'll never give up till they find somethin'."

Benet's face is red from remembering Broadway and Squash. I go back to the original topic, maybe to save myself from feelin' horrible.

"Leave her alone. She'll come around."

"Huh? Oh, OK. When yew talk to her, tell her to come home. I'd visit her at yer aunt Bevlene's, but that might be umcomf'table and inconsiderate. I'm lettin' her have some time alone. She won't even talk to me for more than two minutes."

I wish she would, though. I feel bad for the guy. And she should come home and save me from babysittin' him. Furthermore, Frico's gone back to school and this place is weird without people in it. Funny, I thought the empty apartment with Claire would be lots of fun. Psssh. The mood's been broken to pieces. Ma Campbell's been stayin' with Mrs Thorpe. I know she secretly hopes James will turn up and they can talk him out of doing anything stupider. Worst thing is, when Claire isn't here (the girl is my rock), I can't even hop up onto the roof and just chill and look around my li'le corner of Louisiana any more, cos the place smells sad and there are handprints where Larry hit the roof tiles on his way down. I feel sick. Empty house, empty apartment next door, empty pool, empty parking lot, empty guard house. Damn, the skid really cleaned out this place more than ever.

I did try to call San Tainos, but Claire wasn't here to help me out. So either I'm doing something wrong or San Tainos is a goddamn fairy tale of a place. Someone seems to pick up, but then the phone goes *whoosh*, like rain. I can't get through – and I need to quit before I get a hell of a phone bill handed to me by Valerie when she gets back. Well, suddenly Valerie turns up, and she couldn't even care less about the phone bill if I told her. She just comes in and drops her bags and locks the door behind her and hugs me and asks if I'm OK. You'd think she hasn't seen me in a hundred years.

The swamps have stopped burning. But a family of four water-spouts appeared on the lake before the end of November. Those things are still out there searching. The first one apparently hollered for backup. The city got tornado warnings going off every few hours, but none of these things are comin' ashore. I've got to talk about this before it gets worse. But Mattis is far away in Wherever-Land, and the last thing Moms needs right now is to think I'm goin' nuts again. The woman has set herself a long cleaning roster, and she's goin' at it like a menace. That's what she does when she's under stress. She cleans. The whole place is scrubbed from top to bottom. Usually after the bathroom is done she's OK again. Not this time.

"I went to Larry's wake last night."

"Oh."

"Good man. Great family. People loved him. But they left early. Nobody wants to stay out late at night."

She's been sighing a lot since she came back. "Oh Terence. I don't know what's gonna happen to us. Everything is all over the place."

Oh man. Hearin' my mother melt like this just makes me so disappointed in myself for messin' with that magic seal in the first place. She warned us about meddling with hoodoo for years. I wouldn't feel any worse if someone said "Skid Beaumont, you're a selfish bastard" and kicked me in both knees, cos they'd be right. Doug always had the right idea: *Money is his kind of magic.* A goddamn credit card is much safer than magic seals, for godssakes.

"Benet wants you to call him."

"Yes, I know."

"He said he's goin' to look in on Mrs Thorpe and Ma Campbell. Maybe he'll find out if they heard from James."

"Maybe."

It's been less than ten minutes, and the phone has been makin' more noise than an ice-cream van comin' up Hayne Boulevard.

For the first call Moms was sittin' at the kitchen table where Pa's ashes used to hang out. It was a short, quiet call. You could tell it was Ma Campbell. Moms leantd forward and rested her elbows on the table like she needed support. Then she put the receiver down for a second on the tablecloth and put her glasses on. When she hung up, the phone slipped out of her hands and prob'ly fell the last half-inch onto the cradle. Maybe Ma hung up at the same time too. Whenever that happens, you hear a bell. One ring.

The second phone call caught her at the sink sighing. Ma Campbell again. Moms told her to come home. Lord knows I got a full bladder, but I'm not leaving this kitchen. I'm curious like hell, but you know when it's not time to ask questions yet. Valerie Beaumont settles into the same tangerine fake-leather chair she was in that morning when I snuck in from Lafayette cemetery. She only gets up to cup the back of the phone and trail it across to where she's sittin'. Almost like she expects it to ring again.

For the first two rings she's lighting a cigarette. "Hello" comes out in fumes. Long distance. She's covering one ear to hear clearly, and the person has to keep repeating stuff. And Valerie Beaumont just sits there in the slices of sunset slippin' through the blinds again with gold smoke curling around her words. She looks at me once during the three conversations, and I understood everything through her eyes before she hung up again. At least I think I did.

They found the urn, caught up against the breakwaters. The lid was off, and inside was washed clean. So it bounced up against the rocks and the tinny sound brought the searchers down. The police could tell that James took it from the vehicle and tried to swim with it. He didn't get far before he had to let it go. He lost his trousers and strength strugglin' to swim with his injured self while holdin' on to the ashes. They think he let go at the last

264

minute and then crawled out bleeding. He made it all the way across the street and into Chalk Park Fair. That's where they found him, stone-cold at the foot of the roller-coaster. A quarter-ounce of gold in his shirt pocket wrapped in aluminum foil. His denim shirtsleeves still buttoned all the way down to hide the old scars. He had some new ones too. Pa's turquoise ring was still on his finger, but his hands were lacerated, they say. Defensive cuts. Seems like a barracuda had set in on his face in the water, so he was a mess. Maybe the fish got attracted to the metal urn and the fight made James let go.

The cops searched Chalk Park and found my goat, in pieces, being smoked over hickory. Some other strips of meat sat in salt inside an old Igloo. The ice container was half-buried in the ground like a deep freeze, hidden by a mini-mountain of appliances and old computer motherboards. Then there was a surprise in the old bathroom. A charcoal sketch, six feet high, signed with the name "Couyon". It was from an old photograph of four-year-old James sittin' on a swamp dock beside Pa Campbell, baiting fish hooks.

"Looks like something from the best artists out on Royal Street" is what they said about it. If I know James, he was trying to take the urn there. I can relate to a guy like James Jackson. Always chasing your old man but forever ending up just one step behind the bastard. It's like you spend your life clutchin' at the air that comes off his goddamn heels.

"Moms?"

She wants me to keep quiet, but I've got to fess up right now. She understands these things, the forces at work. And she needs to know that hell came from her house and broke loose across the city.

"I know what happened. I mean – why all of this happened."

She's squinting through the smoke.

"Why all of what, exactly?"

"The accidents: Doug, James, Peter's car, your car – everything. I know why everything has been happening this year."

I told her the whole story about the seal. Took me six minutes. That's almost an entire cigarette. She crushed it out early and fanned the air. She always does that when she's fixin' to make everything perfectly clear.

"OK, Terence. First of all, I feel like all your life I've had to tell you again and again not to play around with folk magic. I'm so tired, Terence. I got a hundred and one medicine bottles in that bathroom and I never once worry about my children being stupid enough to play around with 'em. But magic, yeah. That's the stuff you always go for. And it's dangerous stuff when you abuse it, these seals and grimoires and hoodoo spells and chants, no lie. So maybe you're right. Maybe that Angelic Order Seal that you've been toyin' around with in your wallet, maybe it did cause three accidents, one attempted robbery and a kidnappin' all on the same night. Maybe that's why someone stole my car in the summer. Maybe your brother broke both arms because you rode with him. Maybe the Tapas truck went up in smoke because it crossed your mind that you could start a fire in a food truck. Maybe you jinxed every one of those vehicles. Maybe you jinxed everything in this town. Perhaps angels *were* churnin' up the lake these past few days looking for their names that you felt you could just tuck away in your back pocket for months and then dump like it was a bubblegum wrapper or something. Who knows?"

"Everything that crossed my mind happened, Moms. Then Mattis told me—"

"George Mattis told you what?"

"He told me he saw the reaper angels searchin' San Tainos when he was a kid."

"Oh, my Lord."

"So I had to get rid of it. And all these waterspouts, it's not even the time of year for them. They're comin' out of nowhere."

"Yes, they are. So. Maybe you ruined your mother's wedding, boy."

I know she's just pausing for drama. She and Ma Campbell should have been actresses, I always say. So I try to break the silence, but she sticks a finger in the air to stop me, cos her lips are wrinkled around a filter.

She pulls the smoke deep. Nothing comes up when she starts talking.

"Or maybe..."

She's shaking the damn cigarette at me, just like Claire does. Matter of fact, all smokers do that. That thing gives them power, you know, like it's a blazin' wand or a sceptre of sort. She's really gettin' into it now.

"Maybe James Jackson, maybe he got out because someone posted some kind of hundred-thousand-dollar bail bond for him – someone like Tracey Benet. Maybe Tracey Benet also lent him a lot of money when he got out. Maybe James couldn't pay him back, so he asked James to do him a special favour to repay the debt. James wouldn't kill you and Frico, so he tried to pay Benet back. Seems like half an ounce o' gold's as far as he got. Maybe Doug fell off the damn motorcycle cos he was chasin' James that night still trying to collect Tracey's money. Doug had no clue about the favour Tracey asked James to do. So he wouldn't leave James alone. So let's say he spent weeks searchin' the swamp and the city and the river. Meanwhile James is livin' right next door in an amusement park. Funny, isn't it? Maybe on that crazy night, James went to buy a knife to scare your brother off, but maybe Dougie had a handgun and James ran him off Paris Road with your friend's car and took the gun once Dougie's arms wouldn't move any more. Maybe that's when he ran up on y'all having a good time in Mrs Thorpe's God-blessed vehicle – and you know the rest of what happened that night. What you don't know is that Mattis ran away from here and wanted you to avoid his niece cos he knew that Benet was plannin' some kind of mass murder. Benet asked him to do the same job and he refused. Ran for his life. Larry Lou should have. Benet got desperate. He let y'all have his house and his bar because he wanted all of you to be as drunk as ever driving into the swamp with a container that he deliberately left in this house. Maybe kept his fingers crossed for a bad accident. All these years, Benet blamed your father and Pa Campbell for the death of Herbert and Orville. He swears it was a plot between your father and Pa Campbell at that time to sabotage the footbridge over the creek in the swamp so he could fall in. But they got his sons instead. Now, whether or not you dump Angelic Order Seals into the lake or simply stop carryin' them around in your pocket, I reckon you're still gonna have waterspouts and storms and tornadoes and satellites fallin' and sinkholes in the swamp for ever. That's how I feel. So now that I told you another side of it, and I'm upset, I'm goin' to have to clean the house again."

She's walking away. I jump to my feet, hyperventilating right now.

"So why were you fixin' to marry Backhoe, then?"

She starts talking over her shoulder, then turns around to face me. Tears like crazy. She's a little girl again.

"I guess with all the dreams I have at night, I still don't see everything comin'. Or maybe sometimes between your heart and your head you listen to the one that hollers louder, I don't know.

"So you didn't know what he was up to the whole time?"

"Had hunches... recently. That last phone call just now was Mattis. He helped me fill in all the blanks. He said he was return-ing your five long-distance calls to San Tainos. I'm going into my room. Turn the key twice. Make sure the door is locked."

Thirty-One

Concrete has no real colour, y'know. You might want to think it's grey, but it's not. And it's not beige or white or greenish neither. And unless you paint it, then the colour of concrete is what you call *cold*. Matter of fact, the only thing colder is the scene we're lookin' at right now at Tracey Benet's office building, in the rear underground parking lot on Poydras Street. He's not down here. Police detectives are questioning him upstairs at Earnest-Benet. That's cos under here, sittin' on cold concrete, they found a 1981 Toyota Tercel. Yessir. The car is facing in, tucked in between two broad columns with black-and-yellow stripes at their bases. When the guard flips the switch beside the elevator, hummin' fluorescent lights flicker all the way up the row of cars, and the whole place looks like a slightly brighter version of a prison cell. From the street, wind is coming through some decorative blocks and turning into a hollow sound. They pull the car cover off the Tercel and Moms catches her breath. Not because of the dust. It's cos in the back seat you can see a brand-new toothbrush, fresh clothes and a neatly folded towel. Pop open the trunk and you'll see some sturdy grass rope, gaffer tape, cinder blocks, a small axe and a rectangular space where an Igloo used to be. Moms' hand goes over her mouth. She's grabbin' on to me as if she just found me after long search. One of the officers, a real jerk, he thinks now is a good time to do jokes.

"You'd imagine that he'd arrange a better getaway car for the guy. Couyon wouldn't get to Mexico in this thing."

Moms is keeping her cool – or her sanity. He's not worth it. Furthermore, whoever stole this car is gonna end up somewhere much hotter than Mexico.

It's a whole month before the end of the year, but Valerie Beaumont doesn't think it's too early to post our New Year's resolutions on the refrigerator. Makes you wish you didn't have a damn fridge. She reckons it's a good thing to get an early start. You know how parents love that "New Year, new rules" kind of thing. As if it's goin' to change the fact that what's gonna happen is just gonna happen. Like Frico says, that's just how the Blue Wheel wobbles. But never mind me. I'm just stalling. I still have until tomorrow to write that fridge list anyhow.

At least I know what I can be thankful for. Here, near to the end of November, I'm above ground and still breathin'. Thanksgivin' was on the twenty-second this year, so with all that happened, we missed celebrating it by three days. By the way, in my house we don't do Halloween. Wait. To be exact: *Valerie Beaumont* does not do Halloween. No sir. My mother does not want anybody representing dead people turnin' up at her door. So Heaven help the poor li'le kid who's bangin' on the front door in a Count Dracula suit, cos he's gonna get a Holy Ghost lecture that's bound to make him vanish like *poof*.

Anyway, to make up for missing Thanksgivin', she's plannin' a big ol' party with lots of food prepared by herself and Mrs Thorpe. She was very sensitive about doin' somethin' so soon after James's cremation, until Ma Campbell said she should stop the foolin' around and put on the best damn party ever in honour of her son and husband. So we're gonna have it outdoors with trestle tables and Japanese paper lamps and lots of decorations all over. All the neighbours are invited and involved. There's gonna be Indian, West Indian, Greek and New O'lins food under blue umbrellas like a taverna. I'm busy planning a Pepto-Bismol station, but I don't think ol' VB's goin' to allow it, that lady. She will also not have anybody talkin' about triple funerals, criminal investigations, freak accidents, magic spells or the fact that Bo's might have business trouble because of Benet.

"Once people can bounce, they won't break. We're bouncin' back," is what she says all day.

There's a smoky-grey wash that comes with autumn days and the light leaves earlier in the evening. I got some sleep after painting the edge of the pool and scrubbin' the sadness off that part of the roof where Larry Lou landed.

I wake up much too soon though, cos Moms was watchin' a silly soap opera and it crawled up through my ears and got caught up in my criss-crossing dreams and couldn't free itself. I open my eyes and, I swear, I really want to tell her that the TV doesn't need to be so loud when I'm sleepin'. But right now is not a good time for an argument. She's in a good mood in spite of everything. Furthermore, we'll have lots of cussin' to listen to once Aunt Bevlene gets here and her ex-husband Tall Horse arrives from Atlanta in his eighteen-wheeler. First of all, that damn truck's gonna take up the whole parking lot, and she's goin' to be glad for the opportunity go off on him like a siren. Never mind that the man owns the apartment we live in. Lord knows, family gatherings are only good for me in small doses – like medicine. People put on fresh cologne and brand-new clothes to come sit around and dredge up old grievances. Mattis and his wife will be dropping in. They're back from San Tainos, but even with Benet under investigation, I'm sure they'll leave early. They always got lots of stuff to do after dark anyways.

Frico will get here tomorrow, so that he and Doug and Tony can lecture me about life over dinner and in front of my girlfriend.

At least I know that good ol' Claire will be sittin' there doing somethin' juvenile, like lookin' at each of them and laughin' at their noses. You should try that sometime when you're bored in a train station or church or wherever. Just look at about ten people real quick, but focus on the noses. It's really funny stuff, trus' me.

Anyway, Moms thinks hard work and fresh air is the cure for grumpiness, so she sends me outside as soon as I drag myself into the kitchen.

"Go see what the workmen are doin' and come let me know."

Great. Well, I'm thinkin' it's about damn time she trusted me to oversee somethin'. So I get up on the roof – and sure enough, official workmen in fatigues are puttin' up tables and stringing pepper lights along the fence and across the backyard. Mattis hired them as soon as he got back, I hear. Must be his way of smoothin' things over with Moms after taking her down payment for that magic spell and then disappearin'. Now this place is beginnin' to look cool. Cos to begin with, the steady red blaze of the maple tree against the deep-blue restaurant umbrellas in the backyard is something to see. And I can imagine the view when Heaven switches off the sun and all those pepper lights come on. It'll be like somebody plugged in a rainbow.

Before long I see another reason that lady sent me outside. She's up to something. She doesn't know I'm on the roof when she's passin' below with a cigarette in her hand, walkin' the full perimeter of the apartment complex. Now look, while she's walkin', Valerie Beaumont doesn't take a drag of that cigarette even once. When she passes, I can smell why. She took the tobacco out and stuffed it with basil, so she can secretly bless the full length and breadth of the place. They say darkness can't stick to what is blessed by a basil leaf.

* * *

Everybody's here, I swear. Must be about a hundred people or more hobnobbin' in our backyard. Frico's brought some fartsy friends with him. Doug and Tony are sprawled off on plastic chairs sippin' liquor. This must be the first time they've ever dared drink alcohol in front of their mother. And they better make damn sure it's light beer, or they may be in danger of gettin' their ears boxed. Ma Campbell's sittin' with them, grumblin' about the dinnerware as usual. I saw Mattis and his wife earlier at the stuffed-crabs-and-gumbo table. You should see the guy: full seersucker suit, complete with hat and tie, lookin' like a recent lottery winner. He was braggin' how he made a killin' in San Tainos, mostly from American tourists, as if I'm supposed to jump up and cheer. That hustler keeps sayin' I might be interested in what he brought back for me, but I don't wear tourist T-shirts and I'm done with seals and talismans for now.

Anyway, I passed by my boy Peter Grant, who volunteered to be the DJ. I swear, you could hardly recognize the guy without that bleach-blonde Suzy Wilson up under his arm. Must have taken a hell of a long time to get their lips unstuck so Suzy could go off to Canada for the weekend. He says he's on a mission to play somethin' that'll make Auntie Bev and Tall Horse stop the goddamn bickerin' and maybe even cuddle on the dance floor. Good luck, man. You'll be here all night. So far I can identify our Greek, Mexican and Indian neighbours millin' around among all our family and friends. They're the ones who start speaking English when you walk up. But some of these other people are moochers who heard the music, walked in off the street and grabbed a plastic plate. It's OK. Cops are doing more regular patrols of late, and it's been a while since we had some kind of shindig, so this is a beautiful thing.

Well, I got a hankering to taste everything, so any extra social-izing can wait. Now, like I said, this is an international buffet, so by the time I get around to pilin' the entire planet on my plate, I can't find a frickin' seat anywhere. Eventually, I pull up a chair to the corner edge of a table with Frico and his friends. Teesha Grey starts lookin' at me weird, like she thinks I'm gonna say something embarrassin'. She really shouldn't worry about me. She should fret about the fact that 'Zoid and his friends are comparing fresh tattoos on their arms – and here come Moms, Mrs Thorpe, Mattis and his wife, Auntie Bev and Tall Horse saunterin' down the steps. If Valerie sees that tattoo, I swear she'll scrub it off herself. Right quick, Frico and his pals they vacate the table so the elders can all sit and be miserable together. Tall Horse is singin' one of the old hits that Peter's playin'. And he's gettin' an earful for it.

"Lord have mercy, Tall Horse, that song is so old. Cain't you be more current?"

"Bevlene, cain't you be more *quiet*? This is ma song!"

"I think you should let the original singers have their song back, before you get sued for damages."

"Matter of fact this is *our* song, Bev. We danced to it in 'sixty-eight."

"I met you in nineteen seventy-one, Tall Horse."

Now, this conversation is getting all tangled, and it'll be hell tryin' to untie the knots. Tall Horse stuffs a chunk of macaroni-and-cheese into his mouth. Now, this guy is our landlord. But Moms knows that as soon as he's scarfed down a few plates, he's gonna slap the face of his watch and holler "Time, time!" – and she's not goin' to see this guy for about another year or so. So she wants to ask him about fixin' some things in the apartment. The place is still in shambles inside and outside. Matter of fact, at first she wanted to have this whole party out in the parking lot to avoid the shabby backyard and the old eyesore of a pool, even after the workmen bailed out the dirty water down at the deep end. Well, soon as Moms mentions anything about repairs, Mattis jumps in and offers Tall Horse a loan to fix the apartment. I'm sure his wife kicked him under the table, cos he turns to her right away.

"It's OK, baby. Tall Horse here can pay me back a little at a time, eh? I know he's good for it. I predict that lots of things are about to change around here anyway. So we might as well get on it, eh? Matter of fact, I hope you don't mind – Valerie, Tall Horse – but after the workmen finished earlier today, I asked them to stay and take a look around, eh? Do an inventory of what's broken."

"Well that's easy: *everything*!" Something tells me Aunt Bevlene came here to have a fight.

Sure enough you can see three of the workmen, over by the old laundromat. It's the first time I ever saw the doors wide open and all the lights on. They're looking at the nine washing machines. They're a funny bunch, goofin' off more than workin'. One is moving to the music and singin' into a monkey wrench for a microphone. The oldest-looking one is just sittin' down on top of a machine the whole time with a plate in his hand, lettin' the other two clown around while he chows down.

Well, I'm up to my neck in adults cussin', so I take off with my plate and walk over to Claire, who's by the edge of the pool like that night we met. Now look, the pool has been transformed. Moms decided to cover the bottom of the empty pool with about forty Japanese paper lanterns. OK, they're not actually Japanese. We made them from parchment paper wrapped around tiny tea lights. They weren't much to look at during the day, but now that they're lit, it's gorgeous, man. The lights begin at the shallow part of the pool and slope down to the deep end, like houses on a hillside at night. Everybody's oohin' at the spectacle and prob'ly wishin' they'd given up their chair to come sit poolside.

Some are here already, hangin' out, backs to the parking lot and feet swinging over the edge. You can just soak up all that warm yellow glow or look across and watch the comedy goin' on in the laundromat. People shuffle over so I can fit in.

Now, I don't even know if the paint's dry enough for my jeans, but I don't care right now. Peter's cranking up the music. I'm feedin' Claire off my fork while she's laughin' at the noses around the pool. Then, after a giant bite, I look at the girl and there's a moment – you know that one second in your whole life where all the pretendin' falls to pieces and you know you're involved up to your eyeballs? Yeah, don't laugh, man. I swear, the whole year I was so preoccupied with that other girl in my head and all the other stuff that I couldn't see that Claire and I, we're a weird kind of fit. But life took a turn and suddenly, right now, I realize my heart is beating out this girl's name in Morse code. So she looks up and catches me staring at her.

"What?"

I start whispering to her between bites. Her curls are ticklin' the tip of my nose, but she's the one doing the giggling. But it's time this girl really knows how I feel, so I'm droppin' some serious lovey-dovey lyrics in her ear. No matter what colour the pepper lights change to, her face is still blushing red. She can't even eat straight. I'm seeing dimples in her cheeks I never knew she had. And she's tryin' to chew and hold her fork and hide her smile all at the same time, while I'm telling her how every night before we met I'd go to bed and dream that I was flying.

"I used to fly everywhere, babe – all over New O'lins in my dreams. I could draw maps from my head right now, with all the details. That's cos I would sail through my bedroom window and take off down Hayne Boulevard and zip under Connection Bridge and follow the flow of the Mississippi River all the way out into the sea in the dead of night: like a shadow searchin' for the other side of myself. Meanwhile you were playin' hide-and-seek with me, poppin' in and out behind stars and that crescent moon that looks like God's fingernail falling into the Gulf. And then one night you stopped runnin' and I caught up to you sittin' at this pool all by yourself. Now these days I don't fly any more in my sleep, Claire. I've landed. You brought me down to earth. Now if I do any flyin', it's in real life, cos you, you take all my gravity away."

Man, she's lookin' at me with those eyes that say everything. She doesn't need words. But I got more lyrics for this girl. So I tell her I want to be wakin' up next to her for the rest of my life, cos she looks like the type to kiss a guy every time she turns in her sleep, and I could get used to that. But I figure I need to drop some classic lines on her to cement myself as the most romantic guy she ever met in her life. So I borrow Alrick Beaumont's poetry from the back of that 1960s postcard to San Tainos that Moms had asked me to throw out.

Who is this woman?
Who ignites all my desires
and sends my spirit soaring?

I back off to give her space to melt and become a puddle in the pool, but the girl's face is frozen solid. I mean, Claire isn't even listening to me any more. And she won't take her eyes off the auto-fill jet valves over on the other side of the pool wall. They're like some tiny inlets where water used to spray back into the pool from the pump. To be honest, I never noticed them before, but nobody sittin' on the poolside can ignore them now. Cos those rusty old jets are sputtering to life, spittin' out streams into the pool that are as brown and mucky as bayou water during gator season. *What the hell*. They're sprayin' into the pool so fast it sounds like a small riot comin' up the road. People start pullin' their legs up over the side, but nobody really gets up until that dirty water starts drenching Valerie Beaumont's beautiful Japanese lanterns.

You can hear the sizzlin' sound of them dying, and darkness creeps back into the pool. This is not cool. Smoke is everywhere, and people cough a bit. As soon as all the fire is extinguished, the jets stop spraying, leaving the smell of smoke and stagnant water thick in the air. Through the smoke there's a wheelchair rollin' in from the laundromat. Over by the table Moms stands up to her full height, which isn't much, but her serious face makes up for it. She looks in the direction of the wheelchair. The smoke clears just enough for me to see that it's that old guy who was sittin' on top of the machine, one of the dead washing machines now rattlin' back to life in the distance. In the background the other workmen are still celebratin', so the guy rotates the wheels of the chair by himself and wobbles all the way up to the side of the pool.

Peter kills the music. Silence. Except for the laundromat humming. Everybody's lookin' at the wheelchair with this withered white dude in his blue work fatigues with the full beard and only one leg. The peak of his painter's cap is hiding his eyes when he rolls into the light, stops and swings the chair around to face Mom's table. The man is a mess. My bones start up the damn rattling and there's an icicle drippin' down my spine. Mattis starts clappin'. One look from Moms makes him stop the damn cheering. My mother is sure that George Mattis has somethin' to do with the abomination happening in front of her eyes right this moment: Alrick Julian Beaumont rollin' out of the grave and into her life again. And my old man, shabby as he is on the outside, he hasn't changed one bit: he's lookin' around at everyone as if it's his homecoming party. He calls across to Moms.

"Heard you had a funeral, Valerie."

Well, look. I hear those six words and it's like someone hit rewind on the memory machine. In my head all I see is my pops fixin' a refrigerator and tellin' me about the parts. My mother is walkin' back from Lam Lee Hahn in the swamp with my dog Calvin bouncin' up and down around her, beggin' for some of what she just bought... My brothers they're tossin' me into the bayou, cos it's my birthday. Harry T and me, we're on a bicycle goin' to Gentilly again. I'm up front on the handlebars, free as the breeze with spring blooms on both sides of the road. This is where memories come, when you can't find 'em. They're all here alive and fresh inside the old man you thought you buried until he came back. Damn. Rockstar moment. But I can remember all the songs this time. I always thought about the first thing I'd say if I ever saw my father again. It'd be poetic and damn profound, I told myself. I'd hug him whether he had one leg or no arms, and it wouldn't be weird, I said.

"Goddammit! What the hell are you doing here, man?" is not exactly what I had planned to say. Mind and mouth broke up again. Word is gettin' around now. You can see the buzz in the crowd. My mother's still not movin'.

Meanwhile that flesh-and-blood ghost just sits there with his one leg and his arms by his side, more useless than Doug and limper than one of those voodoo rag dolls out in the French Market, complete with a grimace of a smile. Mr Mistake-Maker himself. Mattis's "surprise from San Tainos". I should've known. Mattis snuck him in here and he took all evening to repair the pool pump and the washing machines. And the lights are on again in the apartment Mattis used to live in. But my mother's face is dark. And the off-duty night clouds overhead are starting to look pretty busy again.

Mrs Thorpe is tryin' her best to hold her back, but my mother moves away from her chair and steps out from under the blue restaurant umbrellas. The crowd makes a ragged kind of aisle between my parents. She's there, prob'ly feeling naked in front of the whole world, tryin' to take it all in. Last she ever saw of this man was an alligator-mangled leg in an old Caterpillar work boot. Last she heard of him was his voice breaking up through a CB radio, comin' in from miles away. Last time she saw his face, I was about ten years old. So you can tell her heart is in a hundred pieces and her knees are goin' next. But I swear I'm more worried about my pops right now. Cos she's marching towards him. Now she's running. And there's no tellin' what Valerie Beaumont could do to a man who thinks he can come back and wreck her whole damn life by trying to fix everything.

SKETCHER

The first part of Roland Watson-Grant's Trilogy of the Swamp

ISBN 978-1-84688-312-5 • £7.99

"A wonderfully joyous, eccentric first novel."
The Times

Nine-year-old "Skid" Beaumont's family is stuck in the mud. Following his father's decision to relocate and build a new home, based on a drunken vision that New Orleans would rapidly expand eastwards into the wetlands as a result of the Seventies oil boom, Skid and his brothers grow up in a swampy area of Louisiana.

But the constructions stop short, the dream fizzles out, and the Beaumonts find themselves sinking in a soggy corner of 1980s America. As things on the home front get more complicated, Skid learns of his mother's alleged magic powers and vaguely remembers some eerie stories surrounding his older brother Frico...

Atmospheric, uplifting and deeply moving, *Sketcher* – Roland Watson-Grant's stunning debut – is a novel about the beauty of life no matter how broken it is.